ACCLAIM FOR CO

"Coble's clear-cut prose makes it easy for the reader to follow the numerous scenarios and characters. This is just the ticket for readers of romantic suspense."

—*Publishers Weekly* on *Three Missing Days*

"Colleen Coble is my go-to author for the best romantic suspense today. *Three Missing Days* is now my favorite in the series, and I adored the other two. A stay-up-all-night page-turning story!"

—Carrie Stuart Parks, bestselling and award-winning author of *Relative Silence*

"You can't go wrong with a Colleen Coble novel. She always brings readers great characters and edgy, intense story lines."

—BestInSuspense.com on *Two Reasons to Run*

"Colleen Coble's latest has it all: characters to root for, a sinister villain, and a story that just won't stop."

—Siri Mitchell, author of *State of Lies*, on *Two Reasons to Run*

"Colleen Coble's superpower is transporting her readers into beautiful settings in vivid detail. *Two Reasons to Run* is no exception. Add to that the suspense that keeps you wanting to know more, and characters that pull at your heart. These are the ingredients of a fun read!"

—Terri Blackstock, bestselling author of *If I Run*, *If I'm Found*, and *If I Live*

"This is a romantic suspense novel that will be a surprise when the last page reveals all of the secrets."

—*The Parkersburg News and Sentinel* on *One Little Lie*

"There are just enough threads left dangling at the end of this well-crafted romantic suspense to leave fans hungrily awaiting the next installment."

—*Publishers Weekly* on *One Little Lie*

"Colleen Coble once again proves she is at the pinnacle of Christian romantic suspense. Filled with characters you'll come to love, faith lost and found, and scenes that will have you holding your breath, Jane Hardy's story deftly follows the complex and tangled web that can be woven by one little lie."

—Lisa Wingate, #1 *New York Times* bestselling author of *Before We Were Yours*, on *One Little Lie*

"Colleen Coble always raises the notch on romantic suspense, and *One Little Lie* is my favorite yet! The story took me on a wild and wonderful ride."

—DiAnn Mills, bestselling author

"Coble's latest, *One Little Lie*, is a powerful read . . . one of her absolute best. I stayed up way too late finishing this book because I literally couldn't go to sleep without knowing what happened. This is a must read! Highly recommend!"

—Robin Caroll, bestselling author of the Darkwater Inn saga

"I always look forward to Colleen Coble's new releases. *One Little Lie* is One Phenomenal Read. I don't know how she does it, but she just keeps getting better. Be sure to have plenty of time to flip the pages in this one because you won't want to put it down. I devoured it! Thank you, Colleen, for more hours of edge-of-the-seat entertainment. I'm already looking forward to the next one!"

—Lynette Eason, award-winning and bestselling author of the Blue Justice series

"In *One Little Lie* the repercussions of one lie skid through the town of Pelican Harbor, creating ripples of chaos and suspense. Who will survive the questions? *One Little Lie* is the latest page-turner from Colleen Coble. Set on the Gulf Coast of Alabama, Jane Hardy is the new police chief who is fighting to clear her father. Reid Dixon has secrets of his own as he follows Jane around town for a documentary. Together they must face their secrets and decide when a secret becomes a lie. And when does it become too much to forgive?"

—Cara Putman, bestselling and award-winning author

"Coble wows with this suspense-filled inspirational . . . With startling twists and endearing characters, Coble's engrossing story explores the tragedy, betrayal, and redemption of faithful people all searching to reclaim their sense of identity."

—*Publishers Weekly* on *Strands of Truth*

"Just when I think Colleen Coble's stories can't get any better, she proves me wrong. In *Strands of Truth*, I couldn't turn the pages fast enough. The characterization of Ridge and Harper and their relationship pulled me immediately into the story. Fast-paced, with so many unexpected twists and turns, I read this book in one sitting. Coble has pushed the bar higher than I'd imagined. This book is one not to be missed. Highly recommend!"

—Robin Caroll, bestselling author of the Darkwater Inn series

"Free-dive into a romantic suspense that will leave you breathless and craving for more."

—DiAnn Mills, bestselling author, on *Strands of Truth*

"Colleen Coble's latest book, *Strands of Truth*, grips you on page one with a heart-pounding opening and doesn't let go until the last satisfying word. I love her skill in pulling the reader in with believable, likable characters, interesting locations, and a mystery just waiting to be untangled. Highly recommended."

—Carrie Stuart Parks, author of *Fragments of Fear*

"It's in her blood! Colleen Coble once again shows her suspense prowess with a thriller as intricate and beautiful as a strand of DNA. *Strands of Truth* dives into an unusual profession involving mollusks and shell beds that weaves a unique, silky thread throughout the story. So fascinating I couldn't stop reading!"

—Ronie Kendig, bestselling author of the Tox Files series

"Once again, Colleen Coble delivers an intriguing, suspenseful tale in *Strands of Truth*. The mystery and tension mount toward an explosive and satisfying finish. Well done."

—Creston Mapes, bestselling author

"*Secrets at Cedar Cabin* is filled with twists and turns that will keep readers turning the pages as they plunge into the horrific world of sex trafficking where they come face-to-face with evil. Colleen Coble delivers a fast-paced story with a strong, lovable ensemble cast and a sweet, heaping helping of romance."

—Kelly Irvin, author of *Tell Her No Lies*

"Coble . . . weaves a suspense-filled romance set during the Revolutionary War. Coble's fine historical novel introduces a strong heroine—both in faith and character—that will appeal deeply to readers."

—*Publishers Weekly* on *Freedom's Light*

"This follow-up to *The View from Rainshadow Bay* features delightful characters and an evocative, atmospheric setting. Ideal for fans of romantic suspense and authors Dani Pettrey, Dee Henderson, and Brandilyn Collins."

—*Library Journal* on *The House at Saltwater Point*

"*The View from Rainshadow Bay* opens with a heart-pounding, run-for-your-life chase. This book will stay with you for a long time, long after you flip to the last page."

—*RT Book Reviews*, 4 stars

"Set on Washington State's Olympic Peninsula, this first volume of Coble's new suspense series is a tensely plotted and harrowing tale of murder, corporate greed, and family secrets. Devotees of Dani Pettrey, Brenda Novak, and Allison Brennan will find a new favorite here."

—*Library Journal* on *The View from Rainshadow Bay*

"Coble (*Twilight at Blueberry Barrens*) keeps the tension tight and the action moving in this gripping tale, the first in her Lavender Tides series set in the Pacific Northwest."

—*Publishers Weekly* on *The View from Rainshadow Bay*

"Filled with the suspense for which Coble is known, the novel is rich in detail with a healthy dose of romance, allowing readers to bask in the beauty of Washington State's lavender fields, lush forests, and jagged coastline."

—*BookPage* on *The View from Rainshadow Bay*

"Prepare to stay up all night with Colleen Coble. Coble's beautiful, emotional prose coupled with her keen sense of pacing, escalating danger, and very real characters place her firmly at the top of the suspense genre. I could not put this book down."

—Allison Brennan, *New York Times* bestselling author of *Shattered*, on *The View from Rainshadow Bay*

"Colleen is a master storyteller."

—Karen Kingsbury, bestselling author

DARK OF NIGHT

ALSO BY COLLEEN COBLE

ANNIE PEDERSON NOVELS

Edge of Dusk
Dark of Night
Break of Day (available July 2023)

PELICAN HARBOR NOVELS

One Little Lie
Two Reasons to Run
Three Missing Days

LAVENDER TIDES NOVELS

The View from Rainshadow Bay
Leaving Lavender Tides Novella
The House at Saltwater Point
Secrets at Cedar Cabin

ROCK HARBOR NOVELS

Without a Trace
Beyond a Doubt
Into the Deep
Cry in the Night
Haven of Swans (formerly titled *Abomination*)
Silent Night: A Rock Harbor Christmas Novella (e-book only)
Beneath Copper Falls

YA/MIDDLE GRADE ROCK HARBOR BOOKS

Rock Harbor Search and Rescue
Rock Harbor Lost and Found

CHILDREN'S ROCK HARBOR BOOK

The Blessings Jar

SUNSET COVE NOVELS

The Inn at Ocean's Edge
Mermaid Moon
Twilight at Blueberry Barrens

HOPE BEACH NOVELS

Tidewater Inn
Rosemary Cottage
Seagrass Pier
All Is Bright: A Hope Beach Christmas Novella (e-book only)

UNDER TEXAS STARS NOVELS

Blue Moon Promise
Safe in His Arms
Bluebonnet Bride Novella (e-book only)

THE ALOHA REEF NOVELS

Distant Echoes
Black Sands
Dangerous Depths
Midnight Sea
Holy Night: An Aloha Reef Christmas Novella (e-book only)

THE MERCY FALLS SERIES

The Lightkeeper's Daughter
The Lightkeeper's Bride
The Lightkeeper's Ball

JOURNEY OF THE HEART SERIES

A Heart's Disguise
A Heart's Obsession
A Heart's Danger
A Heart's Betrayal
A Heart's Promise
A Heart's Home

LONESTAR NOVELS

Lonestar Sanctuary
Lonestar Secrets
Lonestar Homecoming
Lonestar Angel
All Is Calm: A Lonestar Christmas Novella (e-book only)

STAND-ALONE NOVELS

Fragile Designs (available January 2024)
A Stranger's Game
Strands of Truth
Freedom's Light
Alaska Twilight
Fire Dancer
Where Shadows Meet (formerly titled *Anathema*)
Butterfly Palace
Because You're Mine

DARK OF NIGHT

AN ANNIE PEDERSON NOVEL

COLLEEN COBLE

THOMAS NELSON
Since 1798

Dark of Night

Published in Nashville, Tennessee, by Thomas Nelson. Thomas Nelson is a registered trademark of HarperCollins Christian Publishing, Inc.

Thomas Nelson titles may be purchased in bulk for educational, business, fundraising, or sales promotional use. For information, please e-mail SpecialMarkets@ThomasNelson.com.

Library of Congress Cataloging-in-Publication Data

Names: Coble, Colleen, author.
Title: Dark of night : an Annie Pederson novel / Colleen Coble.
Description: Nashville, Tennessee : Thomas Nelson, [2023] | Series: The Annie Pederson novels ; 2 | Summary: "USA TODAY bestselling romantic suspense author Colleen Coble continues her new series set in the fan-favorite Upper Peninsula that incorporates beloved characters from her Rock Harbor novels"-- Provided by publisher.
Identifiers: LCCN 2022023805 (print) | LCCN 2022023806 (ebook) | ISBN 9780785253747 (paperback) | ISBN 9780785253778 (library binding) | ISBN 9780785253754 (epub) | ISBN 9780785253761
Subjects: LCGFT: Novels.
Classification: LCC PS3553.O2285 D37 2023 (print) | LCC PS3553.O2285 (ebook) | DDC 813/.54--dc23
LC record available at https://lccn.loc.gov/2022023805
LC ebook record available at https://lccn.loc.gov/2022023806

Printed in the United States of America

23 24 25 26 27 LSC 10 9 8 7 6 5 4 3 2 1

In loving appreciation for my wonderful publishing team, HarperCollins Christian Publishing, for the past twenty years of loving support.

ONE

SHOULD SHE EVEN BE OUT HERE ALONE? MICHIGAN'S U.P. was a whole lotta wilderness. Michelle Fraser's shoulder blades gave a tingle and made her glance back to see if anyone was following her. No one there. But in spite of seeing no movement in the trees and bushes, she couldn't discount her gut instinct. She'd been spooked ever since she left the safety of the women's shelter.

Maybe it was just knowing she was out here with no backup that had her on edge.

The heavy scent of rain hung in the twilight air as she set the last of her wildlife cameras in the crook of a large sugar maple tree. A northern flying squirrel chattered a warning from its nest. The *glaucomys sabrinus*'s agitation made Michelle pull away in time to avoid being nipped.

Thunder rumbled in the distance, and a spooky mist blew through the forest. The sooner she was out of here, the better. Her last set of cameras hadn't turned up the elusive mountain lions she'd been searching for, but a hunter in neighboring Ontonagon County had snapped a picture of a large male reclining on a rock. If she could acquire more data, it would aid her research for the magazine article proving mountain lions inhabited the area. And she had to have pictures.

She'd been obsessed with big cats for as long as she could remember. Even the various names held a fascinating mystique: catamount, puma, cougar, mountain lion, panther.

A mosquito landed on her arm, and she swatted it. Her hands came away with a drop of blood on her fingers. Yuck. She wiped the residue on her khaki shorts and turned to go back to her ATV. A sound erupted to her right, and it sounded like either a puma or a woman's scream. The hair on her neck prickled, and she moved that way.

The scream pealed again, and she removed the lens cap on the camera slung around her neck. Her palms dampened, and her breath came fast. Walking toward danger might not be the smartest thing, but Michelle couldn't help herself. She yearned to see a puma in the wild in all its power and beauty. Her knees shook as she pulled out a bullhorn from her backpack to frighten away the cat if it sensed her as prey.

Queen pumas would be protecting their litters in June, so she needed to be careful. Her lungs labored as she rushed in that direction. Her black belt in jujitsu wouldn't do much against the speed and power of a puma. She seized a large branch to make herself seem bigger as she advanced through the forest. Evergreen needles clawed at her arms as she forced her way through a thick stand of white pine.

She paused on the other side and caught the glimmer of water. Lake Superior's waves lapped at the rocky shore, and she spotted a yellow kayak riding the swells in the shallow surf. A discarded backpack bobbed beside it.

Her sense of unease grew as she observed the scene. Glancing around, she approached the water and snagged the backpack from the lake, then pulled the kayak onto the rocks. Her gut told her someone was in trouble.

Should she call out? If it was wildlife threatening the woman she thought she'd heard, Michelle could scare it off with a flare. But if the attacker was human, she didn't want to give away her presence and put the woman in greater danger. She scanned the area for bear or cougar scat but found nothing.

The sound of oars slapping the water came from her left, and she ducked back into the shadow of the pines until she could tell the intent of the boaters. Two figures partially shrouded in mist paddled a large canoe around a rocky finger of the shore. The glimpse of broad shoulders through the fog indicated they were probably men. She strained to listen through the sound of the wind and water but couldn't hear much.

She couldn't put her finger on why she didn't want them to see her. Maybe because they were men, and Brandon might have sent them after her.

"I know she ran this way. Trying to get to her kayak, eh." The man's heavy Yooper accent carried well over the water.

"Can't see her through this mist," the other man said. "I don't know why I let you talk me into this. Your love life isn't my business."

"You owe me. Let's try on down the shore. There's a deer trail toward the road she might have tried to take."

Their voices faded as their canoe moved past. She didn't get a good look at their faces. Was a woman out there trying to escape an abusive ex? Michelle had seen plenty of that kind of trauma this past year and had experienced abuse personally.

Once they were out of sight, she stepped back into the

clearing. "Hello," she called softly. "Is anyone here? I can help you."

She walked across the green mossy clearing, searching for a sign of an injured woman. The bushes to her left shivered and rustled, and she stepped closer. "Hello? Do you need help?"

The leaves parted as the mist swirled along the ground, and the pale oval of a woman's face emerged. Long blonde hair hung in strings along her cheeks, and her eyelids fluttered as though she might faint. Michelle rushed forward and helped the young woman to her feet. She was in her early twenties with a slight build. Mud smeared her khaki shorts and red top, and she was barefoot.

She seemed familiar, and Michelle reached down to touch her forehead. She nearly recoiled at the heat radiating from the young woman. "Wait, aren't you Grace Mitchell?"

They'd met when Grace first arrived at the shelter, but Michelle hadn't immediately recognized her with the mud and dirt on her face and hair. The woman's fever alarmed Michelle. "You're burning up. We need to get you to a doctor."

"I-I'll be fine. Do you have some way out of here?"

"My ATV is this way." Michelle put her right arm around the woman's waist and helped her stumble toward the trail. "What are you doing out here?"

Grace paused and wiped the beads of perspiration from her forehead. "I spotted my ex driving past the shelter, and I knew he'd found me. That day we met, you mentioned a remote area you liked with a great camping spot, and I decided to try to find it. You know, hide out until I figured out where to go to get away from Roy. But I stopped by to get camping gear from my parents, and he must have followed me here. He's out there somewhere.

He and a buddy." Her blue eyes flashed with fear. "I can't let him find me."

They reached the ATV, and Michelle got Grace situated, but it was a tight squeeze on the vehicle meant for one person. Michelle got water out of her backpack and helped Grace drink some. She grabbed her phone, too, and took a quick photo of the traumatized girl before she dropped it back into the pack.

Michelle started the machine and pulled out onto the trail back to the cabin where she'd been hiding out. She should have gotten out of here earlier since the weather had caused darkness to fall sooner than expected. It would be slow going on the rough trail with only the headlamps pushing the darkness back a short distance.

After only a few minutes, Michelle realized she'd gotten off the trail. She stopped the machine and looked around. Which way should she go? She consulted her compass and decided to push due west. They'd only gone a few feet when the ground gave out under the machine, and they went flying into the air. When Michelle hit the ground, something in her right leg snapped, and the excruciating pain was instantaneous.

She bit back a scream but couldn't stop the moan as she pulled her knee to her chest. The swelling was already starting four inches above her ankle, but at least it didn't appear to be a compound fracture. "I-I've broken my leg. Are you all right, Grace?"

When Grace didn't answer, Michelle felt along the ground until she touched her thigh. "Grace?" She felt up the young woman's body to her face.

Grace wasn't breathing. "Oh no," Michelle whispered. She checked her out in the dark as best as she could. No pulse.

Michelle dragged herself to the machine but it was on its side, and she couldn't right it with her broken leg. No one would be searching for her out here, so she had to find shelter. But how?

The pain made it hard to think. She froze at the sound of movement in the vegetation. Something big was crashing toward her. A deer? A mountain lion or bear?

A man's shoulders moved into sight, and his expression sent shivers up her spine. When he reached down to lift her up, the pain intensified in her leg, and her vision went black.

/ / /

Law enforcement ranger Annie Pederson sat at a table by herself in the small interrogation room at the Rock Harbor jail and waited for Taylor Moore to be brought in for questioning. Maybe it was Annie's imagination, but it seemed as if the beige paint on the walls reeked with the guilt and despair of countless years of interrogations. Even the clean scent of the disinfectant used in the area didn't dissipate the unpleasantness. She didn't like this space and wished she could have talked to Taylor at the coffee shop or somewhere more pleasant.

But this meeting might be the end of her lifelong search, so she would have faced even tigers in this place.

The door opened and Taylor entered. Several weeks ago Annie had hired her to help out around the Tremolo Marina and Cabin Resort and with Annie's eight-year-old daughter, but the woman had been picked up for questioning about the necklace found belonging to a murdered girl. Her claim to be Annie's sister, Sarah—kidnapped from Tremolo Island twenty-four years ago—had turned Annie's every thought on its head. According to Taylor's ID, she was twenty-nine, three years younger than Annie, so that detail matched Sarah.

Annie's heart squeezed at Taylor's ducked head and stringy locks. The bright-red hair dye was fading, and glints of her natural blonde color showed through. Her jeans and tee looked like she'd slept in them for days, and the scent of stale perspiration wafted from her.

Taylor glanced up, and Annie bit back a gasp at the defiance gleaming in those vivid blue eyes that matched Annie's eye color instead of the muddy brown Annie was used to. Jon Dunstan had claimed Taylor was wearing contacts to change her eye color, and it seemed he was right.

Annie had prided herself on her ability to read people in her line of work. She'd always thought she could detect a liar with no problem. Taylor had completely snowed her. After Taylor's impeccable references, Annie had trusted the woman with her child.

Sheriff Mason Kaleva ambled in behind Taylor. He gestured to the chair across the table from Annie. "Have a seat, Ms. Moore."

In his forties, his husky form brought solace to Annie. He'd always been there for her and his town, and his kind brown eyes swept over her in a questioning gaze. She gave him a little nod to let him know she was okay.

Taylor's eyes narrowed. "It's Ms. Vitanen. Sarah Vitanen."

A wave of dizziness washed over Annie, and she bit her lip and eyed Taylor closely. "You claim to be my sister, but do you have any proof?"

The chair screeched on the tile floor as Taylor pulled it out before she plopped onto it. "I should have expected you wouldn't welcome me with open arms. After all, you did nothing to stop my abduction."

Heat swept up Annie's neck and lodged in her cheeks. "What could an eight-year-old do to stop an adult? If you're really Sarah, what was the name of your favorite stuffed animal?"

"Cocoa," Taylor said without hesitation. "It was a brown kitten. I couldn't have a real one because Mom was allergic."

Annie's eyes widened. She caught her breath as she studied the other woman across the table. "Let me see your left knee."

Rebellion flashed in Taylor's blue eyes, and she leaned down to yank up her baggy jeans, then stood with her tanned knee exposed. A faded two-inch scar just below her kneecap matched the one in Annie's memory. Sarah had gotten snagged on a large metal hook under the dock at the marina. It had taken fifteen stitches to close the wound, and Annie had helped her sister hobble around for several weeks.

But was that proof? Kids had scars from all sorts of things. She *wanted* to believe her sister was still alive, but was Taylor really Sarah?

Her breath eased from her lips, and Annie couldn't speak for a long moment. "You really believe you're Sarah? Did you research all that and make sure the details matched?"

Taylor just stared back at her with that same defiance. In Annie's dreams, finding Sarah meant a tight embrace and happy tears, but Taylor's stance with her arms folded across her chest and her jutting chin warned Annie off any displays of affection. Not that she was feeling any warmth toward the other woman in this moment.

When the other woman plopped back in her chair and didn't answer, Annie licked her lips. "Why didn't you tell me when you first showed up looking for work? Why the fake name? I've been searching for my sister for years."

"Have you? Have you really?"

Annie glanced at Mason. "Ask him if you don't believe me."

Mason shifted his bulky form and nodded. "I've been helping Annie search. We've sent DNA samples numerous times over the past ten years. Her parents searched for Sarah, and even hired investigators, until their deaths."

Annie hadn't known that. Her parents' business, the Tremolo Marina and Cabin Resort, operated on a shoestring, so they must have taken much needed money to try to find Sarah.

Annie shifted her gaze back to the woman across the table. Taylor twisted a strand of hair around her finger in a coil. Sarah used to do that too. If this was a scam, it was an elaborate one. With all her heart Annie wanted to believe it, but she couldn't quite accept it. It was so sudden, and the circumstances were bizarre.

Mason cleared his throat. "We'll need a little more proof. We can get the DNA back in a week or so."

"I have nothing to hide," the other woman said.

Annie had spent twenty-four years agonizing over her failure to save Sarah. The guilt had nearly swallowed her alive, though everyone told her she couldn't have done anything. Until a few days ago, she hadn't been able to recall much about that awful night. Maybe she hadn't wanted to remember how she froze in fear when the kidnapper grabbed Sarah.

Annie fingered the scar on her neck where the attacker had wounded her with a knife. She'd been left for dead in the cold waters of Lake Superior, and while logically she knew she was no match for the gruff woman who'd snatched her sister, Annie had struggled to believe it.

"Were any of the things you told me about your life true? Those things you said about your m-mother?"

"I had a rotten life, if that's what you're asking. All those things I said about my mother were true. And it was all your fault."

There was nothing Annie could say to counter that when her own conscience condemned her too. She was only too glad when her boss, Kade Matthews, texted her with a new case. Mason could continue the questioning about the necklace.

TWO

WITH ANNIE OUT OF THE ROOM, TAYLOR LEANED FOR-ward, tucking her head, and hugged herself. While Annie was around, Taylor knew her purpose and how to respond to anything, but on her own, she was a piece of driftwood tossed by the waves. Her hatred focused her.

Sheriff Kaleva shifted in his chair across the table from her. "You planted that necklace in the shed to frame Jon Dunstan, didn't you, Ms. Moore?"

"I told you—it's Ms. Vitanen."

"We won't know that until we get the DNA back, so let's stick to what we know. The necklace?"

She flopped against the back of the chair and shrugged. "I told you I saw it there."

"I don't believe you. When you told me about it, you changed where you'd seen it. And you wouldn't look me in the eyes. The necklace had no dust on it." He leaned forward. "And you know what else it didn't have? Anyone else's fingerprints. Yours were the only ones on the stone."

Her chest squeezed, and heat burned her cheeks. "You don't know how Jon Dunstan treated me. It's not right."

"So he needed to pay for it by going to jail for something he didn't do?"

When he put it that way, it seemed a little ridiculous. "Everyone gets away with stuff. Sometimes justice has to be served."

"How'd you get the necklace?" He slid a can of soda across the table to her.

She popped the top and took a sip of lukewarm Pepsi. The sweet bubbles gave her courage. "I stole it. It was in Sean's glove box along with a jumble of other jewelry. I didn't think he'd miss it."

"How do you know Sean Johnson?"

"He's my cousin." She shrugged. "Well, he's Mother's nephew. He didn't tell you?"

"He's deceased."

The words hit her like a boulder. While he wasn't her blood cousin, he was the closest thing to family she'd had left. And he'd been kind to her. This also meant the cops had no idea of what he did and why. Neither did she, for that matter.

She shifted on her chair. "I didn't know it was important when I took it, but when I heard Annie describing the missing necklace, I knew it matched the one I had. I realized I could make Jon pay."

"So you had the necklace before you saw the photo in the newspaper and realized it was tied to a murder?"

"I've had it since he came to help me with Mother's estate. Such as it was."

"Which was when?"

"December. She died on the second, and Sean came the next day."

"What was your mother's name?"

"Becky Johnson."

"So she was Sean's dad's sister. Did you know Sean well?"

"I'd met him a few times while growing up. He came to our house maybe three times that I remember. He never stayed long."

"Was there anyone else with him? Did he mention any friends he was close to?"

She shook her head. "He's the one who told me—" She stared down at her hands. It was more than she should have revealed.

"Told you what?"

The sheriff didn't believe her anyway. She raised her gaze to stare defiantly in his face. "That I was really Sarah Vitanen."

"How did he know?"

"He saw a picture of me as a little girl, then showed me a picture of Annie and Sarah at about the same age. You couldn't miss that I was that same girl."

"How much do you remember about being kidnapped?" Mason's voice was gentle.

Taylor's throat tightened, and she swallowed past the stricture in order to speak. "I remember screaming for help. I remember *Annie*. When Mother took me, Annie just floated in the water having a good time."

"You must not have seen Annie get knifed by Becky. She still has a nasty scar on her neck. It's a miracle she survived. She lost a lot of blood and had to have several transfusions."

Taylor gave a slight shake to her head. It was hard to know what to believe—her own memories or what she was told. Could she have missed Annie's injury? In her memory, she was sitting with outstretched arms as Annie faded into the misty night, but that's not the way it went down according to her sister.

But Annie would want to hide her neglect. No one would want to admit they'd let someone kidnap their baby sister. Annie couldn't be trusted any more than the others in this town.

Mason uncapped his water bottle and took a swig. "Did Becky ever talk to you about your previous life?"

"I was punished if I ever asked about my sister or the cottage by the lake. Or if I asked for Cocoa, my stuffed kitty. I learned to be polite and well mannered. The few times I mentioned my previous life, she locked me in the closet." Taylor clasped herself and rocked a little. "I don't like the dark."

"I'm sorry she wasn't kind. Do you know why she abducted you?"

"I overheard Mother tell Uncle Clive that she needed a child, and once she told me she'd had three miscarriages. I suspect she took me after the last one."

"She wasn't married? You didn't have a father?"

Taylor shifted the Pepsi can on the table. "Mother never even had men over. She must have given up trying to have a baby once she abducted me."

Mason gave a slight whistle through his teeth. "So you came here after realizing this is where you used to live? You wanted revenge on Annie? Or did you hope she'd recognize you and welcome you back with open arms?"

"I took steps to make sure she didn't recognize me." She touched her fading red hair. "Hair dye and brown contacts. I wanted to find out more about her before I admitted who I was. And it was a good thing—she didn't seem overjoyed to find out I'm Sarah."

In spite of her anger, pain pierced her heart. It wasn't a sin to want to be loved by her sister. But it clearly was not to be.

Mason rose. "I'm charging you for falsifying evidence. And I'll be watching you. Don't even think about hurting Annie or her little girl. If you give me information that leads to an accomplice

Sean might have had, I'll see about dropping the charges. Did you ever see anyone with him after you arrived? Or overhear any phone conversations? Did he have more than one phone he might have used to send texts?"

She wished she could do more than shrug and shake her head. Spending any time behind bars wasn't something she wanted to do.

/ / /

Thick foliage along the narrow fire trail in the Kitchigami Wilderness Preserve hid most of the cream-colored BMW. The same spruce and oak trees encroaching against the paint also nearly obstructed the path down the lane, and Annie doubted anyone had been down this trail since the car had nosed into the leaves. The pungent scent of pine swept down the hillside on the summer breeze.

Kade pulled back a heavy oak branch to reveal the back window. Orange tow warnings carpeted the glass. "The first one of these is from a year ago."

Annie peered closer. "Whisper Creek Condos issued the tow warnings. They wouldn't have towed it out into the wilderness. Who called it in?"

"A hiker thought it seemed suspicious."

"Is there any other info you've uncovered about Sean targeting Sophie Smith and Penelope Day? Do you think he could have had anything to do with this?"

The case had brought national attention, but Sean's death over the edge of the cliff had stopped Mason from interrogating the man.

"Mason and I haven't found any evidence that Sean was involved with any other deaths. We've gone through phone and computer records, but unless we discover another computer or a cache of evidence, we're dead in the water."

There had been several suspicious disappearances in the forest in the past year, but authorities hadn't been able to discover what had happened to the campers. They could have fallen in the cold water and drowned or gotten lost and never made their way back out. Annie had hoped the discovery of Sean's guilt in the deaths of the two teenagers would lead to more.

She started to run a finger through the thick dust coating the car, then thought better of it in case they needed to dust for prints. "I'm not a car person, but this has to be an expensive ride."

Kade nodded. "At least sixty grand." He forced his bulk through the foliage to examine the front. "No collision damage or anything. It's strange."

Annie peered through the dusty windows. She pulled on latex gloves. "I'm going to see if the car is unlocked."

"Okay."

With just the tips of her fingers, she tried the handle and the door popped open. "I'm in."

She poked her head into the tan interior, which still held the aroma of new leather. In spite of the dust on the outside, she didn't think the car had been used much. She opened the glove box and withdrew the registration. "Belongs to Michelle Fraser. Address is that new condo complex in Rock Harbor out on Whisper Road."

"Pop the trunk," Kade said.

She pressed the button and listened for the trunk release before she got out. Kade reached the trunk first, and she heard his quick intake of breath. "What?"

"A bloody sheet. Someone lost a lot of blood."

She joined him and saw the crusty blackish-red mess on the sheet. It was the only item in the trunk. "Maybe not enough blood loss to be fatal. We need to see what we can find out about Michelle and how this car got out here."

"I think we start by talking to management at Whisper Creek Condos. And we can check out her residence. I'll call Mason. If it's foul play, this is his case."

Annie always hated to give up a case, but Kade was careful to follow protocol, which was why he was the boss. She'd be likely to plow ahead with an investigation and circle back to Mason later.

Kade withdrew his phone and placed the call. "Got a situation here, Sheriff."

Annie listened with one ear to Kade's explanation. She walked around the car and inspected the ground to see if she could spot any footprints or other clues in the loose gravel and soft dirt, but it was hard to say how long the car had been parked here.

Taylor's claims broke through Annie's efforts to focus on the task at hand. Could her search for her sister really be over? And did Annie even want to believe it when the woman clearly blamed her for the circumstances of her life? But everything in Annie wanted to fully understand what had happened and what Sarah had gone through. Her doubts would be resolved in a week or so, but in the meantime, what could she do?

Kade's wife, Bree, had offered Taylor a place to stay until more was known about the situation. Annie's first impulse had been to let her use the cabin where she'd been living, but she couldn't risk Kylie's safety. If Taylor/Sarah hated her enough, she might use Kylie as a weapon. And they still didn't know how Taylor got that necklace she planted in the shed of the property Jon's father owned. Had she been involved with Sean? The questions meant she couldn't be trusted yet.

The hostility in the woman's eyes during the interrogation had been all too telling. While Annie held loving memories of her sister, Taylor felt nothing but rage and contempt.

Kade ended the call and walked over to join Annie by the hood of the car. "Mason is going to the condo at eight in the morning. He said if you wanted to join him, he wouldn't say no. He's shorthanded today. I need to get back to the office, so it's your baby."

"I'll meet him." She grimaced. "Honestly, I need something to occupy my head while I wait for the DNA test to come back."

He nodded. "I get it. Let me know what you find out."

She followed him to the SUV for the drive back to town, then shot Jon a quick text about meeting him for dinner later. His perspective on Taylor's claim would be interesting.

THREE

JON DUNSTAN'S FACE HURT FROM SMILING AS HE DROVE back from Houghton. He'd sent his references and résumé last week to Houghton Orthopedics, and at their first meeting, he and Dr. Mike Willis had connected right away. Mike had called all the references and had spoken to patients and to other area doctors.

Jon found a spot in the gravel lot at Tremolo Marina and Cabin Resort and parked. The scent of a wood fire from the RV park burned his nose, and the dulcet tones of someone playing a guitar outside one of the cabins and the hum of motors out on Lake Superior added a relaxing backdrop on this beautiful June day.

He got out and headed for Annie's cottage. How should he tell her? Just blurt it out or wait for the appropriate time? Maybe telling her in front of Kylie wasn't a good idea. Her daughter had kept him at arm's length ever since they'd met.

He still found it hard to wrap his head around the fact she was *his* daughter.

It wouldn't be news Kylie would want to accept. Jon was trying with the girl, but it was hard when she couldn't stand him. He'd never been around kids much, and bonding with her wouldn't be easy.

The back door was open, and he saw Annie and Kylie through the screen as he stepped onto the stoop. A large apron covered Annie's white shorts and navy top, and her blonde hair was up in a messy bun. The aroma of lasagna made his mouth water. He'd barely managed a bite or two of lunch before meeting with Mike, and he was ravenous.

He let his gaze linger on his daughter for a long moment. She was a replica of her beautiful mother, but maybe she had his hairline. Or was he being stupid to look for bits of himself in the little girl?

He rapped his knuckles on the wooden screen door. "Knock knock."

Annie turned toward him with a smile that didn't quite reach her eyes. She'd never been able to hide anything from him, and his elation dimmed. He suspected it had to do with her confrontation with Taylor. He'd shot her a text asking what had happened, but she'd put him off until tonight.

Her bad news might overshadow his good news. He'd bide his time and see what she needed from him.

"Come on in. You can butter the garlic bread. Kylie is crazy about the Sami's bread you got her."

Kylie lifted slim shoulders. "It's okay." She didn't glance his way as he entered the kitchen.

He exchanged a long look with Annie, who shrugged and handed him the loaf of bread, then gestured to the kitchen table where the butter dish sat. He washed his hands, then grabbed a knife from the drawer on his way and settled down to coat the bread for the broiler. Everything he needed was on the table, including garlic salt and a baking sheet.

The puppy scrambled over to greet him. "Hey, Milo," he

said. The little guy was growing fast, and his curly tail swished frantically when he pounced at Jon's shoe. He was a brown-and-black mirror of Samson with his mix of German shepherd and chow.

"Kylie, you can have your iPad until dinner," Annie said.

Kylie shot from her chair like an arrow released from a bow. "Thanks, Mom," she called over her shoulder as she went. Moments later, the music from *Pokémon Go* wafted behind her as she crossed through the kitchen to the yard.

At least she was out of earshot. Jon waited for Annie to spill what was bugging her before he gave her his news.

Annie's blue eyes studied him when he handed her the bread for the broiler. "You look happy."

"And you don't. What happened with Taylor? You didn't seem to want to talk about it."

She took the baking sheet and put it under the broiler, then set the timer. "Tell me your news first. I need some good news, and I can see it on your face. You got the job?"

"I anticipate an offer later in the week."

"That's wonderful!" She moved into an embrace and rested her cheek on his chest for a long moment. "I can't believe this is really happening."

He smoothed the stray wisps of blonde hair falling from her bun, then brushed his lips across her sweet-smelling hair. His love for her had never wavered in the nine years he'd been gone. It had just gone underground and erupted the moment he saw her face again. "Me neither. Now what's wrong?"

She lifted her head and moved back a step. "Taylor claims to be Sarah. And she knew things only Sarah would know. Mason took DNA, and we should know the truth in a week or so."

"I didn't expect that shadow on your face. Aren't you happy you might have answers after all this time?"

She stared up at him. The trepidation in her eyes deepened. "She hates me, Jon. She blames me for not saving her."

"You were a child! That's not fair." His voice had risen, and he took his agitation down a notch. "What were you supposed to do?" He touched the scar on her neck. "The woman who took her nearly killed you. She knifed you and left you for dead. There was nothing you could have done."

"I think Taylor had a terrible life with that woman. I want to make it up to her, but I don't know how."

He palmed her face in his hands. "It's going to take time, love. You can't expect to pick up where you left off. Do you really believe she is Sarah?"

She pressed her lips together before nodding. "It's possible. If she isn't Sarah, she somehow found out a lot about her. What would be the point? And she didn't hesitate about getting a DNA test. Mason texted me after he interrogated her. Sean's dad was her mother's brother, and he was the only family she had. She says she found that necklace she planted in his car when he was helping her settle the estate."

"Where is she now?"

"Probably in Bree and Kade's guesthouse. Mason was going to turn her loose after finding out what she knew about that necklace. Kade wanted a chance to keep an eye on her."

"Better not to have her around Kylie until you know for sure."

The timer went off, and she backed away to get the bread out of the oven. "There are so many things I'll have to explain to Kylie."

"One thing at a time," he said.

He was in no hurry to face his daughter's wrath when she found out Nate wasn't her birth father.

/ / /

The quiet cottage felt like a welcoming hug. Jon sat next to Annie on the sofa with the aroma of buttered popcorn hanging in the room. Only a few handfuls of their snack were left in the bowl. Tonight they decided to embark on a *Matrix* marathon, but he couldn't keep his mind on the movie. Not with his life about to take a dramatic change.

There were no guarantees with this life change. Questions about the future remained unanswered. He knew he loved Annie, but was it enough to overcome the obstacles? Kylie might never accept him. If she didn't, he couldn't see Annie putting their happiness ahead of her daughter's.

No, *their* daughter. It was a reality he still struggled to accept. He'd missed out on her first tooth, her first step. She called someone else *dada*. It would take the right timing to broach the subject with her. He hoped Annie had a better idea of how to break the news than he did.

Annie scooped up a handful of popcorn. "You're quiet tonight."

"Just thinking about Kylie. When do you think we should tell her?"

She scooted away a few inches. "Not yet. I can't deal with that right now when I'm waiting to hear if Taylor is really Sarah."

He could accept that. After searching for Sarah for so many years, this had to be all-consuming. He wanted it to work out, but he had his doubts about Taylor. She'd tried to frame him—all because she was jealous he was in love with Annie. He'd tried to let Taylor down easy, but he'd only succeeded in angering her.

His face must have radiated his skepticism because Annie stared at him. "What? You don't think Taylor is Sarah?"

The pain in her eyes told him how much she hoped he was wrong. "I have no way of knowing that, but Taylor hasn't been exactly truthful. She tried to implicate me in the murders, and for all we know, she participated in Sean's plot. Others probably know about the stuffed animal and Sarah's scar. Neighbors, friends of your parents. Sarah was part of the fabric of life here for five years. I'll bet you still have that stuffed kitten, right?"

Annie nodded. "Kylie has it now. She loves Cocoa, too, but it's getting a little ratty looking after all these years."

"So even her friends would have heard the name. And Kylie might have told her where she got the plushy and how it got its name."

"That's true." She sighed and looked down at the popcorn bowl. "At least the DNA will tell us the truth."

"And what if she *is* Sarah? You welcome her into your life in spite of the character flaws we've already witnessed? You let her still have access to Kylie? I'm sure there are other things we still don't know about her. While it's a terrible thing she was stolen at such a young age, that experience would've shaped her."

Tears leaked from the corners of Annie's eyes, and he felt like a heel for causing her pain. But he didn't trust Taylor not to hurt Annie and Kylie. Even if the DNA matched, Sarah wasn't the same little girl who was taken away. Annie would open her heart and life to the other woman, and that scared him.

He pushed away his feelings of guilt. "She came here resorting to subterfuge. That's never a good thing."

"Maybe she wanted to get to know us before she told us the truth."

"And maybe she had a more sinister motive."

Annie's nod was reluctant. "She admitted she blames me for what went wrong in her life."

"Maybe she wanted revenge. She could harm Kylie."

"She could've done that already if that was her intention."

"Unless she's biding her time. I don't want you to trust her, Annie. Can you at least be on your guard?"

She didn't meet his gaze. "If Taylor's really Sarah, I have a lot to make up for. Half the resort would belong to her too."

"So give it to her and move into another place. The marina is a drain on your resources and your life. Without it, you could concentrate on the job you love and on Kylie. You only try to keep it afloat because of your parents."

She shrugged. "There's an element of truth to that. There are so many times I've wished I could close it and forget it. But if I gave it to Taylor, she wouldn't know the ins and outs of running the place. I'd have to help her. I don't think it would be that easy to sign it over and move on."

Jon could see how this was going to play out. Annie's life would be totally entwined with Taylor's. "What if she's not Sarah?"

"Then I need to find out why she came here and who fed her information. But I just don't know, Jon. She twisted her hair around her finger the same way. And that scar. She would've had to have inflicted a wound on purpose to have a scar just like Sarah's. It's an old scar, too, Jon. That injury didn't happen last month. Or even last year."

He saw the hope and fear twisting her insides. What good

could come from this with Taylor's animosity? He moved closer and embraced Annie. Her shoulders stiffened a moment before she relaxed against his chest.

"I'm so scared," she whispered. "Be patient with me."

"Always," he murmured against her hair. "I'm not leaving you or letting go, Annie. We'll figure this out. I won't let her hurt you."

Taylor had a bad motive for coming here on the sly. She'd already proven she couldn't be trusted. They had the deck stacked against them in so many ways, but this new wrinkle might be even worse than the situation with Kylie. And that wouldn't be a fun thing to try to straighten out.

FOUR

MICHELLE TRIED TO KEEP THE SCREAM BUBBLING IN her throat locked down, but the pain in her right leg was overwhelming. She rolled on the surface—a cot?—and tried to see in the gloom. How long had she been unconscious? Hours? Days? Her mouth was so dry, and she felt weak and shaky.

She ran her fingers down to her leg and found massive swelling. She'd broken an ankle in volleyball when she was in high school, and the snap her leg had made was unmistakably the same as then. The swelling and pain were more confirmation that her leg was broken. And where was that man?

That poor girl had died too. At least Michelle thought so. There'd been no pulse. Maybe she'd broken her neck in the ATV's tumble over the hillside.

A sliver of moonlight poked through the naked windows, and Michelle saw rough cabin walls and a pine floor. The space was small—maybe ten by ten. She desperately needed to use the bathroom, but was there even one here? And how would she get to it? Maybe she could crawl.

Squinting in the darkness, she spotted what appeared to be a darker area along the wall opposite the cot. It could be a door that opened to another room, and it was her best shot at finding a bathroom. It was possible there was an outhouse somewhere, but she didn't want to try to crawl outside in the dark.

She swung her feet to the floor, and the metal cot rattled. Her leg immediately screamed with the influx of blood to the area. She waited until the agony ebbed a bit, then extended her leg in front of her as she eased down to the floor. The floor smelled like mouse and raccoon, and she heard the scuffling of tiny claws to her right. The original occupants were still here. Keeping her right foot extended, she dragged herself backward across the rough wood toward the opposite wall. It was too dark to be sure there was another room that direction, but all she could do was try.

As she neared the darker area, she paused and saw a glimmer of light coming through a small window above what appeared to be a composting toilet. In spite of the dire circumstances, her spirits lifted a little that she'd been right about this one small thing. It took some finagling and pain to relieve herself and yank her shorts back into place, and she had to lie on the floor until the pain eased a bit.

When she got a little strength back, she went in search of water. Though her stomach growled, her parched mouth was her main priority. She kept close to the walls since she suspected a hand pump would be somewhere near the outside. She found a cabinet with a dry sink and a hand pump, but she couldn't get onto her feet to try it. The only thing in the room was the cot.

She made her way back to the cot, and her hand touched something plastic near the foot of the bed. A water bottle! After making sure there was only one bottle around the bed, she uncapped it and sniffed. No odor, so she could only pray it was good. She forced herself to just take a few sips in case it was the only fluid she would have.

She crawled back onto the cot and felt around for something to prop under her foot. Elevating her leg would help ease the pain, but there was no pillow. Though she was chilly, Michelle took the rough wool blanket and rolled it into a bolster, then stuck it under her leg.

The pain was almost more than she could bear. If only she had some ibuprofen.

Gritting her teeth, she tried to power through by thinking about something else. Who was the man who'd come toward her before she fainted? She'd been too fuzzy with pain to remember anything other than a dark form. The fact that he'd brought her here instead of taking her to the hospital wasn't a good sign.

No one would be searching for her. Only her former boss knew she was working on a magazine article, and she wouldn't be expecting to see her anytime soon. Going off grid had its negatives. So if she was going to get out of this mess, she'd have to do it on her own.

A sound outside caught her attention. The growl grew louder. It was an engine. Maybe an ATV. Her pulse fluttered and she sat up. Her jujitsu could be helpful. She might be able to disable an attacker from her place on the cot with a chop to the throat or a kick to the groin with her good leg, but she couldn't run while the guy was on the floor.

Her leg raged with pain again, and she inhaled as she tried to deal with it. The engine cut off outside the cabin, and heavy steps approached the door. A key grated in the lock, and moonlight flooded the interior as the door swung open. Her heart tried to jump from her chest as she struggled to see the face of the man in the doorway.

"So, Michelle, you have something I want. Where are your belongings?"

His question made her freeze. He knew her name, so this wasn't some random abduction. She'd been targeted. She swallowed past the lump in her throat and licked her parched lips. She couldn't think.

"Cat got your tongue?"

"I don't know what you want."

"You can't answer a simple question?"

"If you know my name, you know I was living at the women's shelter. Did my husband send you to kidnap me?"

"Just answer the question. Your belongings—where are they?"

She didn't intend to tell him anything. Giving him what he wanted was likely to end up with her dead. "Do you have any ibuprofen? My leg is broken."

"It will heal eventually." Something thumped on the floor. "Let's see if a little more time will loosen your tongue."

The door clicked behind him as he left with a finality that made Michelle want to scream. What did he want from her? Whatever it was, it couldn't be good. She had to get out of here.

/ / /

Annie had always found the Whisper Creek Condos picturesque. Built three years ago, the condo complex spread along the banks of the creek and had velvety grass with a beautiful heated pool. A microbrewery was at one end of the property along with a hockey rink for the residents. Several ice-fishing huts matching the architecture crouched along the water with gear for the residents' use.

She followed Mason through the office door, front and center of the complex. The leasing agent behind the reception desk looked up with a perky smile. She appeared to be in her thirties with bright red hair pulled up in a ponytail. Two candles burned on her desk, which accounted for the apple scent in the air.

The news anchor was nattering on about how hackers were taking control of vehicles and how to stop them. Annie barely registered the brunette on television before focusing her attention on the woman at the desk.

Her smile faded when she recognized Mason. "Sheriff Kaleva, what can I do for you?"

Mason slid the car registration across the desk to her. "We found this car abandoned in the forest. Ms. Fraser appears to reside here?"

The woman glanced at the slip and nodded. "I noticed this morning she'd finally moved her vehicle. We've sent notices and left stickers on the car for about a year. She's never answered her phone or stopped to take care of the situation."

"When was the last time you saw her?" Annie asked.

Mason sent her a look that ended her questions. This wasn't her investigation.

"It's been ages. Her rent is paid by mail, and she never answers her phone. That car hadn't been moved out of the parking garage in all that time. It was covered in dirt." The leasing agent leaned forward. "I don't think she's living here. I told management I believed she was using this residence as a cover for something. Who leaves an expensive car like that in the parking garage that long? Something's fishy about it all."

"Did you ever meet Ms. Fraser?" Mason asked.

"Just when she leased the apartment. Young, probably

twenty-four or twenty-five. Long brown hair, brown eyes. Around my height of five four. She seemed skittish and scared when she checked in here."

"Was she alone?"

The woman nodded. "She kept glancing out the window. I think she was afraid of someone."

"Did you see anyone with her?"

"No, but she was really jumpy."

Mason waved the car registration. "Did she drive here in this car?"

"Yes, and that was the last time I saw it moving."

Kade had said the vehicle was easily worth sixty thousand. Who would leave a vehicle like that and never drive it?

Mason glanced out the window. "Could we do a wellness check on her?"

"Sure." She reached into the drawer and fished around. "Here's the key card."

The woman was much too curious herself to turn them down. Annie and Mason followed her out of the office and down the hall to the elevator. They took it to the top floor. Mason rapped on the door and called out his identity.

When no one answered, he stepped back and nodded toward the door. "Go ahead and open it."

The leasing agent swiped the card and opened the door. She stepped out of the way and let them go first. Annie caught a glimpse of fear in her brown eyes. Maybe she was afraid they'd find the Fraser woman dead inside. Annie had the same worry.

The air inside the condo felt stale and dusty. With the drapes pulled, it was hard to see, so she felt along the wall and flipped on the light switch. With the overhead chandelier throwing out illumination, she could see the place looked unlived in. No knick-knacks, no personal photos out. The thick coating of dust showed clearly on the dark wood floors. Annie walked through the entry and living room to the kitchen. The cabinets and drawers were empty. She peeked out onto an empty deck.

"She's never lived here, Mason." Annie swept her hand around the space. "There isn't a single dish in the kitchen. No skillets, no canned goods or utensils." Opening the refrigerator revealed a brand-new, never-used interior.

"Very strange," Mason said.

The leasing agent had followed them in, and a frown darkened her face as she glanced around. "It looks like it did when she moved in."

Annie trailed behind Mason down the hall with the other woman bringing up the rear. Annie checked out the hall bathroom first. No toothbrush, no deodorant. Nothing but dust. The guest room was completely empty. The main bedroom held only a bed covered by white bedding. The adjoining bathroom was a repeat of the hall bath—empty of everything but dust.

Had Michelle ever slept here, or had it been for show from the beginning?

The leasing agent stood in the hall with a shocked expression. "I saw a moving truck arrive with the furniture. I had no idea she wasn't living here. Her rent payment has always been punctual. Why would someone pay for a home and not live there?"

The question of the day.

Not expecting to see anything, Annie opened the closet. Two boxes were stacked on the left, back against the wall. She flipped on the closet light and leaned down to examine them.

"Mason, this might be some personal stuff."

He knelt beside her. "Let's see what's in here." He opened the first box to reveal a jumble of clothing. The second box held old picture albums.

"Can we take these to try to track down where she might be and what's happened to her?"

"Not without a warrant." Mason put the lids back on the boxes. "I'll get one, though, if we can't find her soon. With that bloody sheet in the car, I have good reason to be concerned for her welfare."

Annie stepped out of the closet and followed him into the hallway outside the condo. She was very concerned about Michelle's well-being.

Mason glanced up and down the hall. "Let's see if any neighbors are home. You take the north side and I'll take the south."

He told the leasing agent they didn't need her assistance any longer, but she loitered longer than necessary on her way to the elevator. Once the elevator doors closed, Mason and Annie began knocking on doors.

The last door on Annie's side opened, and an older woman with her hair in pin curls opened the door. Her faded blue eyes held curiosity. "Hello, young lady, what can I do for you?"

Annie gestured down the hall. "Have you ever met the resident in 5C? Michelle Fraser?"

"The people in and out of there were never very friendly. And always different. Young women, all of them, and they never stayed more than one night. I tried to chat with a few of them, but they scurried off like mice."

Annie frowned. What had Michelle been up to?

FIVE

WAS JON DOING THE RIGHT THING? AS HE GOT OUT OF the car, he eyed the converted lighthouse owned by Bree and Kade. A breeze blew in off Lake Superior, and it held the scent of moisture. The sound of children's laughter floated up from the rocky shore, and he walked to the slope that led down to the water to glance at the youngsters splashing in the waves. The Matthews children tossed a beach ball with their mother at the water's edge while Samson, tail held high, ran back and forth barking.

Perfect. He could confront Taylor with no onlookers. He hadn't decided what he wanted to say yet, but he'd figure it out.

He retraced his steps, then went past the big house with its lighthouse tower until he came to a small guest cottage overlooking the big lake. A bike leaned against it by the front door, and he hoped that meant Taylor was inside.

He saw movement through a window and rapped his knuckles on the door. Taylor opened it, and her face went rigid when she saw him.

She stepped into the opening as if to prevent him from coming inside. "What do *you* want?"

"An apology from you would be a nice place to start this conversation." He pitched his voice into a mild tone so she didn't get her back up any more than it already was.

She folded her arms across her chest. "Fine. I shouldn't have tried to frame you."

"Why did you?"

It was disconcerting to see her blue eyes now when she'd masked them with the brown contacts for so long. With those eyes, he could see a resemblance to Annie. Could she be Sarah?

He wanted to know her reasoning. Why had she lied? What had she hoped to gain?

She lifted her chin. "It's not right that people like you hurt people like me. Annie has everything, and I have nothing. I wanted to level the field a little."

"By getting me locked up? You must be very unhappy to want to ruin someone's life."

Her lower lip quivered. "I already said I was sorry."

The word *sorry* hadn't crossed her lips, but he let it pass. "Did you want to hurt me or Annie?"

She shrugged. "Both, I guess."

She wasn't going to give more of an explanation than she already had, so he moved on. "Why didn't you tell Annie who you were when you first got here?"

"I remembered her, you know. I might have been little, but I remembered the way she didn't run to help me. I screamed her name over and over, but she just splashed around in the water and didn't scream or anything."

"She'd been injured. The woman knifed her in the neck. She was a little girl—Kylie's age now. Do you think Kylie could protect a smaller child from an adult?"

She blinked. "She could have at least screamed."

"She was fighting for her life too. Since you hate her so much, why even tell her who you are?"

Taylor chewed her lip. "I didn't think you would press charges if you knew who I was."

At least she was being honest. "So it was all about getting out of trouble? You didn't care to get to know your sister?"

"Why are you interrogating me? This isn't your business. It's between me and Annie."

"I love her and don't want to see her hurt. She desperately wants to find Sarah, and if you are Sarah, you plan to twist the knife in her chest, don't you?"

"Someone should pay for what happened to me," she shot back.

"What that woman did was terrible, but bad things happen in life. You think Annie has had it easy? Her dad was an autocrat, and he never forgave her for not saving you. Money was tight, and she worked hard to get where she is today. It wasn't given to her. Every person on this planet faces challenges. How you handle those trials determines your character. I think yours needs some work."

Her cheeks went red. He hadn't made the most tactful comment, but he was beyond coddling her. "You need to grow up and take responsibility for your life. No one is going to lead you by the hand to a better life. Get a job and work hard. Take classes in your spare time. There are programs to help with education. Don't sit in the house and cry over the past. The future can be as bright as you want to make it."

"I don't have to listen to this." She stepped back and reached for the door.

He stuck his foot out to prevent her from slamming the door. "Just remember, I won't let you hurt Annie. If you're really Sarah, you wouldn't want to hurt your own sister."

Her blue eyes glittered. "If? You don't believe me?"

"You haven't exactly been truthful."

"I'm Sarah, and there's nothing you can do about it. I'm going to be in her life whether you like it or not. If you know Annie well, you'll know I'm right when I tell you that if there's a choice between you or me, she'll pick her own flesh and blood. All I have to do is drop a few whispers in her ear about you, and she'll listen."

He wanted to shake off her words, but he knew how much Annie valued family. He couldn't let Taylor see how her words had stung. "Don't hurt Annie or Kylie."

"Or what?" she jeered.

He had no answer for that, so he retracted his foot and spun on his heel. The door slammed behind him, and he realized his hands were trembling a little. That hadn't gone well. His meddling might have made her more determined to cause trouble.

One thing was clear—she hated Annie and blamed her for the wreck that was her past life. And Jon wasn't sure how to stop her from destroying Annie's happiness.

/ / /

Taylor stalked outside into the breeze off Lake Superior, but the moist air failed to cool the heat in her cheeks and radiating through her chest. How dare he! This was between Annie and her and was none of his business. She went past the Fresnel lens tower and picked her way down the hillside to the water, where Bree threw a ball with Samson and her children.

Taylor liked Bree and felt she might be sympathetic to her plight. After all, she'd offered her a place to stay while this all played out. That had to stand for something.

Samson, curly tail high, left the ball and pounced on the white foam rolling to the sand. Bree's four-year-old twins, Hannah and Hunter, ran into the waves with the dog while their mother dropped to a beach towel on the shore. The older boy wasn't around, so Taylor headed toward Bree.

Bree's curls gleamed golden red in the sunshine. It was a much prettier color than the one Taylor had used from a bottle. A light, flowery scent wafted Taylor's way, but she couldn't identify the cologne the other woman wore.

Bree was checking her phone when Taylor approached, and she put it down when Taylor stopped beside her. "Good morning." Her smile faded when Taylor scowled. "Something wrong?" She patted a place beside her on a *Moana* towel. "Have a seat and tell me about it. Did you sleep well?"

"I slept fine." Taylor dropped beside her and clasped her denim-clad knees. "Jon Dunstan showed up at my door. He doesn't believe I'm telling the truth about being Sarah. I admit it's hard for me to think of myself as Sarah after being called Taylor all these years, but I know the truth."

Bree tucked a wayward curl behind her ear. "Do you remember much about those early years?"

Bree's careful tone stiffened Taylor's spine. Did she have doubts as well? Was no one on Taylor's side—no one in town who wanted her to take her rightful place? Her eyes burned, and the beautiful blue water blurred. She wasn't about to give anyone the satisfaction of seeing her pain, so she turned her head and blinked.

"I remember a little. Mother used to sing songs in the kitchen. I remember some of them. One was something about a playmate."

Bree sang a few stanzas in a clear soprano, and Taylor nodded. "That's the song."

"I wasn't living here when you went missing, but I remember hearing the story," Bree said. "It was a sad thing all around. Annie's parents wore haunted expressions for as long as I knew them, and they spoke of their search for their missing daughter. That incident never seemed relegated to the past. That should bring you comfort. And you can't blame Jon for being cautious. He doesn't want Annie's hopes dashed if the DNA doesn't come back with a match."

"It will match."

Bree turned her head and locked gazes with Taylor, who put as much confidence in her expression as she could. It had to match. If it didn't, it meant Sean had lied to her. It meant Taylor was still rudderless and without an anchoring identity. She couldn't bear that, not when she was certain of who she was. Once she'd seen that picture of herself as a child, she'd had a goal for the first time in her life. And it felt good to have direction.

Bree stood and shouted at the children, "Don't go out any farther! Come back this way." When they complied, she dropped back down to the towel. "Do you remember the cabin where Annie lives now?"

That was a sticking point. Taylor didn't remember much about the inside of the cottage. She remembered the water, the pier where they watched the loons, and a playground. The playground in her memory was different from the one at the marina now, but she'd heard it had been redone a few years back. That had to be the only reason it wasn't familiar.

"I remember it," she lied. "Everyone needs to get used to the idea that I'm Sarah."

"Do you think of yourself as Sarah?"

"Not yet, but I will once a few people have the courage to use the name."

"I'm sure Annie is hopeful."

Taylor let out an unladylike snort. "She'd like to deep-six me again. Then she wouldn't have to share any of the property or money. It would be all hers."

"Money has never meant much to Annie. She'd gladly give anything she owned to have her sister back."

Taylor didn't answer when it was clear she'd never convince Bree of Annie's part in the kidnapping. Her one vivid memory was of an older sister's blue eyes in the water as she did nothing to help. That couldn't be a false memory. It just couldn't.

But as much as she reassured herself, she realized the imprint could have been a movie she watched as a child. That's what her mother had always said when she mentioned that specific memory. One thing Taylor knew for certain—the woman who raised her wasn't her real mother. There were too many holes in Taylor's early life. Too many missing spots. Like what had happened to her favorite stuffed animal, Cocoa the kitty. Annie's face had changed when Taylor pulled that name out. She wasn't exactly sure how she remembered it. She hadn't consciously thought of it, but the memory sprang from the shadows as soon as Annie asked the question.

But thinking about it now, she remembered that Kylie had an old plushy cat named Cocoa. Was it Sarah's favorite toy?

Taylor had to cling to the small clues she had to her identity. She had purpose when she came here, and she didn't intend to lose her focus. Someone had to pay for what had happened to her. While she didn't want Kylie to suffer, it might be necessary.

SIX

THE SUMMER FESTIVAL WAS IN FULL SWING ALONG Rock Harbor's streets. The booths of vendors hawking homemade candles, essential oils, paintings, and Finnish art lined Houghton Street with offshoots of fewer stands branching out along Pepin Street and Kitchigami Street. Down along Negaunee Street past Bree's lighthouse, Annie knew she'd find displays of agate jewelry, pottery, copper items, and thimbleberry jam. People dressed in Finnish clothing milled around as they prepared for the parade. The town had been settled by Finns back in the copper-mining days, and it still held the flavor of its residents.

It was a week Kylie looked forward to every year, and Annie had already let her daughter burn off energy at the park bouncy house and playground before they perused the festival offerings. The aroma of *panukakkua* and *pulla* blending with the rich scent of beef pasties made her mouth water, and even Milo lifted his nose and sniffed at the air.

Kylie had a plea in her blue eyes. "Couldn't we have panukakkua just this once, Mommy? It's not like I can't ever eat gluten for the rest of my life, right?"

"Honey, you have celiac disease. That's never going to go away. But I'll get the ingredients and see what I can do about making a gluten-free version, okay?"

Tears flooded Kylie's eyes, and her mouth went mutinous. "Maybe some Fazer chocolate?"

"That we can do." Annie steered Kylie toward Nicholls' Finnish Imports. Anu carried all things Finnish, and the chocolate was one of her hottest-selling items.

Annie glanced down at Milo, who trotted along at Kylie's heels. "You have a very good puppy. I can't believe how quickly he's learning."

The words were no sooner out of her mouth than the puppy shot forward, yanking the leash from Kylie's hand. He barked and ran to sniff noses with Samson, who lay at Bree's feet as she stood outside Nicholls' talking to Anu Nicholls and Naomi O'Reilly, her best friend. Milo crawled on top of his father with a blissful expression in his dark eyes.

Annie and Kylie ran to retrieve Milo before he took a notion to dart out into the street. "Well, he was doing great until he saw Samson," Annie said as Kylie chased Milo.

Bree bent and rubbed Milo's ears. "Good boy," she crooned. "He's missed us." In her thirties, her five-three frame was compact but muscular from her search-and-rescue career.

Pink-cheeked and breathless, Kylie reached Annie and the dogs. "Bad Milo." The puppy ignored Kylie's scolding tone and burrowed deeper into Samson's fur. Kylie scooped him up and held him until he quit struggling to get back to his father. "Oh no, you don't."

The puppy subsided against her chest and whined. Anu moved close enough to rub his ears. Milo's whine grew louder, and he lunged for Anu, who caught him before he could wiggle out of Kylie's arms.

"What's gotten into you, little fellow?" Anu tried to hang on to the wiggly body as he tried to move down her chest. Once Milo reached Anu's belly, his whine grew even louder, and he licked at her stomach. "What on earth has gotten into you?"

Annie took the puppy and cradled him in her arms. "All this excitement. Settle down, Milo." The puppy continued to try to lunge at Anu. "Maybe I should take him to the park and settle him down."

"Leave Kylie with me," Anu said. "I think I see her eye on a Fazer chocolate bar."

Kylie's eyes gleamed. "Yes, please."

Smiling, Annie took the still-protesting puppy across the street to the park, where she set him in the grass to do his business. Keeping a tight hold on his leash, she glanced around for Jon. He was supposed to pick up his dad and meet them in town, but they hadn't set a firm place or time. They'd planned to text and arrange a meetup to get ice cream and shop.

This should have been an afternoon off, but Annie's thoughts kept running back to the strange case that had dropped into her lap. It was Mason's responsibility, but she wanted to find out why a woman would rent a high-dollar condo and leave it empty. And the car situation was equally strange.

She spotted a familiar set of wide shoulders and waved at Jon, who was getting out of his red Jaguar in the parking lot by the park. The breeze ruffled his brown hair out of its usually smooth style, and he waved back and went to help his dad out of the passenger seat.

With his cane firmly in hand, Daniel Dunstan appeared more frail than the last time she'd seen him. Her palms went damp as she pasted on a smile and moved to greet them.

Would he blame her for Jon's decision? Giving up a prestigious medical partnership wouldn't be what he'd want for his son. This hadn't been an easy decision for Jon, and she still wasn't sure where their relationship was leading. Trust was slowly coming back, but the key word was *slowly*. Jon had left her once, and she still half expected him to cut and run now that he knew Kylie was his daughter.

Mr. Dunstan's green eyes crinkled in a smile below his bushy white eyebrows. "There's the girl who upended my son's life." His voice was still a little slurred from his stroke.

Her heart slammed against her chest, and she stopped a few feet away from him. Her gaze made a quick detour to Jon's face before landing back on his father's. "I'm sorry, Mr. Dunstan. I didn't know what he was going to do until he did it."

"I think it's a fine decision, Annie. He should never have left here in the first place. He hasn't been happy, but I expect that to change now that he's home." His gaze slid over her shoulder. "Have you seen Martha's booth? She's selling pies, and I want to buy every one of them that are left so she has time to wander around with me."

"The pastries are that way." She pointed toward the Suomi Café.

"I'd better hustle then." He patted her shoulder and made his way across the street.

"Is he okay by himself?" she asked Jon.

"He has to feel he's got some independence. I think he'll be all right." His tanned fingers touched her elbow. "Where's Kylie?"

She tried not to show how her pulse sped up at his touch, and she resisted the temptation to run her fingers along his square jaw. "At Anu's shop. I brought the puppy over to potty. Have you told your dad about Kylie?"

"Not yet. I'm waiting for the right time. He'll be thrilled."

"I think it's a good idea to wait. We have a lot going on."

When the full story came out, she wasn't sure what her friends and neighbors would think of her. Would Jon's dad blame her that he had missed all those early years? This whole situation was such a mess.

/ / /

The sweet aromas of waffle cones and ice cream wafted to Jon's nose as he pushed open the belled door to the shop. Kylie had shot him a mutinous glare when he joined her with Annie at his side. She'd brightened at his suggestion of ice cream, but she didn't have much to say to anyone except Milo on the way to get the promised treat.

"What would you like, Kylie?" he asked in front of the glass display.

Annie was chatting with the teenager behind the counter, and Jon realized the pretty brunette was Donovan O'Reilly's daughter, Emily. Donovan owned the local hardware store and was married to Naomi.

Kylie took her time perusing the offerings. "Chocolate delight in a waffle cone."

Maybe this hadn't been a good idea. The place was a minefield for people with celiac disease. "Um, that has gluten in it. How about a chocolate sundae? Then you can choose the things that go on it."

Kylie's eyes filled with tears. "Before you came along, I could eat whatever I wanted."

Annie turned around at her daughter's distressed tone. "Jon

has a great idea. How about chocolate ice cream with hot fudge and nuts?"

"Can I have whipped cream?"

Jon spied the Reddi-Wip container. "All the whipped cream you want."

He exchanged a long look with Annie. There was some truth to Kylie's complaint. It *was* his fault she was dealing with this disorder. She'd inherited the celiac gene from him. Once she realized that, it wouldn't endear Jon to her. The whole relationship was a swamp of possible pitfalls that could suck them into more anger and resentment.

He had no idea how to win over Kylie. Ice cream had seemed the way to her heart until the quicksand of her dietary restrictions opened in front of them. He watched Emily prep the sundae and ordered the same for himself. Annie chose a strawberry sundae and ordered a small cone for the puppy.

The bell jangled, and he turned to see Glenn Hussert enter with a stack of papers. He wore his ever-present green John Deere hat over his brown hair.

Glenn stopped when he saw them and smiled as he handed one of the flyers to Jon and another to Annie. "I'm running for state rep. I hope I can count on your vote, eh."

His Yooper twang sounded forced to Jon. He took the flyer and glanced at it. "Thanks."

Glenn owned Bunyan Fisheries outside town, but Jon didn't know him well enough to promise him a vote.

With Milo on leash, Kylie took her sundae and headed for the door to grab a table outside. Annie mouthed for him to follow Kylie while she waited on the rest of the ice cream. Jon's palms grew moist at the thought of trying to hold a conversation with the hostile girl. It shouldn't be this hard, should it? He thought back to his growing-up years and how easily he'd chattered to his parents about anything and everything. He hadn't been around kids much, so the distance was probably his fault.

He'd always believed he'd never be a father, and he hadn't made any effort with children. He saw them in his practice, of course, but he talked mostly to the parents about surgery and recovery. While he might smile and say hello to a juvenile patient, he didn't spend any time getting to know them.

That had been a mistake—one he regretted now that he faced Kylie's adversarial attitude.

Kylie plopped down in an iron chair at a metal-and-glass table with the puppy at her feet. Milo sat on his haunches and whined up at her expectantly. "Your ice cream cone is coming." She licked the chocolate from the handle of her spoon and didn't look at Jon.

"So, you excited about going into second grade?"

"*Third* grade. Second grade is for babies."

Messed up again. "Sorry, of course. Third grade. Do you know what teacher you'll have yet?"

"No."

Did she like any sports? Soccer, maybe? What did kids that age do? Jon wasn't used to feeling so inept and unprepared, and it was like he'd teleported back to that awkward phase in middle school. It wasn't a time he wanted to revisit.

Kylie shot out of the chair. "Taylor!"

Jon turned to see Taylor stop at the sound of Kylie's voice. Taylor's gaze flicked to Jon, and the triumphant glint that sparked in her eyes didn't help his dislike. In spite of the fact that he'd warned her off just this morning, she sauntered over to join them.

She touched the top of Kylie's head. "Hey, Bug."

Kylie didn't reject the nickname from Taylor the way she always did when anyone else but her mother used it. She grinned up at Taylor with unmistakable affection. Would Kylie ever smile at him like that? And what should he do about Taylor being here? Annie had made it clear she wanted some distance between them until they got the DNA results back. It wasn't his place to tell Kylie what to do, though, and if he tried to order Taylor off, he'd alienate his daughter even more.

This parenting gig was hard, especially when Kylie didn't know he was her father.

The bell on the door jangled and Annie came out with her hands full of sundaes and a cone for the puppy. She stopped when she saw Taylor, and color rushed to her cheeks. "What are you doing here?"

Taylor's chin tipped up, and a challenging sneer lifted her lips. "Shopping like everyone else. Kylie called me over."

Annie seemed as indecisive as Jon felt. It was awkward when Kylie had no idea of everything going on with Taylor. How did you explain such complex undercurrents to a kid?

Taylor twisted a lock of fading red hair around her finger. "Does Kylie know who I am?"

Kylie frowned and glanced from Taylor to Annie. "You're my friend. Why aren't you still staying with us?"

If he didn't do something fast, Taylor would tell Kylie more than they wanted her to know right now. He reached over and took Taylor's arm. "I'll get you some ice cream."

He guided her through the door into the ice cream shop, and she didn't resist. Once the door shut behind them, he released her and scowled. "Look, if you have any hope of a future relationship with Annie and Kylie, you need to quit trying to cause trouble. Kylie is too young to understand all that's going on. If the DNA shows you're Sarah, Annie will handle it then. Until then, lay low and don't stir the pot."

"Or what?"

She wanted to push his buttons and was doing a good job of it. He softened his tone. "Waiting until we know the truth isn't much to ask. Annie hasn't said anything bad about you to Kylie. You want Annie to have to tell her how you lied to Mason? About how you used Kylie to get close to Annie? Do you want to destroy the love in that little girl's eyes?"

The anger faded from Taylor's face, and she shook her head. "I like Kylie." She stalked to the ice cream counter and ordered a chocolate twist cone. "Pay for my ice cream and leave me alone."

He was only too happy to defuse the situation with ice cream, but what about next time? This situation needed to be resolved as quickly as possible.

SEVEN

SUNSET TOUCHED THE VICTORIAN BUILDINGS IN DOWN-town Rock Harbor with a golden glow. Jon carried multiple shopping bags and boxes to Annie's vintage red-and-white Volkswagen truck. The musicians were out in full force at the festival. The twang of guitars and the rumble of drums lifted above the murmur of voices.

Annie was tired and ready to put her feet up. Navigating the tension between Jon and Kylie was exhausting. Kylie had begged to have the twins stay with her tonight, and Bree was going to grab their clothes and bring them out to the cottage. How would Jon handle three rambunctious children in the house? The awkwardness between Kylie and him showed no signs of resolving anytime soon, and she didn't know how to help that situation along. She'd never known her daughter to be so hostile to anyone, and she couldn't quite figure out what to do about it.

"You make a great pack mule," Annie told Jon as he stuck the packages into the back seat. "See you at the house in a few minutes." If Kylie hadn't been watching, she would have kissed him.

He hesitated, and his gaze dropped to her lips, so she knew he was thinking the same thing, but Kylie watched them like a hawk as she buckled herself into the back seat.

"Annie!"

She turned at the sound of Mason's voice. He strode across Houghton Street toward them, and her pulse quickened. Maybe he'd found Michelle Fraser.

Mason stopped in front of Jon and her. "Glad I caught you. We found out some interesting details about Michelle Fraser. You have a minute?"

"You didn't find her?"

He shook his head. "She fled an abusive marriage, and in the time she's been missing, she's had five different addresses—all at the same time."

"Wow, she must have money."

"Her ex is part of *the* Fraser family. The one that owns a number of iron mines in the area. The ex lives just outside Marquette."

It clicked for Annie, and she nodded. "That might explain why she didn't go to the police for protection. Maybe she tried and the Fraser money overruled her. What about her parents and siblings? Do they know where she is?"

"I left a message for her mother but haven't heard back from her yet."

Annie frowned. "So no one's looking for her. What if she's out there lost in the forest somewhere? The bloody sheets are worrisome."

"I agree. I think I'll pay the Frasers a little visit. See what the ex knows."

"You're up for reelection, Mason. You sure you want to stir a hornet's nest?"

"I've never let money or politics interfere with doing my job, and I'm not about to start now. Want to go with me? I plan to make that visit in the morning."

"Sure. What time?"

"About ten. I hear my niece and nephew are about to descend on your place. Bree said she'd take Kylie with the twins when she picks them up in the morning."

The relationships were more complicated than they sounded. Mason's wife, Hilary, was Bree's first husband's sister. The twins technically weren't related to Mason and Hilary since Kade was their father, but Bree's oldest, Davy, was their nephew, and they had never differentiated between the children. Bree's first husband, Rob, was Davy's father, but Rob's mother, Anu, claimed all of them as her grandchildren too. Kade had adopted Davy, and while Hilary had objected to the name change initially, she'd seen the writing on the wall and had accepted the situation. To complicate the complex family web even more, Hilary and Mason had adopted Kade's sister's child, Zoe, conceived when his sister was sixteen. So the families were tightly interwoven.

"I'll be ready. How'd it go with Taylor? Did she give you any more information?"

"Not really. I'd hoped she might know who Sean associated with, but she didn't seem to know that much about him. She'd only been around him a few times. I don't think she had anything to do with the murders." Mason sighed. "But I'll keep digging. So far his friends are coming up clean. Maybe he committed the murders by himself, but I'm not assuming anything."

"And what about the missing hikers? And Christopher Willis? Do you think Sean killed Willis, too, or had anything to do with the missing hikers?"

"There's no direct evidence one way or another. I don't have much to go on, but I'm still digging."

She watched Mason stride off toward the sheriff's office.

"What's that all about?" Jon asked.

Annie told him about the abandoned car and condo. "The forensics aren't back yet, but we also found a bloody sheet in the trunk. At the very least, we need to try to get a DNA sample from Michelle's parents to see if it's her blood. We couldn't find so much as a toothbrush at her condo."

"Strange circumstances. Has a search of the forest been conducted?"

"Just the general area around the abandoned car. There didn't seem to be footprints leading into the forest. It was more like the car was dumped there. If the blood is Michelle's, the first thing is to figure out where to search. I don't think we've found the right area yet."

"Lot of forest up there. It's going to be difficult to figure out where to look."

That was an understatement. For all they knew, someone had killed Michelle, dumped her body in Lake Superior, then driven her car out to the forest to get rid of it. That seemed a more likely scenario than Michelle herself driving it out and wandering off somewhere. "Hopefully we'll get some information tomorrow. The more we dig, the more convoluted this gets."

Jon glanced at Kylie in the back seat. "Mind if I bring Dad along for a while tonight?"

Annie tensed. "You're not going to tell him tonight, right?"

"Not yet. But he likes kids, and I thought I'd watch him interact with all of them. Maybe I can learn something that will help me."

She took his hand. "Don't rush it, Jon. It will come."

Her words sounded hollow, even to herself. Plain and simple, Kylie didn't like him. Annie didn't know what it would take to change her daughter's mind.

/ / /

Was this what married life would be like? Jon couldn't tear his gaze away from the homey dinnertime scene in Annie's living room in all its messy kids' glory.

The gluten-free pizza had been a big hit. Did kids always talk with their mouths full and consume that much food? Jon watched Annie navigate the questions and demands with a smile and a calmness he admired. He scurried around handing out juice boxes as the three children scarfed down a large pizza all by themselves. It was a good thing they'd ordered an extra one for the adults.

Martha Heinonen had driven his dad out to the cottage and had stayed with him. Jon couldn't decide if it was because she couldn't bear to leave Dad or if she was trying to be helpful. Either way, watching them interact with the children was eye-opening. His dad's gaze never strayed far from Martha's elegant figure, reminiscent of Queen Elizabeth when she was in her middle years.

After dinner, his dad challenged the kids to charades. Jon remembered playing it when he was a kid, and the children were eager to play. By the time the girls' team beat the boys, Kylie was sitting on his dad's lap, and Bree's twins were nestled on each side of him. Of course, they had probably seen him some since they lived next door to Martha's bed-and-breakfast.

What kind of magic had they used to reach the kids like that? Jon didn't understand it. Both his dad and Martha had a natural ease around them. They teased, laughed, and joked with the children almost like they were kids themselves. Jon didn't know if he could ever emulate it. Was it too late to learn?

Maybe he'd missed the window of opportunity when he was in his twenties.

While his dad turned on a new kids' movie, Jon moved to the kitchen to scoop up the paper plates with the remains of pizza and empty juice boxes. He shoved it all in the trash and bagged it up to take outside. Annie followed him into the attached garage, where he stashed the garbage bag in the can. The garage was as clean as the inside of the cottage. Neatly organized shelves held paint and cans of oil. Bikes hung on racks on the walls, and the painted concrete floor was swept clean. Annie seemed to do everything well. He didn't deserve her.

"You seem a little sad tonight, Jon. You okay?"

He put the lid back on the can and turned toward her. "I don't think I'm getting anywhere with Kylie. Did you see how she's already smitten with my dad? She flinches when I touch her shoulder, but she's in there sitting on his lap watching TV right this minute. If I tried that, she'd glare a warning at me to keep my distance. If I only knew the secret. I'm a failure as a father."

Annie moved closer and stepped into the circle of his arms. The sweet scent of her hair wafted to his nose, and he drew her close against his chest. He felt so right with her in his arms, complete and whole. His inability to get close to Kylie had to bother her as much as it did him. Would she turn away from him when she realized what a failure he was?

"You're not a failure unless you give up. And you're not a quitter. I know it's hard when she makes you feel rejected. Things will get easier the more you're together."

He pressed a kiss against her hair. "It hasn't gotten better so far. It took my dad and Martha about fifteen minutes."

"Kids are naturally drawn to the grandparent types. I think

it's that the older generation enjoys kids for who they are—they don't have to live up to anything special to feel appreciated. There's a relaxed attitude most of them have around children. They experience the wonder of childhood all over again through the kids' eyes. It's hard to explain, but watch them and notice how they enter into a kid's world without judgment."

"Parents have to correct and guide, right? So how do you do that and still have your kid love you?"

"Unconditional love," Annie said. "Kylie knows even when she messes up, I'll still love her. She knows the only reason I discipline her is to help her in the end. I've told her many times that it's my job to make sure she becomes a good human. One who cares about other people and has good character."

"Easier said than done."

Annie pulled away and stared up into his face with intent blue eyes. "You could take her on an outing, just the two of you."

"What kind of outing?"

"Maybe surfing. Or fishing. She's asked to go kayaking at Pictured Rocks for a long time, but it's a full day to do it, and I haven't had time. Maybe visit a copper mine. Or go out to Isle Royale. That's another place I've wanted to take her."

The thought of being all alone with Kylie and trying to keep her happy made his forehead bead with sweat. But he had to try, didn't he? Annie was right—he'd never quit anything in his life. He'd finished college and med school in record time. If he could do that, he could win the heart of his own daughter.

"Let me do some research and figure out what she might like. I'm starting to get to know her better. I'd like to think about it and pick the perfect day."

She hugged him again. "Just don't think everything rises or

falls on one day with her. I've had a lifetime with her. You missed out on so much, and it wasn't your fault."

"It was, though. I was young and stupid. It's hard to get past the mistakes I've made."

"I've made the same mistakes. We share the guilt equally."

Nice of her to say that, but Jon didn't buy it. He was older and should have manned up. Lack of communication had nearly destroyed them, but he was determined to make sure it didn't happen again. Not with Annie and not with Kylie.

EIGHT

ANNIE HADN'T BEEN TO MARQUETTE SINCE NATE HAD died. It was the largest city in the U.P., but Annie thought it still held on to its small U.P. flavor with its local shops and breweries. It was a major shipping port for iron ore, but she had always loved it for its outdoor beauty. She often brought Kylie here in the winter to marvel at the northern lights glimmering along Lake Superior. There were no northern lights out in June, but the luxurious green everywhere was nearly as compelling.

The Fraser home was a palatial marvel of turrets and curved windows that surveyed the blue waves of Superior. Eyeing it, Annie guessed it to be at least ten thousand square feet with a quarried stone exterior and a copper roof. The gardens were massive, and the fragrance of roses and lilies filled the air. There were no vehicles in the circle drive, but then the place boasted a four-stall garage with another detached building out back. The rumble of a riding mower came from somewhere in the area.

She got out of Mason's SUV and followed him to the double doors that appeared to be handcrafted walnut. "Did you call ahead?"

Mason reached for the doorbell. "Nope. Surprise questions are usually more truthful."

Before he could press the bell, the garage door to their left opened, and a red convertible backed out into the sunlight. Annie wasn't one to recognize hood ornaments, but it seemed expensive. The driver was a blond male in his thirties, and he frowned when he spotted them in front of the door. At first Annie thought he might drive away without speaking to them, but Mason lifted his hand and hurried down the steps to block the guy's drive with his burly form.

The man's scowl deepened, but he put the car in Park and leaned his elbow on the window opening. "Sheriff Kaleva, isn't it? What can I help you with?" His congenial tone was at odds with the caution in his hazel eyes.

He had the chiseled good looks of a male model or a movie star, and Annie didn't see a wedding ring on his tanned left hand. His gaze sharpened as it settled on her, and a shiver went down her back at his predatory smile. She'd run into her fair share of male attention, and she was immune to his type. But she could see where he likely succeeded when he set his mind on pursuit of a woman.

Mason glanced at Annie and nodded for her to take the lead. "I'm LEO Pederson." She stepped closer to read the man's expression. "You're Brandon Fraser?"

"Obviously."

"We're investigating an abandoned car in the Kitchigami Wilderness Preserve. It's a BMW registered to your wife, Michelle Fraser."

"In the Ottawa National Forest? That's a ways from here." A slight twitch and widening of his eyelids were the only indication he gave of surprise. "We're separated."

"Not divorced?"

"She disappeared and couldn't be served with papers. I decided to let it ride until she showed up again."

"Seems generous of you. Was there ill will between the two of you?"

He fixed her with a stare. "There usually is when people get a divorce."

"When did she disappear?"

"She left me a year ago." His clipped voice held forced boredom.

"Have you heard from her at all during that time?"

"If I had, I'd be divorced by now."

Annie made a mental note to ask Mason to check with Marquette police about any domestic incidents. There was a barely restrained fury and contempt in his manner that put her back up. The whole thing puzzled her.

"Any idea why she would rent a condo and never live in it?" Mason asked.

Brandon flinched. "She wasted money like that? Typical Michelle. No thought for how hard I work. She has never learned the value of a dollar. Nice cars, designer clothes, expensive shoes—that's all she has ever wanted."

He spoke of her in the present tense, which Annie took as a positive sign that Michelle might still be alive. "What about her relationship with her parents, siblings?"

"Her mom is still alive, and she gets along fine with Michelle. Too well. She's always babied her. Her dad died in a mining accident, and she doesn't have any siblings. That's how we met seven years ago. I went to her house to tell her mother about Adam's death. Michelle was eighteen, and I was twenty-one, but she acted so responsible and mature. At least at first. It wasn't until we were married that I realized she only married me for my money."

Annie didn't want to assume anything since this was Brandon's version of the truth. "Could we get her mother's address?" Mason had already tracked down her mom, but she wanted to see how much Brandon would cooperate.

He snatched his phone from the car's console and swiped through it. "I'll text you the info if you give me your number."

Annie rattled off her phone number, and he punched it into his phone. Moments later, her message alert dinged. "Got it, thanks."

She spared a glance at the entry. The woman lived in Munising near Pictured Rocks. They could make a run over that way. They could all go kayaking after she spoke with Michelle's mom. Maybe it would be some bonding time with Jon and their daughter.

She dragged her thoughts back to the man in front of her. "What about your family? Has anyone heard from Michelle? A sister, your mom, her best friend?"

"She didn't get along with my family, and she's always been a loner. We had some friend couples, but she didn't go out to coffee or lunch with anyone special that I know of."

His gaze cut away, and she immediately knew he was lying. Why would he want her to think Michelle had no friends? Would a friend contradict his version of events? Maybe Michelle's mother would know.

She noticed a flicker of movement and saw a woman at an upstairs window. The woman disappeared before Annie could make eye contact.

She glanced at Mason to see if he had any other questions,

and he gave a slight shake of his head. She took a step back. "Thank you for your time. If you think of anything else, you have my number."

It was only after his car vanished through the gate that she realized he hadn't asked if they'd found any evidence that Michelle might be hurt. Did he simply not care, or did he know more than he let on?

/ / /

Imprisoned for thirty-six hours.

The sunshine slanted through the dirty cabin windows, and Michelle sat up with a slightly clearer head. She'd awakened on Wednesday night, and it was now Friday morning. How long would it be before she lost track of time? The pain had kept her tied to the bed most of yesterday, but she had to move past it somehow. The packages of jerky the man had left pushed away her hunger pangs for a while, and she tried to conserve them since she didn't know how long they would need to last.

The man hadn't returned, and she had three jerky sticks left along with two bottles of water. What happened if he didn't come back? What if he decided to let her die out here by herself?

And why had he even taken her? He mentioned her belongings, but she had nothing of real value.

She'd prayed for deliverance, but sometimes God expected action too. She couldn't lie here on this cot and expect help to come to her. The past year of hiding from her husband had taught her that she was stronger than she knew and that she had the courage to take the next unknown step.

She had to figure out a way to make a crutch. This area was

too vast and wild to be able to crawl out, especially when she had no idea where the man had taken her. Without a compass or anything to guide her, she could wander in the wrong direction too. She'd peered out the window a couple of times yesterday, but the thick forest prevented her from seeing any kind of landmark that might indicate her location. She'd have only the sun to guide her, and it wouldn't tell her which way to go to find civilization.

But she couldn't lie here and wait to discover her fate.

There was nothing inside the cabin to use as a crutch. If she could get out into the forest, maybe she could find a tree branch that would work. And a clearing where she could find a landmark.

She'd tried the door countless times without success. And without being able to stand, she couldn't crawl out the window. This morning she felt stronger, though. Maybe she had the upper body strength to pull herself up the wall and through the window.

Gritting her teeth from the pain in her leg, she slid down to the floor and crawled to the window a few feet away from her cot. She managed to get onto her good knee and reached for the windowsill above her head. Her fingers just grazed it, and she grabbed hold to pull herself up. For a moment she thought it might work, but the wood gave way under her fingertips, and the rotted windowsill came away in her hands. She fell back and wrenched her broken leg as her knee twisted.

The pain pulsed up her leg to her knee, and she groaned as she bit back a scream. She tasted blood and realized she'd bitten her tongue. She lay on the floor inhaling the stench of small rodents and dirt until the agony ebbed. Once she could think past the pain, she sat up and looked around.

Now what? Her legs stretched out toward the cot, and she

eyed it. What if she could move it under the window? Sitting on it on her knee might let her crawl through the window. She moved around until she was sitting with her feet under the head of the bed. She gripped the cold metal with both hands and drew it toward her. The cot legs scraped across the pine floor. She managed to move it toward her by six inches.

This might actually work. She scooted toward the window on her behind and tried again. A few inches at a time, she drew the cot with her toward the window until the length of it was centered under the window. It was still a few feet from the wall, so she maneuvered herself along the wall and pulled it closer to the window. She had to stop a foot out from the wall so she had room to get out from behind the cot.

She scooted out until she was at the head of the bed again, but her strength was gone, and she had to lie on the floor until her panting eased and she didn't feel so shaky and spent.

The sunbeams were at a different angle, and she thought it must be close to noon by now. The man had come in the night last time, and she suspected he'd continue that if he even came again. He wouldn't want her to see his face. So she had time to rest and regain her strength. She crawled to her provisions and consumed half a bottle of water and one stick of jerky.

Her progress lifted her spirits, and for the first time, she thought she might get out of here. She returned to the side of the cot and heaved herself back onto it. Her lids were heavy, so she closed them for a few minutes to rest. Drifting off to sleep wasn't an option, though, not when time was ticking away. Her eyes popped back open, and she sat up.

She got on her good knee again and winced at the tweak of pain. It was the wrong angle for her leg, too, and the pain escalated quickly, but the height now was perfect for her to be able to struggle with raising the window. Years of dirt and grime made it sticky, and she was sweating with exertion and pain by the time she raised it a few inches.

She got her fingertips under the edge of the window and managed to force it open. She put her arms all the way through to the outside of the cabin and pulled her body up onto the ledge. She teetered on it with her head and shoulders out into the wind and her legs still in the cabin. If she fell through onto the ground, she'd never be able to get back inside if she failed to find help.

If she went out there, she had to be prepared to stay there, and the fall might do more damage. Tears burned her eyes, but she wiggled back inside and onto the cot.

She'd have to prepare to be on her own first. That included figuring out a way to take what little food and water she had. Her escape wasn't something she could do on a whim.

NINE

KYLIE SAT ON THE DUNSTANS' PIER BEHIND THE CABIN with her legs dangling above the blue waters of Lake Superior. She had been quiet and standoffish since Annie dropped her off on her way to Mason's office this morning, and Jon wasn't sure how to bring a smile to those blue eyes, so like Annie's.

His dad approached with two fishing poles, and his gaze slipped past Jon to Kylie out on the pier. "I thought a little fishing might cheer up her gloomies. Fishing always fixed yours."

Gloomies was a word his dad had used ever since Jon could remember. It aptly described Kylie's expression and Jon's own state of mind. Some mountains seemed insurmountable, and Kylie's disdain was one of those.

Jon pulled a hand-tied fly out of his pocket. "I thought I'd see if she wanted to try this."

"You still have your touch. Good fly."

"I made it this morning. I wanted to show her how to tie them, but she wouldn't look at me so I didn't ask."

"You have to ignore a kid's bad humor and go for the jugular with something interesting. Like fly-fishing." His dad took the fly and tucked it into the pocket of his chambray shirt. "Come with me. I'll show you how it's done."

Not that it would do Jon any good. He already knew Kylie liked his dad and Martha. But he bit back his objections and grabbed a chair to follow his dad out onto the pier.

Kylie shot a glance their way before going back to watching the water.

Jon set down the chair for his dad, who awkwardly lowered himself onto it. He wanted to say something to Kylie, but he didn't want to be humiliated in front of his father, so he settled on the pier a few feet away so he didn't crowd her.

"What are you looking at out there? Mermaids?"

She tipped up her chin. "Mermaids live in the ocean, not Lake Superior."

"I don't know. I've always thought the Bete Grise Beach maiden was a mermaid." The beach wasn't far, farther on up the Keweenaw Peninsula. He could take her up there sometime.

She turned her attention to Jon. "What maiden?"

"According to legend, she was an Ojibwa maiden who loved a warrior across the Gitche Gumee, but they were never able to marry. When she wanted to connect to him, she'd walk the sand at the beach and sing to him. After she was gone, supposedly you can rotate your hand on the sand and hear her singing to her lost love."

"Have you ever heard the singing sand?"

"She doesn't like me." Her gaze said she understood that sentiment, and he suppressed a grin. "I can take you up there sometime."

"Maybe. But I'd like to see the ocean."

Jon made a mental note of her comment. Maybe they could all go to Pelican Harbor or Hope Beach one day soon. He could get her scuba lessons when she turned ten.

Jon's dad held out a fishing pole. "Let's see if the fish are biting."

She brightened and took the pole. "I don't know why Mom had to leave me here. I could have gone with her or to Anu's when Bree had to conduct a search."

Jon bit back the explanation Annie had already tried. Mason was on official sheriff business. A little girl had no business going along on something like that. And she already knew Bree hadn't gotten called out on an emergency search.

"What kind of fish do you like to catch?" his dad asked.

Kylie examined her pole. "The bass are jumping. I saw a couple of them."

"I've got the perfect fly." The older man handed her the fly Jon had tied.

She examined it, then attached it to her pole. "Did you tie it?"

"Jon did. He started making flies when he was your age."

Jon thought he saw a hint of respect in her eyes when she glanced his way. He smiled at her, but she looked away. So much for that.

"I could teach you," he said.

She pressed her lips together. "Not today." She tossed her line in the water, and the red-and-white bobber bounced in the waves twenty feet away.

His phone rang, and he glanced at it. A call from the office manager back home was unusual enough that he rose and walked toward shore to talk. "Good morning, Norman. How's it going in Rochester?"

"Sorry to bother you, but we've got a problem you should know about." Norman had been part of the orthopedic practice since the beginning, and he believed in speaking his mind.

The business wouldn't have been so successful without his management.

"Okay." Jon glanced back toward Kylie and his dad, but they were working on getting a bass to shore. "What's up?"

"Olivia has been arrested for murder."

"What? No, that can't be."

Olivia Thompson was the last person Jon would have guessed would do something like that. In her fifties with a husband and a gaggle of grandchildren, she was a patient favorite. She'd been the one who first invited him to be part of the practice.

"She was caught on video giving a bone cancer patient a fatal injection. When she was arrested, she claimed she wanted to spare him pain."

Jon sank onto a tree stump. "I can't wrap my head around it."

"The news will be all over the papers tomorrow. I'm not sure the practice will survive. The other two partners are already distancing themselves, and the police are all over the place combing through records. Brace yourself, Jon. The police may show up with questions for you as well. You worked closely with Olivia."

Norman didn't have to say what this meant. The funds Jon had invested in the practice were likely gone. This kind of scandal would rock the community. No one would trust their practice. They would all be guilty by association.

He thanked Norman for the call and hung up. If the practice up in Houghton offered him a spot, he might have to turn it down.

/ / /

Annie buckled her seat belt and scrolled through her phone as Mason drove his SUV out the gates of the property. No missed calls, so at least Jon wasn't having too much trouble with Kylie. She dropped it back onto the console. "What did you make of Fraser?" she asked Mason.

"He's lying about something. The question is what."

"I think he was definitely lying about her having no friends. He glanced away when he said it. And there was a woman at an upstairs window watching him talk to us."

"We'll see if he filed a missing person's report or if there's any record of a domestic violence incident."

"What if we wait until he leaves and go back? Maybe we can find out more from whoever that woman was."

"I didn't see her, but I'm game." He pulled his SUV into a parking place along the tree-lined street and glanced in the rear-view mirror. "There he goes now."

She twisted in her seat and saw his sports car speeding away in the opposite direction. "I thought he might hang around and warn whoever was there."

Mason pulled onto the street and did a U-turn. "He still might have called or texted with a warning. She might not talk to us."

"Maybe." Annie wasn't ready to give up yet. She smelled something very off about Brandon Fraser. "We could talk to neighbors too. See if they know anything."

"Good idea." He returned to the Fraser mansion, but the gate was locked this time. They'd evidently arrived after Brandon had opened it for his departure.

Mason ran his window down and pressed the buzzer. There was no answer at first, so he pressed it again.

A woman's voice came over the speaker. "Who is it?"

"Sheriff Mason Kaleva. We wanted to ask some questions about Michelle Fraser."

"You already talked to my brother, and he'll kill me if I speak to you."

Annie exchanged a glance with Mason before leaning over to answer in the speaker. "Were you watching from upstairs? We won't tell him you spoke to us."

"I can't take the chance. Go talk to some neighbors. They might tell you something."

"Which neighbor?" Mason asked.

Only silence followed, and even though he pressed the button again, the woman didn't answer. "Guess that's all we're getting. Any idea which neighbor to go to first?"

"The closest place is down the street on the corner," Annie said.

Mason nodded and turned around to go back. She pointed out the house as they approached. It wasn't as large as the mining magnate's place, but it was plenty grand enough for the neighborhood.

Mason pulled into the drive, and they got out. This place wasn't gated, and they approached the front door to the hum of a vacuum from inside the house somewhere. Annie pressed the doorbell, but the vacuum continued to rumble. She pounded her fist on the door, and the noise stopped.

A fresh-faced woman in her twenties with a baby on her hip dressed in pink opened the door. A red headband held back the woman's tight black curls, and her dark eyes widened when she saw Mason's badge. "Can I help y'all?" Her southern accent was one that wasn't heard often in Yooperland.

"Sheriff Mason Kaleva, ma'am, from over in Rock Harbor. Sorry to take you away from your cleaning, but I had a few questions about your neighbors."

She shifted the baby to her other arm. "My neighbors?" Her glance went to the house across the street.

"The Frasers. We're looking for Michelle Fraser."

She nodded. "Come on in. There's lots to say about sweet Michelle."

Annie exhaled. This must be who Fraser's sister wanted them to talk to.

The woman swung the door open and led them past a toy-strewn hall into the living room, where she plopped the baby down by the vacuum. "I'm Brayonna Day."

"Your baby is darling." Annie wanted to scoop up the pudgy cutie, but some people were careful about letting others touch their babies.

Brayonna picked up the baby and deposited her in Annie's arms. "You can hold her. Her name is Jesalynn. She's six months old."

It had been a while since Annie had held a baby. For just a second she imagined carrying Jon's baby again with him by her side. She shook the thought away. There was a lot to resolve before she could let herself dream of a future. She inhaled the sweet scent of infant and rocked little Jesalynn in her arms in a soothing motion.

"Have you found Michelle's body?" Brayonna asked. "When she quit answering her phone, I was sure Brandon killed her."

Annie's pulse jumped. "No, we haven't. Why do you think she's been the victim of foul play?"

"He was always hitting her in places where others couldn't see. She showed me bruises. She left him a year ago, and we were supposed to meet for lunch. I was going to help her find a safe place, but she didn't show up. And she never answered her phone again, not in all this time. What else could it be? I'm her best friend. She wouldn't disappear without telling me."

"Did you know she had rented a condo at Whisper Creek in Rock Harbor?" Annie asked.

Brayonna frowned. "Where's Rock Harbor? I'm not familiar with it."

"West of here, out near Ontonagon."

"Near the Porkies. That makes sense. Michelle started working on her wildlife biology degree against Brandon's wishes about a year before she went missing. Her passion is the big cats—mountain lions."

The baby began to fuss, so Annie handed her back to her mother. "So she didn't tell you she was leaving the area?"

"No, but I knew she needed to get away before Brandon found her."

"Did he threaten her before he hurt her?"

"He'd been stalking her. Two weeks after she left him, he broke into her hotel and left a dead rat with a note that read: *You're next.* She recognized his handwriting, so she knew it was him."

Annie shuddered. Creepy. "Did she file a police report?"

"No, she wanted to get away, and she'd have to give an address to the police. She didn't want Brandon to find out where she was, and he knows people in high places."

"Did she have any contacts for women's shelters or anyone who might have helped her find the place over in Rock Harbor?"

"I'd given her the card of a shelter in Houghton. Wait a second, I have another card." She sprang up from the sofa and rummaged in a drawer in the desk against the back wall. "Here it is." She handed it to Annie.

Annie glanced at it but didn't recognize the name. "Thank you. Did you file a missing person's report when you didn't hear from her?"

Brayonna shook her head. "I thought for sure she was dead anyway, and with a baby to care for, I didn't want to draw Brandon's attention."

Mason's phone sounded with a message, and he glanced at it. "It doesn't appear her husband filed a missing person's report, and there were no reports of any domestic disturbances at their home."

"She didn't want to escalate things, and it doesn't surprise me that he didn't file a report. Not after that knifing."

Annie leaned forward. "Knifing?"

Brayonna shifted the baby on her lap. "Michelle tried to downplay it on the phone. He cut her with a knife. I think her mom might know more."

Fraser just went to the top of her suspect list. Annie passed along her card. "If you think of anything else, please give me a call."

A dead rat and a knife. Annie would have run too.

TEN

JON SAT IN THE MARINA PARKING LOT AND STARED AT his phone's screen. The amount in his bank account didn't change no matter how long he stared. Annie had picked up Kylie, who at least was jubilant about the fish she'd caught. He should get out of his car and go inside, but his heart wasn't in trying to maintain the facade that everything was fine when it wasn't.

He'd been counting on the money from the sale of his partnership in the practice to make a fresh start here. He'd wanted to buy the three of them a beautiful new home on the water. He wanted to get Annie a new truck, one that could take the beating these roads dished out. A gorgeous ring had caught his eye in a Houghton jewelry store, too, and he wanted to put it on her finger when the time was right. There were so many things he wanted to give her, to provide for them in the future. He'd make a good income as a hospital surgeon, but it wasn't what he'd wanted to do with his life.

And what if the police showed up now after he'd finally gotten his name cleared from the murder some nine years ago? He didn't want to go back into that fog of suspicion.

He glanced at the time on his phone. It was late, after six. He got out and shut the door to his Jag, then stood staring down at it. He could sell it. He owned it free and clear. It should bring in ninety thousand. He had some equity in his place back in Rochester, but it probably wasn't more than fifty thousand. A hundred forty thousand would buy a place here outright. Maybe not the grand home he'd wanted, but he could get a mortgage after he held his job for two years.

It wasn't the end of the world—it only felt like it.

As he approached Annie's cottage, he heard Kylie laughing and spotted her on a tire swing attached to a large oak tree. Her blonde hair streamed behind her as Annie pushed her higher and higher. Pure joy lit Kylie's face as the puppy tried to pounce on her feet with every swoop back to earth. Would she ever be that carefree with him, or would they have to go forward with her guard constantly up around him?

He'd messed up so many things. If only he'd handled things differently back then. If only he'd never left. He'd let pride and ambition get in the way of what really mattered. And maybe he was on the cusp of doing it again. He needed to be careful, to pay attention to what was important instead of what screamed for attention.

Kylie spotted him, and the glee ebbed from her face. She dragged her bare feet in the dirt until she came to a stop. Annie turned and her smile broadened.

She walked toward him. "There you are. I was beginning to give you up for lost."

Milo barked and ran to greet him too. Jon knelt and let the puppy sniff his fingers. "Good boy."

He rose as Annie stopped in front of him. His hands moved toward her, but he saw the warning in her blue eyes and let his arms drop back to his sides. Kylie hated any display of affection between them, but he wasn't sure how long he could go on hiding his feelings when she was around.

"Sorry I was late." For a moment he was tempted not to tell her what had happened, but that was how he'd ruined things nine years ago. No more secrets, no more lies. "I had a disturbing phone call." He told her what had happened with Olivia, and dismay dropped onto her expression.

"They can't think you would have been doing that too."

He shrugged. "I'd like to think not, but Norman said the cops might show up with questions. And my practice is dead there, Annie. Kaput. My investment is gone."

She took his arm. "I know it's a blow, Jon, but it's only money. You'll hear from the practice in Houghton and can start over. It's not like you'll be destitute. You'll still be making an excellent salary."

"You're right, but it's upended everything I thought was going to happen. I've always been a planner, Annie. I don't do well with seat-of-the-pants life changes."

She slipped her arm around his waist, then jabbed him in the side with her elbow. "You're not telling me anything I don't know. Maybe God is teaching you about trust. You don't have to plan out everything. Leave some room for surprises. This could be a blessing in disguise."

He didn't see how, but it wasn't worth arguing about. "Anything I can do to help with dinner?"

"You can cook the fish and the corn. I've got the grill hot and ready on the deck. The salad is ready, and I made cherry cobbler for dessert with that almond flour you got. I think it came out great."

"Sounds delicious." He smiled at his daughter. "Are we eating the fish you caught, Kylie? That one was a beauty."

The edges of her lips lifted, and she nodded. "Mommy wanted to mount it, but I wanted to eat it. Is your dad with you?"

He caught the hopeful note in her voice. "Sorry, he was tired so I took him back to the Blue Bonnet. He told me to invite you to go agate hunting tomorrow if you didn't have anything else to do, though."

"Maybe not tomorrow," Annie said. "What if we take a trip to Munising together? I have some business there, and I thought maybe we could go kayaking at Pictured Rocks."

"That sound good, Kylie?" Jon asked.

She nodded and ran off toward the house. She left too quickly for Jon to decipher her expression.

"I think you're making headway."

He wanted to tell Annie she was dreaming, but he didn't want to spoil the evening. It all felt off-kilter to him, and he didn't know if anything could right it.

/ / /

Munising was small but mighty with natural beauty. It served as the gateway to Pictured Rocks National Lakeshore, and Annie had spent many summers exploring the waterfalls and lakeshore with her family. Her dad had grown up here, and he knew every lane and pond in the county. She'd hoped to give Kylie the same sense of belonging Annie had felt here, but life was always so busy that she hadn't brought her over often.

It was nine o'clock when she drove her old red-and-white Volkswagen truck past the brick storefronts to Elm Avenue. "There it is." She pointed out a 1920s white two-story with a wraparound porch.

The manicured yard and garden added to its charm, and the gray paint on the steps and porch felt welcoming. She parked in the drive and rolled down her window. "Wait here. I won't be long."

Glued to her iPad game, Kylie nodded. Jon took out his phone. "Take your time."

The porch seemed freshly painted and baskets of geraniums swung in the breeze from the ceiling. Even the porch swing was just like her grandma's. Annie didn't have to ring the bell because a woman spotted her through the screen door.

"Coming," she called.

The woman had one of those faces that made you feel accepted immediately. Tiny lines around her brown eyes crinkled when she smiled and stepped out onto the porch. Her salt-and-pepper hair was in a casual, windblown cut that ended at her round chin.

A Yorkie trotted out with her, and the woman scooped her up. She spotted Kylie and Jon sitting in the truck, and her expression softened even more. "What can I do for you?"

"Are you Mary Berlin?"

"Yes."

"I'm law enforcement ranger Annie Pederson from over near Rock Harbor. I'm the one who found your daughter's car in the forest. I need to ask you a few questions."

Mary's smile faltered. "You found Michelle?"

"I'm sorry, but no, we haven't. Her case is peculiar, and I hoped you might shed some light on her activities. When did you see her last?"

Mary gestured to the wicker chairs on the porch before she dropped into one with her dog on her lap. "A little over a year ago. She brought me flowers for my garden for Mother's Day and told me she was planning to leave Brandon. I told her it was about time."

Annie settled in the other chair. "You didn't like Brandon?"

"He was very controlling when they were dating. Always wanting to know where she was if she was a few minutes late, and he even checked her text messages. It got worse after the wedding until she felt like she could hardly go to the grocery store without questions. That was bad enough, but when she showed up here with bruises on her stomach from his fists, that was the last straw. I begged her to leave him before he killed her. But she was afraid he'd come after her."

"Did she call you before she left him?"

"Yes, of course. She called and told me she'd found a women's shelter that would help her. She said she'd try to get in touch, but that she'd been told it was better to cut off contact with family for a few weeks so Brandon couldn't find her."

"What triggered her leaving then?"

"He cut her with a knife the night before. She told me she kept the sheet with all her blood on it. And she took a picture of it."

That explained the bloody sheet. "When did you start to worry after not hearing from her?"

Mary soothed the squirming dog with a rub on the ears. "While I haven't seen her in a year, she's called regularly on a burner phone, just to reassure me that Brandon hadn't found her. But a week ago, she left the shelter and decided she was ready to enter normal life again. She called the day she left, but I haven't heard from her since. After three days had passed, I was getting antsy. By yesterday, I was terrified. I returned the call from that nice Sheriff Kaleva, but he said there was no sign of her."

"We discovered Michelle had rented a condo in Rock Harbor,

but she never lived there. She'd left her BMW in the garage for about a year too."

"She hated that car. Brandon gave it to her, and she suspected he planted a tracking device on it."

Annie leaned forward. "Why did she think it was bugged?"

"He made a few comments about places she'd been. She didn't see how he could know unless there was something on the car."

"Did she have it checked?"

Mary shook her head. "Michelle didn't know who to ask for help. She examined it but never found anything."

"The tracker could have been on her phone too."

"I guess that's true. She felt like the car was a chain around her neck. Brandon gave her plenty of things but never the love and acceptance she wanted."

Annie remembered Brandon's comment about Michelle liking to shop. "Did she spend a lot of money?"

Mary huffed and shook her head again. "She despised spending any of his money. She only spent the money she earned working at the coffee shop. Brandon hated her being a barista. He thought it reflected poorly on him that his wife was working a menial job, but Michelle loved it. She was attending classes at Marquette University part time and was working two days a week."

"Where did she work?"

"Front Street Brew."

Annie had been to the coffee shop a few times. Had she ever met Michelle? "Do you have a picture of her?"

Mary dug in the pocket of her red capris and pulled out her phone. "Sure." She swiped through her pictures and turned her phone around to show Annie. "This was the last time I saw her."

Annie studied the smiling young woman in the selfie with Mary. She resembled her mom with the same warm brown eyes. Her brown hair lay in a smooth curtain on her shoulders. "She's beautiful."

"Inside and out."

"Would you send me that picture? And did she happen to send you a picture of the injury?"

Mary nodded. "I'll send that one too. What's your number?"

Annie rattled it off, and Mary texted over the pictures. Annie heard them arrive. "What about other enemies? Did she have any conflict with people at work or school?"

Mary's brow wrinkled as she thought. "There was a guy at school who had a crush on her. Michelle laughed it off, but I was never sure it was as innocent as Michelle thought. The guy was always showing up places, like maybe he'd been following her. I didn't like it."

"What was his name?"

"Chad Smith. I have a picture Michelle sent me from a school outing to the forest." Mary scrolled through her pics again. "This is Chad."

In his midtwenties, the man wore a camo jacket and stood next to Michelle with his arm extended for the selfie. His thatch of brown hair was unruly and in need of a trim.

"I'll send this to you too," Mary said. "Oh, and her best friend was a neighbor—Brayonna Day."

Annie handed over her card. "Thanks, we've spoken with Brayonna. She said Michelle never called after she didn't show up to lunch a year ago. Do you know why she didn't contact her best friend?"

"The shelter told her she'd be putting people in danger. If

Brandon came after them to try to get them to spill her whereabouts, he might hurt them."

"But she told you."

"She didn't. Just that she was in a shelter and safe. I didn't know where."

That made sense. "Please call if you think of anything else. I'll let you know if we find any more information about your daughter."

The last photo arrived on her phone. She forwarded all the photos to Mason with a short description of what she'd learned. Annie didn't like the proprietorial expression in Chad's sidelong gaze at Michelle. He was someone to check out.

ELEVEN

PICTURED ROCKS NATIONAL LAKESHORE WAS ONE THE U.P.'s wonders, but Lake Superior was never to be trusted. Kayaking in its frigid waters always required being alert and prepared. The tour company Jon had booked would provide whistles, spray skirts, and flotation devices, but he had packed wet suits just in case as well as bottles of water for all of them.

The tandem sea kayaks meant one of them would need to travel with another kayaker, so he volunteered to be odd man out so Kylie could be with her mother. He was paired with a woman in her sixties, and he suspected he'd be the one doing most of the work so he had her sit in the bow. As they started off, he discovered she was a surprisingly strong paddler.

The sun shimmered on the blue water, and clouds drifted overhead. God had provided perfect weather. Jon tried to paddle close enough to Annie and Kylie to be able to converse with them. With Kylie in the bow, Annie did most of the work since the little girl was busy taking pictures of birds and the amazing scenery of Pictured Rocks.

Sweat beaded his forehead from the warm sun on his wet suit, and he began to rethink the decision to wear them. The scent of the water made him wish he could plunge into the cold depths.

Kylie leaned over the kayak and splashed her head. She shook her wet hair like a dog, and he laughed, so she did it again.

"Come closer and splash me with that nice, cold water," he called.

Her smile seemed genuine, and she smacked the surface with her paddle to try to hit him with the water. He smacked his, too, and managed to send a stream shooting at her arm. She shrieked when the cold hit her, but it was a happy sound.

"No fair," she called. "You're stronger."

He paused and looked out over the blue water. "Right through here there have been multiple sightings of *Mishipeshu*."

"I heard about it in school," Kylie said. "That's the big lizard fish. Pressie."

"Two steamer crews in 1890 reported seeing it. Supposedly it's seventy-five feet or more long and has scales on its tail. Its panther-like head is topped with copper horns."

Her blue eyes huge, Kylie nodded. "And a long, greenish-black neck."

It might be best to change the subject. He pointed to the shore with his paddle. "Bridalveil Falls."

She turned to admire the waterfall cascading down the colorful rocks. This area of the North Woods held the magic of sandstone cliffs, beaches, and wild shoreline, and there was no more iconic spot than the falls. In a few more weeks the water flow would slow to a trickle, but the recent rain filled the falls to a roaring beauty. It plunged seventy feet over colorful sandstone cliffs into the cold waters of Superior.

Her mouth dropped open. Kylie sat still in the bow of the kayak as they paddled past.

It was turning out to be a great day. Maybe he'd bring Annie back here once he had that ring in his pocket. He could propose right here when things started to go right with Kylie. A guy could dream, right?

A scream echoed over the water, and he jerked around to see Kylie standing up in the kayak. She began to peel off her flotation device. He spotted a writhing snake drop into the water as she flung away her PFD.

"It was biting me!" She flailed her arms. "It was Pressie, and it bit me!"

"Kylie, sit down!" he yelled. There were no poisonous snakes in the cold U.P., so it couldn't hurt her. He probably shouldn't have been talking about the mythical creature in the lake.

Annie reached out her arms toward her daughter as Kylie pirouetted on the seat, and in the next moment, she plummeted toward the water. A sickening *thud* sounded as Kylie's head hit the side of the kayak and her eyes closed. She disappeared into the water without another sound.

Jon was on his feet and dove overboard in a flash. The cold water hit him like a blow, even with his wet suit on. He treaded water while he kicked off his shoes, then dove down to find his daughter. She was floating lifelessly in the water under the kayak with her head occasionally hitting the hull. He grabbed her arm and pulled her out from under it and then kicked up toward the sunshine.

When his head broke the surface, he spotted Annie in the water on the other side of the group of kayakers. The guide was in the water as well, and neither of them saw that he'd found her.

"I've got her!"

He didn't wait for them to come his way but towed the little girl toward the beach. It was the longest two hundred yards he'd ever experienced as he kept looking anxiously to see if Kylie was breathing. He had to get her to shore. CPR couldn't be performed out here if she needed it, and so far, he'd detected no rising and falling of her chest. Her lashes rested on her cheeks, and she was pale and blue.

As he swam he prayed for her to open her eyes and yell at him. For her to try to jerk away. He'd even take some mean words right about now. Annie couldn't lose her daughter. Not now, not like this, not ever. She'd been through so much. And *he* couldn't bear to lose Kylie when he'd just started getting to know and love her. And he did love her. Prickly or not, she was his daughter. She'd come to love him if the Lord gave them time together.

His knees hit sand, and he struggled up to his feet, then pulled her into his arms. The waves hit his legs, and he nearly fell, but he staggered on to drop onto the beach with his daughter.

She wasn't breathing. He grabbed a nearby piece of driftwood and draped her over it on her stomach. He had to get the water from her lungs before he tried CPR.

"Come on, honey, stay with me," he begged.

Was it too late? It couldn't be. This beautiful day couldn't end this way. She had to live.

/ / /

Kylie lay limp on the sand at Mosquito Beach with Jon on his knees beside her. Annie was immobile, her heart nearly pounding out of her chest. Her breathing labored, she couldn't think or force her frozen limbs to move.

Please, God, don't let my baby girl die.

He rolled Kylie over a nearby log and water ran out of her

mouth. "That's it, honey. Get it all out." He rolled her onto the sand again and gestured for Annie to come help. "I'll do chest compressions, and you breathe for her. You know CPR, right?"

She nodded, but in that moment, she couldn't remember when she'd last had to perform it. Surely Kylie was breathing. She had to be breathing. But Annie saw and heard no signs of air from her daughter. This couldn't be happening. She couldn't lose Kylie.

She knelt on the other side of her daughter and tipped her head back to begin CPR. She clamped Kylie's nose shut with one hand and administered two breaths, then waited for Jon to do the compressions.

"Wake up, Kylie, open your eyes," she whispered as she leaned over her daughter's face.

She blew into Kylie's mouth and watched her chest rise. Again. *Breathe, Bug, breathe.*

Jon, his face intent and focused, started compressions again. On the third compression, Kylie gasped. Jon quickly rolled her to her side again, and more water ran from her mouth and nose. She began to cough and cry.

Tears filled Annie's eyes, and she patted Kylie's back. "Cough it up, honey. You're okay. We're on the beach." She was barely aware of the others on the tour coming ashore and the guide rushing to help them.

"I'm a doctor—I've got her," Jon told the guide, who tried to make him move away.

The guide nodded and corralled the rest of the onlookers away from the scene. "Everyone, give them some space. I'll unpack lunch now. Come with me." He looked back at them. "It was a garter snake. I turned it loose. It won't bother her again."

The sounds of the other people faded as Annie helped Kylie

sit up. The more she coughed, the more color came back to her pale cheeks. Her blonde hair hung in wet strings around her face, and she shivered. Her teeth chattered, and her lips were nearly as blue as the sky.

"Let's get that wet suit off and get her dry." Jon lowered the zipper and began to peel the neoprene from Kylie's shoulders.

Annie moved to help. The numbness encasing her began to fade, and she tugged the wet suit from Kylie's waist and down off her legs until she was sitting on the sand in her swimsuit. She glanced around for a towel, and Jon had already retrieved one from another kayaker.

He rubbed Kylie briskly until her skin started to turn pink. The action brought more color to the little girl's face, and the blue began to fade from her lips.

Jon stopped when he reached her neck. He peered closer at the marks on her clavicle. "There's where the snake bit her."

Kylie clasped herself and shuddered. "I told you it was a snake!" She cried again—huge, gulping sobs—and she threw herself against Annie.

Annie clasped Kylie's shivering form and pulled her onto her lap. "It's okay, honey. I've got you. You're going to be just fine."

Thanks to Jon.

Her gaze locked with his, and she tried to signal her love and gratitude to him with her eyes. *Thank you*, she mouthed.

His sea-glass green eyes were somber, and he gave a slight nod. Were those tears in his eyes too? She thought so. They'd both come so close to losing their daughter. Annie wouldn't have wanted to go on if something had happened to Kylie. If not for Jon's quick actions, the cold water could have carried her to the depths, and they never would have found her body.

Jon rose and went to their kayaks. He rummaged in the hold and removed a Michigan Tech sweatshirt that he brought over and yanked down over Kylie's head.

She thrust her arms into the sleeves and sighed as the warmth enfolded her. "I'm so cold." She held her hand over her eyes to shade them from the sun as she stared up at him. "You jumped in after me."

"Well, I needed to make sure I had a chance to defeat my Yahtzee opponent."

His grin went a little crooked, and she knew the incident had terrified him too. This little girl was his too. Kylie might not know it yet, but Jon loved her. He hadn't tried to back away from her after the truth came out but had moved in to try to build a relationship with her. He was a good man. The best. She was blessed that he loved her.

Annie's vision blurred again, and she pulled Kylie into a tight embrace. "Don't ever do that again, okay? You've kayaked enough to know not to stand up."

"Um, Mommy, it was Pressie! You couldn't expect me to sit there and let it chew off my neck. You would have done something too."

"It was a garter snake," Jon said.

"All I knew was it was biting me. I didn't think about how dangerous it was to jump up." She struggled away from her mom and rose to her feet, though she wobbled a little at the movement. She flicked a skeptical stare up at Jon. "I know you like my mom. And maybe I'll get used to it."

"I'll give you all the time you need. But it's not just your mom I care about. I care about you too. I know it's hard for you to believe that, but it's true."

She stared at him for a few long seconds and shrugged. "I'm hungry. Let's eat."

Annie wasn't sure if she wanted to laugh or cry. Kids were so resilient, but this day would give Annie nightmares for a long time. If Kylie hadn't been here, she would have thrown her arms around Jon and kissed him.

Thank God he'd been there. Thank God, thank God.

TWELVE

MICHELLE WAS SORE FROM YESTERDAY'S ACTIVITY, but it had also given her new courage to try again. Sunrise was beaming over the treetops when she got onto her good knee again and inhaled the strengthening aroma of pine and fresh air. She could do this. She had to do this.

She had tied up what food and water she had in her shirt and fastened it around her waist. While the morning air against her skin felt cool in just her bra and shorts, she could tell it would be a scorcher today. She'd warm up soon enough. With a final glance around, she put on her boots, then hauled herself to her good foot until she was standing with her head above the top of the window.

Wincing, she held on to the window with one hand while she supported her bad leg and eased it through the open window. Using both hands, she gripped the top of the window frame and supported herself with her arms while she managed to get her good leg through the window. At one point she nearly lost her grip and fell, but she gritted her teeth and held tight until she was sitting on the windowsill.

Now to ease down onto the porch and hope she could get there without putting any weight on her broken leg. With her head still inside the cabin and her legs dangling over the outside, she gradually began to lower her feet and legs down toward the porch. She'd extended as far as she could, and the next step was to let go and try to protect her broken leg as she plummeted the last six inches or so.

Holding her breath, she reached for the surface below her with her good foot and bent the knee of her injured leg to try to protect it as she fell. Then she let go.

The impact on her good leg traveled to her hip, and she lost her balance with nothing in front of her hands to grab. Her arms pinwheeled, but she couldn't control her forward momentum. *Keep the foot up!* But her admonishment didn't keep her from buckling onto the rotted wooden boards. She fell onto her good side and lay stunned and breathless for a long moment. The pain in her leg was horrendous, and she closed her eyes and breathed deeply until the first wave passed.

Had she done any more damage? Clutching the calf, she supported her bad leg as she struggled into a seated position. A long splinter had pierced the palm of her left hand, and her whole left side ached from the fall. But there were no more broken bones.

She studied the splinter in her palm, then pressed the point of it back toward the entry spot until a small sliver of it stood above the skin. Using her teeth, she pulled it from her hand and spit it out. The thing was like a dagger. Once it was gone, she reassessed her situation. The food and water had survived the spill with her, and the shirt was still attached to her waist.

The forest looked dark and forbidding, and the thought of trying to find her way through there with a broken leg seemed overwhelming. She wanted to sit on the porch and howl, but she blinked back the moisture in her burning eyes and lifted her chin.

She wasn't a quitter. There had to be a way to get out of here.

She scooted down off the steps and crawled toward the forest. The only possible way through it would be to find a branch she could use as a crutch. There had to be something. The scent of the pine needles as she crawled through wafted to her nose, but instead of calming her, it made her reassess the trees. Spruce trees, pine trees. Finding the right kind of branch wasn't likely.

And she couldn't crawl far with her leg banging against the ground with every pull of her arms. It was already screaming in agony. She paused and stared back at the cabin. There had to be another option. She made her way painfully back to the cabin.

The front door was locked, so she couldn't go back that way. She scooted around to the far side of the porch and peered around the edge. An upended bucket caught her eye. Would it give her enough of a lift to get back through the window?

It was worth a try. She dragged herself off the porch and into the dirt. The bucket was five feet down the side of the cabin, and when she reached it, she realized the back end of the cabin was only another ten feet. Would there be a way in from the rear? She continued the laborious journey to the back, where she found a small stoop that had fallen off the structure. At the other end she spotted a door. But from the inside she didn't remember seeing another door. Where could it lead?

Her arms trembled with exhaustion, but she forced herself to crawl around the rotted and splintering stoop until she reached the door. It stood partially open, and it swung easily when she pushed it with her hand. The sun illuminated the space past the opening enough for her to see it led to stone steps down into the earth.

A root cellar. And she had no strength or light to allow her to go down there. She couldn't stop the tears from spilling down her cheeks. Why did this have to be so hard? Couldn't she catch a single break?

Now she'd have to go back around, dragging the bucket with her, and hope she had the strength to get back inside.

/ / /

Kylie seemed bright and alert this morning when Annie dropped her off to go agate hunting along the shore by Bree's lighthouse. Jon had expected the near-deadly ordeal to have suppressed her energy, but Kylie ran along the grainy sand with Milo chasing after her heels. Lake Superior reflected the light of the sun peeking over the mountains.

He hadn't spotted Taylor yet, and he hoped she didn't try to cozy up to Kylie. The stress of waiting for the DNA to come back was pressing in on Annie even though she hadn't wanted to talk about it.

Kylie came racing toward him. "Jon, look what I found!" She unfurled her fingers to show him an orange, blue, and yellow stone. "I've never seen an agate like this. Is it worth a lot?"

At least she was engaging with him in an excited way. Were things about to get better? "It's not an agate—it's jasper. A nice one."

Her jubilation vanished. "So it's worthless?"

"It's all in the eye of the beholder. While it wouldn't bring in a lot of money, a skilled artisan could make beautiful things from it. When I first dated your mom, I gave her a jasper bead bracelet."

"Did it have mostly turquoise-colored beads? She still has it in her special box."

"Your mom has a special box of jewelry?"

Kylie rubbed her thumb over the surface of the stone. "Uh-huh. It's got that bracelet and a couple of necklaces in it. There's a watch in there and some scarves too." She looked up at him and frowned. "Don't tell her I told you. She doesn't know I found it."

He'd given her all those things. It touched him that she'd kept them all this time. "My lips are sealed."

She ran her fingers over her lips. "You mean like with glue?"

"Exactly." He touched her blonde head, and she didn't flinch this time. "But you can tell your mom yourself. She won't be mad."

"I saw her searching through the box after Daddy died. She cried. I thought maybe Daddy gave her all those things, but you said you gave her the bracelet, so I guess it's just things she likes." Kylie gave him a long stare. "Are you going to marry my mom?"

He gulped at the candid question. Kylie wouldn't like his answer, at least not yet. Things between them had been too rough to believe she was now fully on board with how he felt about Annie. "Um, I—"

His phone rang and he snatched it up, feeling as if he'd just escaped a bear trap. The screen showed a Houghton phone number, and his pulse jumped. "Dr. Jon Dunstan."

"Jon, it's Mike Willis. Hope I'm not calling too early."

"Not at all, Mike. I'm at the beach searching for agates and have been up for hours. We surgeons are early risers."

The other doctor chuckled. "You've got that right. I checked out your references right after you left the other day, and wow, you're a talented surgeon. Patients from as far away as United Arab Emirates."

Thank the Lord Mike had checked right away. If he'd called yesterday, he might have heard about the charges against Olivia. Should he tell Mike about it up front or hope it never came up?

He turned his back to the water and paced a few feet back. The right thing to do was to tell him, even if it meant the end of his hopes for a job.

"Could we meet for dinner tomorrow to discuss moving forward together? My wife will join us, so feel free to bring a significant other."

Maybe it would be best to talk about the "wrinkle" in person. "I'd like that. I'll bring my girlfriend."

"Wonderful. About six at Joey's Seafood and Grill? I'll text you the address."

He'd feared Mike would want to go to an Italian restaurant and he would have had to ask for a change to something more gluten-free friendly. "I know it. It's one of my favorite spots."

After the final goodbyes, Jon shuffled back through the sand to rejoin Kylie. How could he even broach the subject with Mike? He was tempted to ignore the issue and hope Minnesota's problems never came to his haven here, but guilt pricked him for considering it. And money would be a problem, too, most likely. Several obstacles to moving forward with Mike existed, so Jon needed to temper his hopes.

What if it didn't work out? What did he do then? He could start a private practice, but he'd have to be associated with a hospital since he couldn't afford to buy all the equipment necessary for a remote clinic. He had never wanted to do that once he'd tasted being part of a prestigious practice.

And why did he always go back to what *he* wanted? Why did fame and money mean so much to him? The opinions of others had always mattered to him, and he wasn't sure why. Was he so insecure that he had to derive his value from other people? It shouldn't be that way, and he knew it. Every time he thought he had his values straight, he was tempted to compromise.

He should have told Mike up front about the problem and allowed him to do more research and think about the situation before he made a formal offer. But Jon knew what Mike would decide if he heard all that. What doctor would run the risk that a partner's name might be tarnished in the newspaper? It would be professional suicide.

Was there a way to make sure he was cleared? Maybe he should fly back to Rochester and tackle the trouble head-on. The police might look kindly on him if he came in willingly to tell them he had no knowledge of Olivia's actions.

He rubbed his forehead. Why did this have to happen now?

THIRTEEN

THIS INTERVIEW WOULDN'T BE EASY. ANNIE PARKED her truck down the block of the modest Houghton neighborhood and got out into a hot and humid day. The nondescript two-story house she approached appeared to be like all the other ones on the block. Built in the thirties, it was a farmhouse style with white aluminum siding and a large porch, where several preschool children rolled a ball. A chain-link fence ran around the perimeter of the property. The windows were all open, which told her the place didn't have air-conditioning.

A middle-aged woman sat on the porch swing with a book in her hand and put it down when Annie reached the fence and opened the gate. "Can I help you?" While not openly hostile, her brown eyes held reserve and suspicion. Her bleached-blonde hair was frizzy from the humidity.

Annie paused at the caution and warning in the woman's tone. "I'd like to speak to whoever runs the shelter."

"How'd you find us?" the woman demanded.

She'd better try another tactic. "I'm Annie Pederson, a law enforcement ranger investigating a disappearance. I have reason to believe the person I'm searching for might have come here for assistance."

"Who is it?"

"Are you the manager?"

The woman went to the screen door and called inside, "Roberta, can you take the watch for a while?"

A younger woman came out and shot Annie a curious stare. "Anything wrong?"

"No." The older woman gestured for Annie to follow her into the house.

Annie stepped past a tricycle and a soccer ball into the warmth of the home. A modest living room was down the hall to the right. The woman led her past that space to double French doors into what had originally been a dining room. It now held mismatched metal filing cabinets and a massive metal desk that had seen better days.

The woman folded her arms and glance at Annie. "We try to keep a low profile, Ranger Pederson. Who gave you our name?"

"A friend of Michelle Fraser's. May I ask your name?"

"Idoya Jones. I handle the books and know all the women here."

So not exactly a manager but an employee with some clout. "Including Michelle?"

Idoya dropped her arms back to her side and went to sit behind the massive desk. "Why do you think Michelle is in danger?"

"We've found her abandoned car. How long was she living here?"

"She was here about a year."

"Were there any altercations with her husband while she was here?"

"Michelle seldom left the premises at first. She was very afraid of her estranged husband and didn't want to be seen. As she gained confidence, she became an employee and was employed to assist me in bookkeeping. She finished up her college degree while she was here. Once she had that piece of paper, it seemed to give her courage. She decided she could handle Brandon and decided to work on a journalistic piece. Did you find her car in the forest? You said you're a ranger."

Annie nodded. "Yes, in the Ottawa National Forest, specifically the Kitchigami Wilderness Tract. The funny thing is, we tracked her to a condo. When we checked it out, it appeared Michelle had never lived there. She'd moved in furniture and had left her car in the parking garage, but she never stayed there. Did she ever mention the condo to you?"

Idoya steepled her fingers together and stared up at Annie for a long moment. "Michelle helped others find new lives. The condo served as a fake address for the women we helped. We used her name on other addresses as well."

"Did the shelter pay for it or did Michelle?"

"We deposited the funds, and the rent came out of her account."

That information opened a new avenue of possible danger. "Were all the women fleeing abuse?"

"Of course. That's what we're all about."

"So a disgruntled spouse might have targeted her?"

The older woman inhaled and sat back. "It's possible. Before she ever started working for us, I warned her it could be dangerous. While she was terrified of Brandon, the other men didn't faze her. She backed down more than one husband who showed up here demanding to see his wife."

"Did you know she was leaving before she disappeared?"

"She wanted to be a wildlife journalist. That piece I mentioned she wanted to work on was for *National Geographic.*"

"Do you know what it was about?"

Idoya nodded. "She was crazy about mountain lions. She planned to find proof of a habitat up here, then try to tag one and follow it."

Annie's pulse blipped. The logical first step would be to plant wildlife cameras. One of those might show evidence of what happened to Michelle. "Any idea where she planned to go in the forest?"

"She planned to stay close, so hearing her car was in the Kitchigami Wilderness Preserve isn't a surprise. If it were me, I'd start near where her car was found."

The only problem with that idea was that Annie suspected Michelle didn't leave the car there. She hadn't been driving it, and it was last seen in the garage at the condo complex. Why would Michelle suddenly start driving her long-abandoned car?

She handed the older woman her card. "Please call me if you think of anything else. If you could take a look at the irate husbands she dealt with, I'd appreciate it."

"If you find her, have her call me. She left some of her belongings, and I'd like to know what to do with them."

"Will do. Do you know who Michelle contacted at the magazine?"

"I don't think so. Oh wait, she sent the initial query from the office computer. Let me see if it will automatically log her on and show that email."

"You have access to all her email?"

Idoya nodded. "There were no secrets between us, and she didn't have many messages. She didn't use her real name on her email account. Hang on." She jiggled the mouse and the iMac sprang to life. "Here it is." She grabbed a sticky note and jotted down the name and contact information. "The woman said she'd like to see what Michelle came up with. You could check and see when she was last in contact with Michelle."

Annie glanced at the note. "Thank you. I appreciate your help."

Idoya showed her out to the porch, and Annie hurried back to her truck. She pulled out her phone and called the editor at the magazine. Yuriko Davis didn't even remember the contact. No help there.

But the wildlife cams were a definite new clue.

/ / /

The back of Annie's neck prickled when she left the shelter, and she glanced around to see if someone was watching her. Children played in the yard, and two women chatted on the porch. Nothing seemed out of order, so she shrugged and got in her truck.

She called Mason and told him what she'd found. "Can you get me an address for Chad Smith? I'll run over to talk to him."

"I'll text you. Good work. And I have more information on Michelle's car. I accessed all the cameras around the condo complex, and it appears two teenage boys took the car from the parking garage for a joyride. I was able to identify them, and they've done it before. I picked them up, but they were clueless about Michelle."

"I think I know the incident that caused the blood on the sheet we found." She told Mason what Michelle's mother had said about the knife incident. "But I'm still concerned she's not contacted the shelter where she was working. And why hasn't she been in touch with her mother now that she felt comfortable enough to leave the shelter? And where has she been living since she left there a week ago? It's clear she wasn't staying at the condo."

"Lots of questions and very few answers. Let me know what you find out from the Smith guy. I've already got the address. Sending it now."

Her phone pinged. "Got it. I'll be in touch."

She ended the call and glanced at the address in her text messages. Chad Smith lived in L'Anse, only half an hour away. If she found him home, she wouldn't have to drive all the way to Marquette. As she pulled from the curb in front of the shelter, she saw a white panel van pull out of a driveway down the street.

She didn't think much about it until she turned onto M-41. The van let another vehicle in front on occasion but kept pace with her. She pulled into a service station to see what would happen, and the van continued on past. She went inside and bought a bottle of water, but when she got back on the highway, she saw the van parked along the side of the road. When she passed, it pulled out behind her again.

It was clearly following her. Could it be a disgruntled husband who knew she was trying to find Michelle? She wasn't working on any other case right now, so it seemed the most likely explanation.

She sped up until the van fell behind, and in the curve around L'Anse Bay, she took a sharp right into an area she knew was protected from sight by trees. She waited fifteen minutes before she pulled back onto the highway. She didn't see the van again until she drove down Chad Smith's street.

And there it was, parked in Smith's driveway. She cut the engine and got out as a young man in his midtwenties fumbled with a key in the lock of the house.

"Hey!" she called.

He turned around and blanched when he saw her beside the distinctive red-and-white Volkswagen truck. His gaze darted from right to left as she started toward him.

"Chad Smith?" she asked from the bottom of the porch steps.

A defeated expression settled into his hazel eyes. "Yes."

She stared him down. "Why were you following me?"

"I don't know what you're talking about." His protest was feeble.

She fisted her hands at her side. "You followed me from the shelter. How'd you know Michelle was staying there? Did you follow her home one night too? Were you *stalking* her?" Her anger rose at the thought.

He held up his hands. "No, no, I wasn't stalking her. I'm worried about her."

Annie didn't buy it for a minute. "Why would you worry about her? She's been protected in a shelter."

"But she's been gone a week. No one has seen her."

"How do you know?"

A dull red crept up his face. "I had a tracker on her ATV. It hasn't moved."

Stalking her just like Mary had said. Annie wanted to punch him. "When did you last speak to Michelle?"

He shrugged. "The last day of school?"

"How well did you know her?"

"Well enough to know she was crazy about mountain lions."

"Did she see any for herself?"

He shrugged again. "She had a favorite spot she watched for them, but all she'd seen was scat and tracks. They're there, though."

"Where was this place?"

"In the northwestern part of Kitchigami Wilderness Tract. The tracker stopped there, but I couldn't find her ATV. I can give you the coordinates. That's all I know."

Annie knew the place and had seen signs of the big cats herself. She had him text her the coordinates then sent them on to Mason.

Mason needed to find out what he could about this guy. Annie sensed he might be dangerous. She checked her watch. There was time to go out and search for the wildlife cams.

FOURTEEN

MICHELLE'S CHEST BURNED WITH THE EXERTION OF pulling the bucket behind her, and she paused to catch her breath. Her arms ached, and the muscles in her good leg felt strained and fatigued. She wasn't sure she had the strength to get back inside the cabin even if the bucket was tall enough to help.

She rounded the corner of the cabin and crawled up on the crooked porch. Her hand throbbed where she'd had the splinter, and her broken leg screamed to be elevated. Why hadn't she thought this through? Her predicament was her own fault.

She paused to rest. The window was still five feet away, but she was so tired. She laid her cheek on the rotting wood and closed her eyes. The sound of a truck engine made her open them fast. She sat up as movement through the opening in the brush caught her attention. She glimpsed a blue truck, then a figure got out.

Should she hide or cry out for help? Her decision was made for her when she spotted a ski mask on the man's face. No one would wear a ski mask in June unless he wanted to hide his identity. She shrank back against the cabin's front wall. Too late to hide. He'd seen her, and she couldn't escape.

He came up the steps and put his hands on the waistband of

his camo pants. "How'd you get out of the cabin, hmm? I thought I had you safe and sound."

He unlocked the door before coming to grab her. As he scooped her up, she screamed and flailed to try to get away from his hateful touch. He reeked of perspiration and blood. She could only hope it was animal blood smeared on his camo shirt.

His fist looped out of nowhere and clocked her on the left cheek. The brutality of it left her reeling and barely aware as he carried her into the cabin and dumped her on the cot. He went outside, then returned with a toolbox as she was regaining her full senses.

He took out a hammer and nails, then slammed down the window and nailed it shut. "That should take care of any further escape plans."

The satisfaction in his voice made her want to scream. Why hadn't she tried harder? But no, he would have tracked her. She would have made drag marks through the vegetation as she searched for a stick. And once she'd made a crutch, he could have followed her path with no trouble.

She sat up and pushed her hair out of her face. "Just let me go. I haven't seen your face. I can't identify you."

"I don't think so. You know too much."

But she couldn't identify him. "What are you going to do with me?"

"That's up to you. Where are your belongings?"

"I can't tell you where it is. I'd have to take you there, and my leg needs surgery."

"How do you know?"

The displeasure and threat in his voice made her shudder. "I've broken an ankle before. I had to have a plate and screws inserted. This might need that kind of repair too. Please, I need a doctor."

"Surgery. I'll have to think about what to do."

He left her again, and she listened for the truck to start, but his steps came back her way, and he entered with a case of water and bags of food. He dumped the supplies in a corner.

Her gaze lingered on the jerky on top. She'd been rationing what little she had, and her belly ached with hunger. Her lips were dry from dehydration, too, but she didn't intend to give him the satisfaction of seeing her dive into the supplies.

Were his eyes blue? He wasn't close enough for her to be sure, but she thought so. She memorized the set of his shoulders and his rangy build. He was about six feet tall, and she would guess he wore a size eleven shoe. Maybe she'd recognize his figure, but she didn't know a single feature of his face.

He moved back toward the door, this time slamming it behind him. The key clicked in the lock, and a few seconds later, the truck engine roared to life. The forest swallowed up the sound in short order, and she was left listening to the distant sound of birds chirping from the trees.

She scooted to the edge of the bed and down to the floor. She hurt so much she could barely drag herself to the supplies, but hunger and thirst propelled her. She tore into a package of jerky and gobbled up several pieces before she uncapped a bottle of water and swigged it down.

How long would this last? She eyed the stash. If she was careful, it would last a week. And she planned to be very careful. Would he take her need for a doctor seriously, or would he decide to cut his losses and kill her? She suspected the latter. He had to know that if he took her in for surgery, he'd never get her back.

She'd scream for the police the first chance she got. But would they protect her? Once she was home recuperating, he might break back in and haul her out.

What could he want that badly? Pictures on her phone incriminating Brandon? She couldn't think of any.

/ / /

The Kitchigami Wilderness Preserve was full of twittering birds and the blended scents of leaves, mud, pine, and wildflowers. Jon walked through the pines with Annie and Kylie in the shadow of the thick overstory of oak and sycamore trees. He whistled for Milo to come back before he slipped out of sight.

"The cams are probably on branches of deciduous trees," Annie said.

"What should I be looking for?"

"Her ATV might be around here somewhere. Either that or she found the tracker and tossed it away. And look for cams in the trees."

Jon nodded. He knew Annie had to check it out, and it was a beautiful day for a hike in the woods.

A jaybird scolded them from a nearby spruce tree before flying off in a flurry of blue. He scanned the branches, searching for a glint of a camera's eye, but he saw nothing.

"Let's go toward the water," Annie said. "Most animals congregate around water, and she might have set up cams at the nearest watering spot."

He was lost in this dense brush, but Annie led the way with confidence. They broke through the thickets onto a small beach with Superior's waves rolling onto its pebbles. It felt like a spot all their own, as if no other human had ever stepped foot here. Until he spotted a candy wrapper and a half-empty water bottle.

He picked up both and scrunched them in his hand. "Litterbug."

Annie nodded and went to study the trees lining the beach. "There's one!" She disappeared into the woods.

Milo yipped and raced over to throw himself at Jon's feet. He was trembling and crying as only a frightened pup could, and Jon reached down to comfort him. "Easy, boy, what's wrong?"

As he ran his hand over the puppy, he felt something wet on the side of Milo's muzzle. Jon stared at his fingers. Red. He sniffed the metallic odor. Blood. "Are you hurt, buddy?" He knelt and examined the puppy for a cut or injury. Nothing.

"Is Milo okay?" Kylie fell to her knees beside her puppy. "Is he hurt?"

"I don't see anything, but he has some blood on him. Did you see where he was playing?"

Kylie pointed to a rock pile near the water. "Over there." She scooped Milo up in her arms and hugged him close to her chest.

Jon approached the rock pile and began to kick things around. All appeared normal at first. Until he found a boot lodged between two rocks. It was small, like it belonged to a woman. His gut clenched, and he rose to hail Annie.

She heard his call and came to join him with a cam in her hand. "You find a cam too?"

"Milo had blood on him. He was playing around over here, and I found this." He held up the boot. "We should both explore a little more in case someone around here is hurt."

Or worse.

If only they hadn't brought Kylie out here. They'd found some gruesome sights this summer so far. Neither of them said it, but he saw the worry spring into Annie's blue eyes. While she went north with Kylie and Milo along the beach, he went south. When he found nothing, he moved into the tree line a couple of feet and scuffed his boots through last year's leaves.

He saw something red in a low bush and bent to look. A young woman, in her late teens or early twenties, lay curled into a ball under the vegetation. She was missing a boot, and blood trickled down her leg from a gaping wound. Her lips were cracked and her skin appeared dehydrated beneath her tangled mass of straight black hair. Her backpack was discarded a few feet way. How long had she been out here?

She flinched when he touched her arm. "Don't hurt me anymore," she whispered.

"I won't hurt you." He rose and yelled Annie's name before kneeling beside her again. He pulled out an unused bottle of water, then slid his arm under her and helped her to sit up. "Have some water."

She opened dark-brown eyes and pushed her black hair out of her face. He put the bottle to her lips for her to take a sip. "Not too much at first. I don't want you to get sick."

She raised a feeble hand and grasped the bottle to drink more. "So thirsty."

"How long have you been out here?"

"I don't remember. Forever," she whispered.

He heard thrashing through the underbrush. "Over here, Annie!"

Annie and Kylie came into sight with Milo on their heels.

Annie saw the girl, and her eyes went wide as she hurried to join them.

She knelt on the other side of the girl. "Are you Michelle Fraser?"

"No, I'm Shainya Blackburn."

"Are you injured?" Annie spotted the blood and winced. "That's a nasty cut. Let me see what I can do." She shrugged off her backpack and unzipped it to get to a first aid kit.

Jon moved in and took the pack. "I'll do it." While Annie was competent, he was the doctor. The girl winced when he began to clean the laceration. "What happened?"

"Two men. They chased me." The girl reached for the water again and took a gulp. "They might still be out there."

"When was this?" Jon asked.

"Yesterday, I think. Or maybe the day before. I got lost, and I can't remember. I was so scared."

"Did they hurt you?" Annie asked after a sidelong glance at Kylie, who stood a few feet away.

"N-not like you mean. They laughed while they chased me and threw rocks at me. One kept telling me to run so it was more fun. I think they might have been teenagers. Or in their early twenties."

This was sounding all too familiar with some of the other things that had gone on this summer. Jon checked his phone. No bars. "We'll need to transport her from here by ourselves."

"The truck isn't that far. Maybe we can make a travois."

Jon handed her his backpack. "I can carry her out if you take this."

"You sure?"

He nodded. "Let's get her to the hospital. I think she'll need stitches on that leg."

And Mason needed to know there were still a couple of thugs out here terrorizing people.

FIFTEEN

THE SCENE AT THE HOSPITAL WAS SO HECTIC THAT Annie was glad they'd dropped Kylie and Milo off at Anu's. There'd been a car accident with multiple injuries, and the small facility in Rock Harbor was bursting at the seams when they brought in the girl. She'd told them she lived on the Ojibwa reservation by Baraga. Annie thought it likely her love of nature had helped her survive whatever had happened out there.

Knees hugged to her chest, Shainya sat in a waiting room chair. She was looking better. Annie had used her own comb to remove twigs, leaves, and mud from the girl's dark hair, and her color was improving. She was a beautiful girl with high cheekbones and dramatic coloring.

Annie returned the comb to her backpack. "Can I call someone for you—your parents, maybe?"

Shainya chewed her lip before answering with a slow nod. "We're not on the best of terms. I moved out a couple of weeks ago, but they'll need to come get me."

"Where are you living?"

"I was with my boyfriend, but we broke up a couple of days ago. I found him with another girl, and I took off. Nature always helps center me."

Annie nodded. "I feel the same way. What is your ex-boyfriend's name?"

"Joel West."

Annie jotted it down so she could tell Mason. She glanced at Jon in the chair beside her. "Would you call her parents?"

"Sure." He pulled out his phone. "Number?"

Shainya rattled off her mother's number, and he put it in his phone.

Jon rose to step out of the noisy and chaotic waiting room. He exited into the late-afternoon sunshine, and Annie watched him pace and bite his lip as he placed the call. He always did that when he was agitated. Mason appeared behind Jon, then passed him to proceed to the waiting room.

He spotted Annie and came to join her. He stared at Shainya, and his gaze softened. "I'm Sheriff Kaleva." He took out a notepad and squatted in front of her. "Can you tell me what happened?"

Tears glistened in Shainya's eyes, and she launched into the story about two men chasing her.

"What were you doing when they started chasing you?"

"I was camping. I'd just gotten my tent up and was cooking a burger over the campfire. It was nearly dark, probably nine. A rock came flying out of nowhere and knocked the iron skillet out of my hand. Then there was a gunshot and laughter. Some guy yelled, 'Run, little rabbit.' So I did."

Annie suppressed a shudder. That had to have been terrifying. No wonder Shainya was traumatized. Annie took her hand, and the girl clutched her like a lifeline.

Mason wrote in his notebook. "How long did the chase go on? Did you see the men well enough to describe them to a sketch artist?"

Shainya shook her head. "It was too dark. I know the area so I was able to hide in small caves and behind rocks. They kept tracking me, though. I'm not sure how since it was so dark."

"They might have had infrared goggles," Mason said. "Lots of hunters use them."

Hunters. Just like Eddie Poole had reported. What was going on in the North Woods? They had one dead camper already, and she still suspected Sean Johnson had a connection there.

A nurse called Shainya back, and Annie gave her hand a comforting pat. "I'll be right here. Jon is coming back now too. I'm sure your parents will be here soon."

"Thank you for everything." Shainya limped away with the nurse.

The automatic entry doors opened for Jon, and he joined Annie and Mason. "I got her mom. She was running for her truck when we hung up. She and her husband both work at the casino. She was going to grab him on her way out. I'd guess it will take them an hour or so."

"I want to wait and make sure Shainya is okay."

"I wouldn't have it any other way," Jon said. "The mom thought I was calling to tell her Shainya was in jail. The boyfriend sounds like a piece of work. Drug sales, breaking and entering, poaching. Even when I told her Shainya had been injured, she wasn't going to come until I mentioned they'd broken up."

"She must really hate the guy."

"His name is Joel West," Annie said. "Maybe he's got a rap sheet."

Jon sat beside her and leaned forward. "That's not all she said. The poaching thing I mentioned? She said she suspected him of bringing in out-of-state people for illegal moose hunts. Out to Isle Royale of all places."

"That's outrageous!" Annie hated poachers.

Moose had nearly disappeared from the state after World War II, but the Department of Natural Resources had worked hard to grow the population. She loved the magnificent beasts.

"One of the hunters he brought in went missing and was never found. A seventeen-year-old girl who came with her dad. The assumption was that she fell off a cliff or something and wolves disposed of the body. But it sounded suspicious to me, knowing what's been going on this summer."

"When was this?" Mason asked.

"August of last year," Jon said.

"I'll see what I can find out." Mason jotted it down and put his notebook away. "I'll head back to the office. If you hear anything else, let me know. Where's Kylie?"

"Anu has her at the store. Bree was out on a search for a missing cat."

The search team conducted searches for all kinds of things, so this was nothing unusual. Annie glanced at her watch. "Anu will be closing up shop in a few minutes. I should let her know I'm still tied up."

"Want me to grab her?" Jon asked. "I could take her to the shore and look for agates down the hill from the lighthouse. She likes that."

"Sure, if you don't mind. We can meet there." At least Kylie seemed to tolerate him now. Annie was thankful for the change.

Jon nodded and rose to walk out with Mason. "Text me when you're on your way."

She nodded and sat back to wait. With any kind of luck, Mrs. Blackburn would have more information.

/ / /

Anu's shop was still open when Jon pushed through the door to the interior filled with various aromas of wool, candles, and craft items. He spotted the dwindling stock of Annie's woven rugs in a window display. She'd be glad to know they were selling well.

Kylie was sitting on the floor in a corner playing with a kantele, a stringed instrument similar to a ukulele but longer.

He didn't see Anu or Milo as he went to join his daughter. He settled on the wood floor beside her. "You're pretty good at that."

"Anu has been teaching me for a long time. This is her kantele, and she said I can have it one day." Kylie ran her fingers over the smooth birch surface.

"Where is Anu? I don't see Milo either."

"Milo won't leave her alone. She's in the break room getting me a piece of Fazer. That's okay, isn't it? I know I haven't had dinner yet."

"It's fine. There's no chocolate in the world better than Fazer. Think she'd give me some if I ask?"

"If you ask nicely, I will, *kulta*," Anu said from behind him. She had a candy bar in her hand.

Max Reardon was with her, and Jon got up to shake hands with him. He'd been the first man Anu had dated in the decades since her husband had disappeared.

"Good to see you," Max said. He turned to Anu and brushed a kiss across her lips. "I'll meet you at the restaurant in a few minutes."

She nodded as he went out the door. Milo whined at her feet.

Jon noticed how agitated the puppy seemed. "What's with Milo? Doesn't he know he can't have candy?"

Anu handed blocks of chocolate to Kylie and him, then placed the remaining bar on the counter before she scooped up the pup. "He has been like this since they arrived. He's very distressed, but I do not know why."

The dog nuzzled her chin, then tried to worm his way down to her belly. He'd done that the other day, and Jon couldn't figure it out. He stared at Anu's stomach, which looked distended. She'd always been so thin that it was noticeable. But the middle-aged spread got to most everyone, even women as active and slim as Anu.

But was that all it was? There was something he'd heard at a doctor's seminar recently that nudged him, but he couldn't quite put his finger on it. Something about dogs . . .

He frowned as he stared at Milo's agitation. It would come to him. The more he tried to grasp it, the more it danced away. The chocolate melted smoothly on his tongue, and he picked up the partially eaten package of Fazer. "Mind if I have another piece?"

She put down the puppy before she turned to fold some sweatshirts. "You may eat it all."

Without the puppy in the way, Jon could see her stomach more clearly. He tried to tell himself the distension meant nothing, but he couldn't dispel the unease. His gaze fell on the purplish rash between the folds of her fingers. Dermatomyositis? He didn't see any of the muscular weakness that often accompanied the inflammatory myopathy. He'd seen several patients with the condition.

"You been feeling okay, Anu?" He tried to make the question sound casual.

"A bit tired, but there have been many tourists through the shop, and I have been shorthanded." She rubbed her stomach as if she had fleeting pain. "In spite of not feeling hungry, I have gained a bit of weight. That might be adding to my fatigue."

"You look great," he said in case she'd seen him staring at her stomach.

The memory Jon had been trying to grab finally surfaced. One of the doctors at the seminar had mentioned dogs trained to sniff out cancer. Milo wasn't trained for anything like that, but canine capabilities could surface by themselves. Was he totally off track? He wasn't an oncologist or a gynecologist, though he'd had to study the subjects in medical school.

Ovarian cancer caused bloating, and some patients experienced dermatomyositis. The symptoms were often very vague at the beginning. Was it right to scare Anu and ask her to get checked out?

Not yet. He'd do more research and talk to Annie about it. He could even ask Dr. Eckright when she'd last had a checkup and see if he thought there was any cause for concern. No need to terrify her if he didn't have to.

He licked the last of the chocolate from his fingers. "Want to go hunt agates while we wait for your mom? Bree might be home now, and the kids are likely there."

"They are," Anu said. "Bree texted me on her way home to fix dinner."

"Yay!" Kylie rose and grabbed her pup. "Let's go play, Milo."

The dog wiggled and whined to be let down, so she plopped

him back on the floor. He raced to Anu again and his whines escalated in volume.

"You silly puppy." Anu reached down and scratched his ears, but the caress didn't soothe his agitation.

This was getting them nowhere. Jon stepped to Anu and picked up Milo. "We'll get out of your hair. Thanks for taking care of the squirt. How's the closing going on the cabin? I haven't asked Annie lately."

Anu was buying a dilapidated cabin on the Tremolo Marina property. The cabin would have held too many bad memories for him to want to live there, but finding two dead bodies dumped in the closet hadn't seemed to bother Anu. She still thought the place was perfect for her retirement.

"We close in two weeks. I cannot wait to begin renovation."

"Don't be too eager. I'm having trouble finding a contractor now that Sean is gone. I'm not sure Dad's cottage will ever be done. I may be living at Martha's B and B the rest of my life."

Anu walked them to the door. "Martha would not mind. She is enamored with your father."

"I think it's mutual." Jon brushed his lips across her soft cheek. "Thanks again."

"You are a sweet boy." She shut and locked the door behind them.

The lights went out moments later. Jon carried the puppy to his car. Mason had taken him to pick it up at Anu's so he had a vehicle.

It was probably nothing, but his worry escalated as he looked back at the shop.

SIXTEEN

TAYLOR HAD STAYED IN THIS TINY HOUSE UNTIL SHE wanted to scream. But going into Rock Harbor made her feel like a slug that had just crawled out from under a log. She was sure people were staring at her with contempt, even though Bree told her it was her imagination. Bree claimed no one knew about the way she'd tried to frame Jon, but Taylor didn't buy it. She knew how rumors traveled in a small town.

She went to the window and peered out onto the grassy lawn bordered by the blue of Lake Superior in the distance. She often walked on the beach, but she was tired of that too. Still, it was better than sitting here staring at four walls.

She put on a headband to keep her hair out of her eyes in the wind, then went to the door. The fresh scent of the lake hit her, and she inhaled. Maybe there would be a friendly soul walking the sand. She was lonely.

Bree was nice enough, but Taylor could tell she was on Annie's side. Everyone in town was on Annie's side. And why not? Taylor was new here. Of course they'd believe Annie. No one stopped to think about all Taylor had gone through. If only she had a friend. Someone who knew and understood her.

She'd thought Jon might be *the one*, but he'd been just as

faithless as all men. Her mom was right. Taylor should have known better than to trust any man.

The grass was springy under her flip-flops as she made her way to the steps down to the beach. She heard voices and saw Kylie and Jon walking along the water's edge.

She retreated a step and started to go back to her cottage, but no. She had done nothing wrong. The beach was open to everyone. Jon Dunstan didn't own it. And even though she'd been warned to stay away from Kylie, the little girl loved her. It was cruel to keep them apart. They had no right to dictate that she couldn't see Kylie.

Head high, Taylor went down the steps. The iron railing held her steady when her knees trembled with the stress of the coming confrontation. Would Jon order her away, or would he try to be pleasant for Kylie's sake? She was about to find out.

She reached the sand and kicked off her flip-flops, then tipped up her chin and marched toward Kylie. Kylie saw her before Taylor called out to her, and she jumped to her feet.

"Taylor!" The little girl pelted across the sand to throw herself into Taylor's arms.

A rush of pleasure and triumph swamped Taylor as she clutched the little girl to her chest. "I've missed you, Bug."

If Annie could call Kylie Bug, so could she. It felt all kinds of great to be loved like this. A child's love was the purest, most wonderful kind. And even though she didn't know it, Kylie was her niece. They were part of one another.

Jon's gruff voice broke into Taylor's enjoyment. "What are you doing here, Taylor?"

She let go of Kylie and turned to face him. "Just taking a walk."

Jon held out his hand. "We need to go, Kylie."

The little girl grabbed Taylor's hand and hung on. "I don't want to. I've been looking all over for Taylor."

"Your mom texted, and she's on her way. Let's meet her at the road and go to dinner. We can go to the fish house."

"I'm tired of always having to eat something without gluten. I want to go to the Suomi and have pulla."

Taylor recognized the whine in Kylie's voice as a ruse to get her way. Jon probably didn't know the little girl well enough to see she was playing him.

"You know we can't do that, Kylie. I can't either. I get just as tired of not being able to eat what I want as you do. It gets better." He took a step toward them. "Come on, we need to go."

"I'm not going, and you can't make me. Mommy wouldn't make me. She knows I love Taylor and wanted to see her. I'm staying here until Mommy comes. You're not the boss of me."

Color swept up Jon's face, and he pressed his lips together. His eyes narrowed, but he inhaled and stepped back. "Your mom will have plenty to say about your disobedience. You think she'd be glad you talked to a grown-up like that?"

Kylie hung her head. "I'm going to be in trouble." She pulled her hand from Taylor's. "I have to go. I'll ask Mommy if I can come visit now that I know you're here. Are you staying with Bree?"

"I'm staying in that little cottage behind Bree's lighthouse. You can come see me anytime." To retain a shred of her dignity, Taylor turned and walked toward the steps.

She couldn't bear to have her *dear sister* order her away. Or to see Kylie cry about it. Her time was coming. The DNA test would be back on Thursday, just three more days. Taylor couldn't wait to see Annie's face when she read the results. What would she say? Would she apologize or still snub her?

Taylor knew what the test would reveal even if Annie still didn't want to admit it. And the revelation would be sweet.

/ / /

Annie paused to admire the way the sunshine slanted through the prism of the Fresnel lens in the lighthouse before heading toward the water. She spied a familiar figure running away from the steps toward the cottage behind Bree's home. Was that Taylor?

Her gaze went to Jon and Kylie on the beach. Had Taylor spoken to them? She'd asked the woman to stay away from Kylie. It was only a few more days until the truth came out, but what would Annie do if she found out Taylor was really Sarah?

Annie longed for closure, but she didn't want her beloved sister to be someone who would try to frame another person. She didn't want to have to learn to love someone who despised her. Taylor had made it clear she hated Annie. If she turned out to be her little sister, how would she even deal with that? How would they find a way forward through those circumstances?

Jon had seen her, and he lifted a hand in greeting. He and Kylie came toward the steps, and Annie waited for them. Jon carried the puppy up the stairs as Kylie scampered ahead of him. Her cheeks were pink, but her mouth was set in a mutinous pout.

She stopped in front of Annie. "Did you see Taylor? Jon made us leave her, and I wanted to stay and talk to her. I don't know why you won't let me talk to her. She's my friend, Mommy. It's not fair."

"I'm sorry, honey." Annie hesitated. She needed to give her daughter some kind of reason, but the full truth would require more explanation than Kylie could understand. "Taylor lied about some things, and I'm not sure we can trust her now. Mason is checking it out. I want to wait until we know the truth. Her lies could have sent some people to jail. That's not okay."

"To jail?" Uncertainty crept into Kylie's blue eyes. "That's a bad lie."

"Any lie is bad," Annie reminded her. "But yes, that was a bad one. Just try to be patient, okay? I'm trying to do what's best for you."

"But what about what's best for Taylor? Aren't we supposed to forgive? She doesn't have anyone, Mommy. She's all alone, and she looked so sad. She had tears in her eyes when she ran off."

Annie's eyes filled at the thought. Kylie was right—Taylor had no one left in the world. Her pseudo mother was dead, and now so was her cousin. Annie knew about feeling alone, but even after Nate and her parents had drowned over two years ago, she'd had Kylie. And she had friends who loved and supported her. Taylor didn't even have a friend.

"You're right about that." Her gaze went to Jon, whose green eyes were somber. "Give me a few more days to figure this out, okay? We'll see what we can do to help Taylor."

Even if the DNA showed she wasn't Sarah, if Annie helped her, maybe she could help turn the course of her life around. If she had no one, Taylor was apt to go from bad to worse.

Jon took her hand. "How'd it go with Shainya's mother?"

The warm press of his fingers calmed and centered her. "She got there just as Shainya was released. Mason talked with her, but there wasn't any more information than what she'd told me. Shainya was exhausted, so her mom took her home to the reservation. There will be plenty of people around to protect her."

"The guys chasing her probably don't know who she is, and Baraga is an hour away so she's probably safe on the reservation."

"I hope so."

They walked back toward their vehicles. She could tell Jon had something on his mind by the way he kept biting his lip. And his frown came and went. He'd tell her when they were alone.

When they reached the lighthouse, Bree stepped out onto the porch, and her twins scooted past her to see Kylie. Hannah carried a soccer ball, and the three of them began to kick it around.

A worried expression marring her face, Bree descended the steps behind them. "Did Taylor bother you? I've warned her not to approach Kylie."

"She left when I asked her to," Jon said. "I didn't expect that."

Annie took a step closer to Bree. "Would you have time to conduct a search tomorrow? I have some coordinates where Michelle Fraser was last. I'd like to discover any wildlife cams she set up. I have a bloody sheet that belongs to her we can use for the scent article."

"Sure, that's not a problem. Samson will enjoy the outing. What time?"

"About eight? I'll come here."

Bree nodded and punched it into her phone. Annie noticed the speculative stare Jon gave Bree. What was up?

He bit his lip again and frowned. "Has Anu been feeling all right?"

Bree frowned and started to nod, then stopped. "She hasn't said anything. Should I go check on her? What did you see?"

"You know a lot about dogs. Have you ever heard of dogs being able to smell certain illnesses? I read a study about that recently, and I wasn't sure if it was true."

"Actually, yes. Milo's mother was a trained medical dog. She sniffed out cancer, of all things. Why do you ask?"

"Milo has been acting strange around Anu." He glanced down at Annie. "He keeps burrowing into Anu's stomach and whining. He won't leave her alone."

Annie nodded. "I saw him do that the other day too."

"I noticed a purplish rash in the webbing of her fingers. The medical name for it is dermatomyositis. And her stomach looked bloated to me. It's probably nothing, but I'd like her to get her ovaries checked. Just to be on the safe side."

Bree went pale. "You suspect ovarian cancer?"

"I hope not, but it's often hard to diagnose, and I don't like the mild symptoms I saw. Coupled with Milo's reaction, I'd feel better if she ruled it out." He glanced again at Annie. "I wasn't sure how to bring it up to her. She'd think I was out of my mind. I wondered if maybe I should mention it to Dr. Eckright. He could suggest it as a routine checkup."

"That's a great idea. She has a yearly checkup with him next week," Bree said.

"I'll mention it to him then. There's no reason to worry Anu if we don't have to."

"She'd want to know," Bree said. "Anu is strong, and she always meets adversity head-on. I don't think we should treat her like a child."

"It's your call then. Do you want to mention it to her, or should I?"

"You're a doctor. You can explain it better than me."

Jon wasn't looking forward to that conversation, but maybe Bree was right. Anu was strong. She'd handle it.

SEVENTEEN

THE COMFORTING SCENT OF CURRY STILL LINGERED IN the cottage as Jon sat on the sofa and dug into a warm brownie. "I couldn't have done better myself, Kylie. Good job."

The little girl beamed at the praise. "I followed your recipe and only forgot the vanilla. Do you think it made much of a difference to leave it out?"

"I can't taste any difference."

Annie settled beside him. "I didn't even have to help her other than getting it out of the oven."

Kylie scooped up Milo. "Can I play *Pokémon* in the yard before it gets dark?"

Annie glanced at the window. "For half an hour."

"Thanks, Mommy." She grabbed her iPad and scooted out the door with the puppy.

Annie sighed and leaned her head back. "What a day. I'm beat." She lifted her head and stared up at him. "Do you really think Anu has ovarian cancer?"

"I hope not."

"Do you have a feeling one way or another?"

"I'm a doctor. We go by tests and examinations. No one has checked Anu out for it, so there's no way of knowing."

"But you must have some sixth sense you use in cases like this."

He slipped his arm around her and pulled her close. "You mean my Spidey sense?" Even though he made light of his intuition, it kept bumping up against him.

"Exactly."

"I'm concerned. Let's leave it at that." He saw the mutinous tip up of her chin. Better distract her. "What about the cam you found? Anything on it?"

She shook her head. "I'm going to go out and look more. My search got suspended when we found Shainya."

"I got a call from Mike in Houghton."

"The orthopedic surgeon?"

"Right. He invited us to dinner on Wednesday to discuss next steps. Can you get a sitter?"

"I'm sure I can. By *us* you mean he invited me specifically?"

"He told me to bring my significant other. That would be you."

"Where are we going?"

"If you're worried about what to wear, you look beautiful in anything. We're supposed to meet at Joey's Seafood & Grill."

"Dress jeans will be okay then." She clasped her hands together. "You're getting an offer! It's really happening."

"Whoa, don't get your hopes up. I should have told him right away about Olivia's arrest and how that is likely to affect me. I wanted to tell him, but I couldn't get the words out. Once he hears about it, I'm probably sunk."

Her blue eyes softened. "Maybe he'll want you anyway. He's got to know you're an excellent surgeon."

"He checked my references and said he was impressed. But

if the police show up here asking questions, it could boomerang onto the practice."

"You could call the police yourself and offer to answer any questions. Have you talked to Mason about it?"

"No. You think he could help?"

"He could speak with the detective in charge of the case and see if they're investigating you too."

"There's no *if* about it. I'm sure they are. They'll want to see what the rest of us know or saw. I'm surprised they haven't called yet."

"She was just arrested three days ago. It will take time to work their way through everyone."

Annie was right, but it was hard to wait for the next shoe to drop. Every time he saw an unfamiliar car pull up to the bed-and-breakfast, he held his breath. "Maybe I should just call. Get it over with."

"Like right now?"

"It's not that late."

He pulled out his phone and looked up the number of the Rochester precinct. When someone answered the phone, he explained that he needed to talk to the detective in charge of the investigation. A few moments later, he was transferred to Detective Ken Perry.

"Detective, I'm Dr. Jon Dunstan. I heard about the arrest of Dr. Olivia Thompson. I'm a former partner in the practice and thought I'd better check in."

"Former? I heard you were one of the partners." The man's voice was gruff like a smoker's, and he took a long slurp of a drink.

"Technically, I am, but I had notified them last week that I would be moving to Michigan. At that time I had no clue this was brewing."

"Uh-huh. I'm recording this conversation, just so you're aware."

"That's fine."

"Why did you leave the practice? Did you observe Dr. Thompson murder a patient?"

The suspicion was obvious in the detective's voice. "Nothing like that. I had the utmost respect for Dr. Thompson. I find it hard to believe she would do what she's accused of. My father had a stroke, and I brought him to Michigan to take care of business. While here, I reconnected with my former fiancée, and we are getting back together." He kissed Annie's hand. "I don't have a new position here yet, but I'm working on it. I let Dr. Thompson know immediately."

"Did you ever observe Dr. Thompson with a patient?"

"No. We all had separate patients. I never had a case where I needed her consult, and she never asked me for one either. She's been a respected surgeon for a long time. Frankly, I think you're wrong."

"You haven't seen the video, have you?"

"No," Jon admitted.

"There's no question she injected something into the patient's IV. Moments later the man expired. The autopsy found a lethal dose of potassium chloride. We have video of the good doctor taking the drug from the dispensary as well. There's no question it's homicide. The bigger question is, are there other victims?"

The full story shook Jon. How could Olivia have done something like this? Had she snapped mentally? He shook his head.

"Are you there, Dr. Dunstan?"

"Yes, yes, I'm here. Just shocked. It's hard to believe."

"Did you notice a higher number of deaths among her patients?"

"No, she had an excellent track record." He clutched Annie's hand. "Am I under suspicion, Detective Perry?"

"Should you be?"

"No, of course not." Jon pressed his lips together. The guy was being a jerk.

"Thanks for calling in, but don't be surprised if we have more questions. This is a big case and likely to get bigger."

The call ended, and Jon put down his phone. The call might have bought him a little time, but it hadn't resolved anything.

/ / /

Jon immediately liked Dr. Ben Eckright's waiting room. It was as welcoming as the Blue Bonnet Bed-and-Breakfast. Pictures of the doctor's boating adventures on Superior decorated the room, and Jon thought he would have a lot in common with the general practitioner.

The doctor himself appeared in the doorway. His warm brown eyes and grandfatherly manner were the kind guaranteed to put even the most frightened kid at ease. Mostly bald, his scalp still hung on to a few stray ginger strands.

His grin broadened when he saw Jon. "Dr. Dunstan, I was hoping to meet you one of these days. Come on back." He led him down a hallway to a small office lined with antique barrister bookcases. Green file folders covered most of his massive desk, and the computer on one side was old and looked unused.

The doctor dropped into the chair behind his desk. "Glad to have you in town. Rock Harbor can use an orthopedic surgeon. I get tired of having to refer patients to Houghton."

"There's no orthopedic doctor here at all? No one affiliated with your hospital?"

"Nope. It's a crying shame." The doctor steepled his fingertips and stared at him. "I'm sure you didn't stop by for chitchat. Is this about Kylie?"

Did he know Jon was Kylie's father? Jon couldn't see Annie revealing something so personal. Not yet, when so few people knew.

Jon gave a slight shake to his head, and Dr. Eckright grimaced. "Forgive me for prying, Dr. Dunstan. I know you're dating Annie and just assumed . . ."

"Call me Jon." He settled in a chair. "It's about Anu Nicholls."

"That's a surprise. Does Anu know you're here?"

"Not yet. I'm going to tell her." He realized he'd gotten that out of order. Anu should have heard about this before her doctor, but Jon was most comfortable talking about medical issues with other physicians. He dreaded talking to Anu.

"I see. What is your concern?"

Jon told him what he'd observed and suspected. "I was going to ask you to run the tests without worrying her, but Bree wants her to know about the concern."

"Bree has a good head on her shoulders. Anu is a most pragmatic woman. She raised her kids alone and made a success of a business without anyone's help. You don't have to coddle that woman. She can take what life throws her way."

"Should I handle it in a special way?"

"Just lay out what you've seen. Anu will come right in. I've been her doctor for twenty years."

"I thought a CA-125 would be in order as well as an ultrasound."

"I can handle both of those here in the office. Anu won't have to worry about others hearing she might have a problem. I'll do the ultrasound myself and the CA-125 will be part of her screening. I pray you're wrong."

"Me too." Jon rose and shook Ben's hand. "I'd ask to stay in the loop, but that's Anu's call."

"She'll let you know. Anu isn't one to hide her trials." He glanced at his watch. "If you head over to the Suomi now, you'll catch her having breakfast. Enjoy the pulla."

"I have celiac so that's out for me," Jon said without thinking.

When the doctor's smile dropped, Jon realized he'd just let the doctor know he was Kylie's father. The guy was smart. He would put two and two together.

He beat a hasty retreat and headed over to the café, where he saw Anu sitting with Max Reardon at a back booth. Seeing Max there made Jon pause. Should he say anything in front of him? Anu seemed to have stars in her eyes around him.

He started to back out, but she saw him and lifted her hand. The place was bustling as usual, but he saw no one familiar as he made his way to her. "Hi there. Mind if I join you?"

Anu's eyes brightened. "Good morning. It is good to see you. You know Max."

"Good morning." He nodded at the older man and sat across from them in the booth. He waited until he could order coffee as well as scrambled eggs and bacon, no toast. "I have something, um, upsetting to talk to you about, Anu. I hope you won't think I'm prying or am out of line. It's personal, and we can discuss it privately if you want."

Max stiffened, and his brown eyes went flat. Protective instincts or anger?

Anu put her hand on Max's arm. "I have no secrets from Max." Her blue eyes took him in steadily. "I would never think you are prying. What is your concern? Is it about Bree or the children?"

He shook his head and reached across the table to take her hand. He spread her fingers out. "See that purplish rash? It's called dermatomyositis. It's a rare inflammatory disorder. I wouldn't be unduly concerned except for the way Milo has been acting around you and the bloating I noticed in your stomach. It's most likely nothing, but I've asked Dr. Eckright to check you for ovarian cancer, just to be safe."

Max inhaled and leaned forward. "You can't be serious. That seems an unlikely thing to worry her about."

"It's unlikely," Jon agreed. "But it's worth checking out. Milo's mother was trained to detect cancer by smell. I think Milo might have picked up that ability."

Anu still had not spoken, and color came back to her pale face. "What has he done? I have not noticed."

"He tries to burrow against your stomach. That's when I noticed the bloating. I don't want you to worry, but I'll feel better if you get checked. Dr. Eckright can do an ultrasound and a blood test that will tell us a lot. If it happens to be ovarian cancer, we've most likely caught it very early, which is good."

He tried to make his words reassuring, but the shock registered in her face. Her warm fingers held on to his like a lifeline, and he wished he hadn't had to mention it.

She took a deep breath and pulled her hand away to reach for Max's. "I thank you for your concern, Jon. It is very brave of you to intervene. Most people would not have cared enough. I will do as you say and see Ben right away. And I will pray for God's will, whatever that is."

She was such a strong and brave woman. Jon intended to pray along with her for God's mercy.

EIGHTEEN

IT WAS A GOOD DAY FOR A SEARCH. THEY'D COME BACK to the area where they'd found Shainya. Even this morning, Annie had spotted cougar scat and tracks. Maybe they'd get lucky.

Annie had taken the soiled sheet from Michelle's car for a scent for the dogs, and she prayed it turned up something. Bree and Samson took the lead while Annie and Jon followed close behind. Naomi and Charley headed the other direction. The SAR team had been together for over ten years, and the golden's great nose matched Samson's.

Mason had called first thing this morning with the info Shainya's mother had given them about a missing seventeen-year-old girl on an illegal moose hunt. The girl had never been found, but the sheriff up that way discounted the idea that anything sinister had happened. On occasion accidents occurred in the North Woods, and people never came back from an adventure. Nothing strange to see, according to the sheriff.

"Was Kylie okay with being left behind today?" Jon asked.

Annie swatted away a black fly. "Lauri agreed to keep all the kids. They love her. She was going to take them swimming." Kade's sister's maturity had come a long way the past few years, and she was good with the children.

Would the dogs find a scent today, or would this search be

for nothing? Even finding a cam with some images would help them.

The sound of a glad bark came from up ahead. "I think Samson has a scent!"

The dog's prowess was renowned in the US—in the world really. Bree had flown with him to several countries after disasters, and the success of his nose was unsurpassed. Annie tried to temper her hope. There was no telling if they'd find Michelle alive. Or if they'd find her at all.

She and Jon broke into a run to catch up with Bree and her dog. She caught a glint of Bree's red hair before she disappeared into the trees. "That way." She jogged to the left.

Her breath burned in her lungs by the time she was five feet behind Bree. Jon breathed heavily beside her, too, but the exertion would be worth it if they found anything. A long howl came moments later, and Annie's heart seized.

It was Samson's death signal.

She slowed, not eager to see whatever lay in front of them. Bree reached the rock where the dog stood first. She knelt on one knee and comforted Samson who continued to whine and tremble.

The discovery of a body was always hard for a search dog, and Samson had an especially tender heart. Annie reached Bree's side. "Is it Michelle?"

"I don't think so. Blonde hair. An autopsy will have to be done to determine cause of death and identity. Michelle has brown hair, correct?"

Annie stepped around the rock and took a look. She shuddered at the grisly scene. "That's what her picture showed, but she could have dyed it."

"Maybe. This seems natural to me, but the coroner will know for sure." Bree buried her face in Samson's fur. "It's okay, boy. You're okay." She rose and pulled her dog away from the scene. "I'm going to call Mason. He'll want forensics out here."

"I think I'll look around. I'll be careful of the crime scene."

Bree pulled out a handful of pistachios and opened them as she talked to Mason. Samson lay at her feet with mournful eyes.

Jon stood off to one side to allow Annie to do her job, but she caught a glimpse of the sympathy on his face. She beckoned him to come with her, and they began a sweep of the perimeter.

"What are we looking for?" he asked.

"Any scraps of clothing, tracks, footprints. Anything that might help us get a sense of what happened here."

"Got it." He wandered off a few feet and began to scour the ground.

Annie grabbed a stick and poked through bushes and thick weeds, searching for anything interesting. Nothing but leaves, rocks, and bugs. She reached a small crescent of beach on Superior and paused at the tracks in the sand. Several footprints. She counted two large prints likely belonging to two different men as well as smaller prints. It could have been one woman or maybe two.

She pulled out her phone and snapped pictures of everything she saw. Bree and Naomi hadn't made it here, and neither had Jon. The prints could be innocent, maybe fishermen or hikers, but given the nearby body, she wasn't assuming anything. She got out yellow crime tape from her backpack to cordon it off.

Jon saw what she was doing and came to help her. He took one end of the tape and they stretched it around the area. Once it was secure, she went back to searching. They headed away from the beach, and Jon grabbed her hand.

He pointed to her left. "There's an ATV. It's on its side like it's been wrecked."

She couldn't tell that from here with the machine in shadow, but as they neared, she saw he was right. The machine had been mangled from hitting a large rock. "Maybe she had an accident and crawled away before she died. The ATV isn't that far from the body."

He nodded and went back to the search. "The accident could have flung her too. Let's see what else we find."

She snapped more pictures for Mason and turned the other way. Hidden by vegetation, she found a backpack. She pulled Nitrile gloves from her pack and unzipped the backpack. Inside she found a notebook, water bottles, jerky, and a compass. The engraving on the back of the compass had a name: Michelle Fraser.

Was that Michelle's body after all? She could have bleached her hair. Or was this merely a clue that Michelle had been here?

She couldn't wait for Mason to get here so they could unravel this. The notebook might have information. She pulled it out and flipped through. Michelle had sketched cougars in various poses, and she'd made notes about possible sightings. Annie slid the notebook back in the pack and unzipped the front pocket. A phone was nestled there.

Annie turned it on, but it was password protected so she put it away. Mason could deal with that, but it likely held a lot of information. Maybe they were about to find out what happened to Michelle Fraser.

Mason wore a pained expression as he surveyed the scene. Jon stood at the perimeter of the clearing so he didn't get in the way. He loved watching Annie work. Her dramatic hand gestures as she told the sheriff what she'd found kept him riveted. She cared so much about other people and her job.

He glanced at the time on his phone. Well past lunch, and his stomach growled as if to remind him it was empty. Way back in Annie's truck they had a cooler with sandwiches and apples, but it would take half an hour to hike to it, and he doubted he could get Annie to eat even if he went to grab the food.

A twig snapped behind him, and he turned in that direction. As far as he knew, everyone was closer to the lake. Maybe it was a deer or other wildlife. He scanned the thick copse of underbrush hunkering under the oak overstory and saw a flash of green movement.

Someone was there.

On his guard, Jon moved in that direction and saw no one. But a fresh footprint impression in the grass near a log still rose as if the person had just left. It could be another searcher, but the hair stood on the back of his neck.

"Hello? Anyone there?"

No answer. That was worrisome since anyone with a legitimate reason to be here would have replied. He stopped and scanned the area again before moving deeper into the forest. The imprints of a scuffle in the dirt stopped him. Broken branches, deep gouges in the mud, and a discarded flannel shirt lay strewn around the clearing. Something had happened here.

He backed away to go find Mason and Annie and bring them here. They were righting the ATV to look for evidence. They followed him when he explained what he'd found.

Annie circled the area to study the prints while Mason headed closer to the water. "Two women and a man, I think. See the different shoe sizes?" Annie said.

"I found something," Mason called from the other side of a rocky outcropping.

Jon led Annie toward Mason's voice, and they found him at a kayak partially hidden by vegetation. "Looks like a rental." Jon pointed out a label on the hull of an outfitters from Rock Harbor. "Did you check the dry hold?"

"Not yet." Mason pulled it from the shrubs and flipped it over so he could get to the compartments.

Jon bent to help him. "I'll get the one on this end." Reaching inside, he felt through the compartment and found a dry bag. He pulled it out and dumped the contents onto the ground.

Annie reached past him and snatched an item in her gloved hand. "There's a woman's wallet."

She unsnapped it and flipped it open. Her eyes widened. "It belongs to Grace Mitchell!"

Jon glanced at the picture of the girl. Blonde hair. The body they'd found was a blonde. Jon saw the thought flicker across Annie's face as she continued to stare at Grace's picture. They probably hadn't found Michelle at all.

"What about the ATV? Any idea whose it is?" Jon asked Mason.

"I called in the registration number. It belongs to Fraser. I assume Michelle took it when she left him and was using it. I found the tracker on it, too, though it's not working now."

"So both girls have been here." Annie flipped through the other pictures and documents in the wallet, but they held no surprises. "We need to talk to Brandon again and see if she took the

ATV when she first left, or if she came back for it. He claims he hasn't seen her since she left, but where did she store the machine if she took it when she left?"

Mason nodded and went back to examining the kayak. The only things he found in the dry bag in the other compartment were a pair of jeans and a tee. Grace had evidently brought along a dry set of clothes in case she capsized.

"We need an autopsy and ID performed on the body ASAP," Mason said. "I'll let the Ontonagon County sheriff know we might have found Grace."

Jon looked around. "Michelle was here, too, though. Where is she?"

Mason's phone sounded, and he listened for a long moment. "We'll be right there." He ended the call. "Montgomery found tire tracks. It's probably nothing, but I'd better check it out. And the DNA on the bloody sheet came back. It's Michelle's blood, likely from the attack with the knife her mother mentioned to you." He scooped up the evidence he'd found in the kayak. "I'll have Doug retrieve the kayak so we can dust it for prints."

Jon and Annie followed him away from the clearing into a thickly wooded area where they found beaten-down weeds and grass from truck tires. A sprinkle of rain began to intensify.

"I'll need to get a mold of the tires before this rain ruins it," Mason said.

Jon assessed the tracks. "A ton truck."

This scene was only a few yards from the body they'd found. They'd missed it at first because of the heavy vegetation.

But where had he taken Michelle?

With the ATV in the area, Annie walked around staring

up into the trees. "Here!" she called. She spied a wildlife cam attached to a large spruce tree.

Jon retrieved it for her, and she took it and turned it on. "Michelle would have liked to have seen this."

She showed Jon and Mason the picture of a mountain lion, then continued to scroll through the pictures.

Jon peered closer when Annie gasped. "What is it?"

She turned the camera around to Mason and him. "Someone carried her out of here."

The picture showed a man carrying a woman with dark hair toward the area where they'd seen the tire tracks, though no vehicle showed in the frame.

"Any other pictures?" Mason asked.

Annie shook her head. "We need that warrant to examine her personal effects. She was definitely abducted."

Mason nodded and walked away to use his phone. Jon took Annie's hand. "You're amazing at what you do. I'm proud of the way you care about people, Annie."

Color rushed to her cheeks. "Thank you. You take care of people in a different way."

"You're so beautiful inside and out. We have a lot of lost time to make up for."

Tears made her blue eyes luminous. "Not everyone gets a second chance."

He kissed her and silently promised not to mess this up.

NINETEEN

JON'S SPICY COLOGNE WAFTED ANNIE'S WAY AND MADE it hard to concentrate on the task ahead of her. She drove her pickup toward Marquette in a dreary drizzle of rain that made the afternoon seem later than three. Mason had turned her loose to question Brandon Fraser, and she intended to hit him hard.

She glanced at Jon in the passenger seat. "Ready for this? Brandon will likely not be any more welcoming or helpful than he was the first time."

Jon studied the picture on Michelle's phone. "I noticed her leg looks damaged. I'd guess she injured it in the ATV crash."

"You can tell that from the photo?"

"Look here." He traced a finger along the picture. "Appears to be a tibial plafond fracture. It can involve the joint as well. I see these a lot in auto accidents."

Annie winced. "That sounds painful."

He nodded and put down the phone. "They often require surgery. If the guy carried her off without getting her medical attention, it will never heal right. And it might even cause infection. You think there's any chance it's Brandon in the photo?"

"The guy's build seems similar, and I want to see if he owns a one-ton pickup. Those aren't that common."

"No," Jon agreed. "Don't you need a warrant to examine his stable of vehicles?"

"Mason is running a search of vehicles Brandon owns, and I should have that by the time we see Fraser. Could you shoot Mason a text and tell him about the broken leg? He could check hospitals and emergency clinics."

"What about talking to Michelle's mother? Maybe she would recognize the guy's outline."

"Wildlife cams don't take the best pictures at night, and he was walking away. Getting an ID will be tough. But you're right. Mary might have an idea who it could be."

Annie felt an inner urgency about finding Michelle now that she was sure there'd been an abduction. Where had the guy taken her, and why had he left the other woman's body behind? Had he merely seen an opportunity after an ATV crash and taken it? Maybe the abductor hadn't seen the other body.

Annie had lots of questions and no answers.

They reached the Fraser property, and the gate was closed again. After speaking to the housekeeper through the intercom, they were granted access. Annie parked in the circle drive in front of the door, and they dashed to the porch in the rain. She shook the rain off her hair, then pressed the doorbell.

The housekeeper was an older woman with graying hair. "Mr. Fraser has agreed to see you. This way." She made it sound like he was some kind of king granting an audience.

Annie suppressed a wry grin. She and Jon went through the two-story foyer and past an expansive living room to an office lined with books. The space was so large, the massive desk looked small.

Brandon indicated the two armchairs across from a love

seat. "I didn't expect to hear from you again. I told you everything I know." He came around from behind the polished walnut desk and sat on the love seat opposite them. "I only have a few minutes."

A sideswept hairstyle with product replaced his carefree, windblown look from the last time, and he wore a suit.

Annie was tempted to tell him Mason would be happy to haul him to jail for questioning, but she swallowed her response. The guy was used to his word being law, and it rubbed her the wrong way.

"It appears your wife has been abducted, Mr. Fraser." Annie watched for an expression of shock, but his poker face gave nothing away. "I wondered if you might recognize this man." She handed over her phone for him to examine the photo.

Frowning, he took it and studied it. "Who can tell anything from that? If I didn't know it was Michelle, I might not even recognize her."

"I'd hoped something about the man's stance or build would seem familiar."

"So this guy is carrying her. What makes you think he isn't trying to help her?"

"She looks unconscious. And I think her leg is broken."

"Where'd he take her? Have the hospitals around the area reported any broken legs?"

Annie decided to ignore that question since Mason wouldn't have checked it out yet. "We found a wrecked ATV titled in your name."

Fraser scowled. "She wrecked it? It was a gift from my dad."

"Did you give her permission to take it?"

"Nope. It was in a summer storage barn at one of the mines,

and an employee found it missing the summer she disappeared. I never did figure out why she took it."

"Do you have a pickup truck, Mr. Fraser?"

His hazel eyes narrowed. "What kind of question is that? Most households in the U.P. have a pickup. I've got a Dodge Ram 3500."

Annie wasn't all that knowledgeable about pickups, but she knew a 3500 was a one-ton pickup. Unfortunately, he was also right about the many trucks up here. It would make sense he'd need a heavy-duty one in his line of work.

"Would you mind if we checked it out for evidence?"

He held up the phone. "What, you think this is me? I haven't seen Michelle in over a year. I wouldn't hurt her."

"I know you injured her with a knife."

His face tightened. "I suppose her mother told you that. It was an accident. I was cutting up steaks, and she was arguing with me. She fell onto the knife."

That was the most ridiculous excuse Annie had ever heard. "I saw how much blood her injury caused. That seems very unlikely. You've made no secret of your hatred of her. That puts you high on the suspect list."

He threw his hands up. "Fine. Look at the truck all you like. It's new, bought six months ago. You won't find even one of Michelle's hairs or DNA. She's never been in the truck."

"I'll call for a forensic tech. Thank you for your cooperation." She rose, and Jon did the same.

They hadn't learned much, but at least his truck could be ruled out if he was innocent.

The rain pounded against the hood of the truck as Annie drove to see Michelle's mom in Munising. Though it had to be done, she suspected it would be a dead end. The photo simply didn't show enough.

Jon looked at the photo again as Annie drove. "The more I study this picture of Michelle's leg, the more I think the tibia is severely displaced."

She spared him a quick look as she turned onto Mary's street. "What's that mean?"

"A displaced fracture damages more soft tissue along with the joint. It's a very unstable fracture, and she'll be unable to put weight on it."

Annie's phone rang as she parked in Mary's drive. She answered it, then put it on speaker. "Hey, Mason, did you get my text?"

"Yeah, I found the truck in the DMV database. Listen, I've got information breaking all over the place. Brandon's truck tires don't match the imprint forensics took. My tech got into Michelle's phone. There's a picture of Grace in the woods on it. She looks terrified and exhausted. The two women were clearly together at some point. And I got a quick turnaround on the autopsy. It's Grace. She suffered a broken neck, likely from the ATV crash."

"And it was clearly a bad crash," Annie said. "Jon told you he thought Michelle's leg was broken. He's looked at the photo more closely and thinks it's a severe break that will require surgery. Did you hear from any hospitals?"

"Our inquiry came up empty. The reported fractures were other verified people. No unknown woman or anyone with a name close to Michelle's reported to an ER or doctor's office. I checked orthopedic clinics as well."

The dead-end news wasn't what she'd wanted to hear. "I'm at her mother's now. I'll see if she has any idea about the abductor's identity."

"Marquette police have a forensic tech en route to the Fraser house. I'll let you know what I hear."

"Thanks, Mason." Annie ended the call and opened her door into the rain. "Okay, let's see if we have better luck here."

Jon jumped out, too, and they dashed through the puddles and downpour to the porch, and Annie pressed the doorbell.

Mary opened the door almost immediately. "I saw you pull up. You have news?" Her brown eyes held a hopeful shine.

Annie flicked the wet hair away from her face. "May we come in?"

"Oh, sorry." She stood away from the open door. "Get out of the rain."

Annie stepped into the foyer and wiped her wet feet on the rug. The charming blue-and-yellow decor in the living room off to the right felt warm and welcoming. A cinnamon scent wafted from somewhere and added to the homey atmosphere.

She started to take off her shoes, but Mary stopped her. "These old floors have seen more than a little rain. Come in and sit down."

Annie eyed the upholstered furniture and chose a wooden rocker that could withstand the saturation in her clothes. Jon crossed the room and sat on the brick hearth.

"Though we haven't found Michelle yet, we do have some information." Annie took out her phone and called up the photo.

"A wildlife cam got this picture of a man carrying her out of the woods. Is there anything about him that seems familiar?"

Mary took the phone and studied the image. "Michelle looks unconscious."

"There'd been an ATV accident." Annie held back the information about Grace. "We think she might have injured her leg too."

"So he could have been carrying her to get help?"

"She hasn't turned up for treatment, so unfortunately we suspect he took her somewhere."

Mary, eyes wide with alarm, looked up from her perusal of the picture. "You mean, he abducted her?"

"We don't know what happened since we haven't been able to find her. Or him. Is he familiar at all?"

Mary shook her head. "He's much bulkier than Chad, and I don't think any of her friends are that muscular. This guy looks like he works out."

Annie had thought the same. Her thoughts raced to the Wolstincraft brothers she'd questioned about the murders of the teenage girls when Jon came back to town. But being muscular was hardly unique in this area. "I know the lighting isn't great, but I'd hoped something was familiar."

"So you don't have any idea who he is or where he took her?"

"Not yet, but we're working hard on it." Annie rose and retrieved her phone from Mary. "Thank you for your time. If we hear anything else, I'll let you know."

Mary walked them to the door, and they ran back to the truck in the rain. Annie flung herself behind the steering wheel. The rain began to stop, and the sky lightened a bit.

She peered up into the clouds. "I'm starved. I'd suggest we

stop for dinner, but I need to retrieve Kylie. Bree probably has her by now."

"I brought snacks." Jon rummaged in a backpack by his feet and produced a stick of something.

"Jerky?" She'd eat jerky, but it wasn't her first choice.

"Buffalo mixed with cranberries. Tanka bars. Lots of protein and actually good."

"It doesn't sound good." But she was always willing to try new snacks, and it might be something she could buy for Kylie.

She unwrapped it and took a bite. "This is really good."

"Told you." His bar was nearly gone.

She chowed down hers and ate another as she drove. A rainbow appeared in the horizon ahead of them. She hoped it meant they'd find Michelle. Alive.

TWENTY

THE PAIN IN MICHELLE'S LEG WAS AT EXCRUCIATING levels again. Why couldn't the guy at least have brought some Tylenol? Did he want her to get better or not? Every muscle in her body ached as well. The journey through the yard had been tough.

She stared at the window. The nails in the sash mocked her. She had no claw hammer or anything to remove them. When she ran her fingers through her tangled dark hair, it felt greasy and in need of a wash. She'd kill for a shower. It had been nearly a week since she was taken.

And no one was looking for her.

Why would they? She'd vanished off the face of the earth for a year, and even the editor at the magazine didn't expect to hear from her until she had something to show her. Her mom might be wondering, but Michelle wasn't sure even Mom was concerned yet. She would be as the days stretched on with no word, but she might think Michelle had gone to ground again to avoid Brandon. She'd give anything to hear her best friend, Brayonna's, voice right now.

Had Grace Mitchell's body been found? That was her only hope. If someone found Grace, they'd find Michelle's wrecked ATV. And while that wouldn't necessarily lead them to this run-down cabin, it might spark a search.

As she'd stared at the four walls, she puzzled over what the man wanted from her. Did it have anything to do with her work for the shelter? Michelle helped Idoya with the books, and she'd begun wondering about some outside deposits. She'd planned to ask Idoya if she knew who had donated that much money. Michelle had snapped photos of the logbook's pages and had even slipped the logbook into her backpack to take a closer look. Idoya would need it back, and Michelle had thought she'd manage to return it before her boss knew it was gone.

Nosiness had always been her besetting sin, though it was a good trait for a reporter. It was what got her into trouble with Brandon when he'd found her snooping through his office. She hadn't found anything noteworthy, but he hadn't spoken to her for a week.

Would Idoya wonder about her when she didn't check in? Had she tried to call her? Only a handful of people would miss her if she died in this old cabin.

Her phone was in her backpack at the accident scene. If they found that, the police could open her phone, but it wouldn't show them her location now. How would anyone find her? The whole situation seemed hopeless, but she'd thought that once about her marriage. She'd thought she would never have the courage to escape Brandon's abuse, but she'd found the strength.

She could find that same strength now. There had to be a way.

She looked at the window again. He hadn't nailed shut all the windows. Just this one. Maybe she could drag the bed to another window. But after staring around the room, no other spot was suitable. The other two windows in the room had obstructions to positioning the cot properly.

And the door was locked, so there was no escape avenue there.

She pressed her fingers to her temple. *Think!* There had to be something she could do instead of lying here awaiting her fate. And while she didn't know what her kidnapper had planned for her, she was sure it wasn't good. The throbbing in her leg brought tears to her eyes, and she grabbed her calf and rocked back and forth. The movement helped soothe her a bit.

Her jujitsu training had made her proficient in delivering incapacitating moves. If she could disable him, she could take his keys and drive out of here. She'd have to use her left foot on the accelerator, but that was a minor detail.

What advantages did she have? She swept her gaze over the room for the umpteenth time since her captivity began, and she still found no option for a weapon.

She thought through her training. She could use a knife-hand strike to the carotid artery. Or even better, she could blind him temporarily by driving her thumbs into his eyes. But to do that, she had to catch him off guard. If only she could escape when he wasn't here.

She studied the dirty mattress where she lay. The cot itself. If she could take it apart, she could use the metal leg or some other part as a bat. His truck engine was so loud that she had heard him approach from a distance. She could be waiting behind the door and attack before he could respond.

Could she get the bed apart? She slid to the floor with her legs extended in front of her. Once she was there, she dragged the mattress down, too, so she could examine the way the cot was assembled. Multiple bolts held the legs and frame together, and she thought she could get it apart.

For the first time in two days, Michelle felt a sliver of hope. She gripped the closest bolt and began to twist it counterclockwise.

It didn't budge. Was she turning it the right way? *Righty tighty, lefty loosey.* Counterclockwise was correct. But years of dirt and grime had welded it in place. Maybe another one would be easier.

She scooted back three feet to the foot of the cot and tried the next bolt. It moved half a turn but then froze completely. The next one seemed even more immovable than the first. A few minutes later she'd tried them all and only had bloody fingers to show for it. Was there anything she could use as a makeshift wrench? Or some kind of tool?

She'd spent many hours in the past week exploring every nook and cranny of this tiny cabin and had found nothing loose lying around.

She was stuck here at the mercy of that awful man. And she suspected it wasn't just him she had to deal with but more people in the shadows. But she couldn't give up and wait for her fate. There had to be a way. And she would find it.

/ / /

Thunder rumbled overhead, and the smell of ozone wafted and rain slashed at Jon's car. The wind nearly shoved it off the road at the curve onto the marina property. It was so dark it appeared to still be night, even though it was seven in the morning. The back-deck lights glimmered through the storm, and he spotted Annie moving around in the kitchen.

He parked and sat in the lot a few minutes, hoping the storm would abate a fraction. While he waited, he noticed a dark SUV backed into a small opening in the forest. Why hadn't it been parked in the lot? Did the driver need help?

He tried to peer through the curtain of rain to see if there was any movement in the vehicle, but it was too dark. There was no help for it—he had to get out into the raging storm and see if anyone was in trouble in that SUV. He didn't have a rain jacket or even an umbrella, so he grabbed the newspaper he'd bought in town even though he hadn't read it yet. He unfolded it and held it over his head as he got out, then jogged through the mud puddles to the SUV.

As he approached, the headlights switched on and nearly blinded him. He held up his other hand to block the glare as the engine roared to life. The vehicle barreled out of its spot and drove right at him. He barely jumped out of the way to avoid being hit and fell into a mud puddle.

He lay stunned in the muddy water and watched the vehicle vanish around the curve. The glow from the vehicle's lit dashboard showed him the outline of a head. He thought it was a man, but visibility was too poor to be sure.

It had been deliberate.

He didn't doubt the driver had seen him and tried to run him over. Why? And why had the person been parked where he could watch Annie's cottage and the marina? Was someone casing the property? Or was it something more sinister? They'd found Grace's body yesterday, and he'd thought someone was in the woods watching them then too.

He got up and wiped his dripping, muddy hands on his pants. Or maybe it had nothing to do with the body they'd found. If that was the case, Jon had no idea what it was all about. But it made him uneasy.

He was already soaked to the skin. He jumped over mud puddles as he ran through the driving rain. The back door of the cottage was unlocked, and he practically fell into the kitchen. The aroma of cinnamon and maple syrup swirled in the air.

Annie turned from mixing a batch of pancakes. "Jon, what on earth?" She snatched up a dish towel and handed it to him to mop his face. "Let me get a bigger one. There are some in the dryer." She went through the door into the utility room and returned with a fluffy bath towel.

He was shivering, and the warmth from the dryer felt good on his cold skin. "Thanks."

"I've got some clothes of Nate's that should fit you. You were always about the same size. Come with me."

Jon followed her through the living room and to the small main bedroom. The space held no pictures of Annie and Nate together. Had she recently removed them, or had she kept mementos like that out of the sleeping space? It was small, with only enough room for the bed and a dresser. A jewelry box and a picture of Kylie sat atop the four-drawer dresser by the door.

Annie opened the bottom drawer and extracted khaki shorts and a red tee. "You can change in here. Come to the kitchen when you're done."

She hadn't asked what happened, probably assuming he'd only gotten drenched from the storm. He touched her arm when she turned toward the door. "It wasn't just the rain, Annie. Someone in a dark SUV tried to run me over. The vehicle was wedged into a small opening in the trees, and the driver seemed to be watching your house."

Her eyes narrowed. "Tried to run you over?"

He nodded and explained what had happened. "I barely managed to jump out of the way. It was no accident."

Her blue eyes searched his expression. "But why?"

"That's the million-dollar question. I thought maybe it had something to do with finding the body yesterday, but watching you wouldn't change anything. Mason is leading the investigation, and you don't have any evidence here, so what would be the point? I don't like it, though."

"I don't either. Did you get the make and model?"

He shook his head. "The storm was too bad. I could only see it was a dark SUV."

"I'll let Mason know. I'll see you in the kitchen." She shut the door behind her.

He stripped out of his dripping-wet clothes. Even his underwear was wet, so he checked the bottom drawer and found a pair of Nate's, even though he hated to wear his dead buddy's clothing. It felt like he was trying to take Nate's place with everything.

At least Nate had died not knowing Kylie was Jon's. That truth kept rearing its complicated head and surprising Jon around every corner. Kylie had warmed up to him, but he wasn't sure they would ever get to the kind of relationship he longed for with his daughter. And they all had to face family and friends learning the truth. So far he and Annie were the only ones who knew the truth.

Well, and Dr. Eckright, but Jon didn't think the doctor would blab to anyone.

TWENTY-ONE

THE DELECTABLE AROMA OF PANCAKES AND MAPLE syrup in Annie's kitchen pushed away her unease over the SUV incident. A haze hung over the yard as the sun burned away the moisture from the storm. She'd called Mason but hadn't gotten him, so she left a message.

She glanced at Jon. It disturbed her a little to see him in Nate's clothes. When Jon had come back into her life, it seemed there had been no more space to mourn Nate. There were such a lot of changes to get used to.

Jon flipped the pancakes and glanced her way. "This gluten-free sourdough starter is the bomb. How'd you find it?"

"Bree, of course. Bree researches everything."

Jon's gaze went over her shoulder to the back door. "Speak of the devil. Bree and Mason are here." He turned off the stove and put the stack of pancakes on the table. "Good thing we made plenty. I'll call Kylie."

From down the hall, Annie could hear the *Pokémon* music playing. "Wait just a few minutes. There might be an inappropriate subject for little ears. I wasn't expecting them."

She stepped to the door and opened it. "You're out bright and early. Jon just made some pancakes with that sourdough starter you found us. They smell divine."

Bree had Samson lie down on the back deck, and Milo scooted out the open door to join him. "I didn't have a chance to grab breakfast so I'm game."

Mason followed Bree inside and glanced around. "Is this a good time to talk?"

From his tone Annie knew it was something serious. "Kylie is playing in her room. She won't overhear us. Any more information about Grace?"

"The Ontonagon sheriff is on his way to notify the parents. We got lucky with that immediate dental records match."

"That poor family." Annie got out coffee mugs and poured them both a cup of fresh brew. "Have a seat."

"That's not why we're here, Annie." Mason's voice was heavy. "The DNA came back a little early."

Annie gripped her hands together and moved closer to Jon. He slipped his arm around her waist. "And?"

"Taylor is Sarah. She's your sister."

Her knees went weak, and she would have fallen if Jon hadn't supported her. Her throat thickened, and she tried to wet her lips, but all the saliva had dried up in her mouth. She hadn't expected these results, not really. Deep in her heart, she'd been sure Sarah would never have turned on her the way Taylor did.

"Annie?" Bree's voice seemed to come from far away.

Annie barely felt Jon moving her to a chair and pushing her head down between her legs. She took a deep breath at his command, then another and another until her head began to clear.

When she sat back up, Bree was squatted in front of her. Her green eyes radiated warmth and concern. "I know this is a shock, Annie, but honestly, I never dreamed you'd ever have closure after all these years. Think of what a wonderful gift this is—Sarah is alive! She wasn't murdered and left in an unmarked grave somewhere. Your baby sister is here in town."

"I-I've treated her terribly."

"You did what you had to do to protect your daughter. That's all. You were never unkind."

Annie covered her face with her hands. "I should have sensed it. How did I not know Taylor was my sister? It seems impossible. I should have known!"

Jon put his hand on her back. "Annie, think about it. She wore contact lenses to change the color of her eyes. She dyed her hair. How could you recognize Sarah in the remodeled woman who showed up here? She deliberately set out to deceive you. Just because you didn't recognize her doesn't mean her actions were miraculously all right. She came here to make you pay for something that wasn't your fault. You had no control over what happened that night."

She knew he was right, but grief and guilt raged a terrible storm in her heart. If only her parents were alive right now. If only she could have brought Taylor to them and announced she'd found Sarah. It might have made up for the disappointment Annie had been to them, especially her dad.

Her vision blurred again, and she struggled to hold back the tears. "Does she know yet?"

Mason settled into a kitchen chair and reached for a pancake and the syrup. "No, we came straight here."

"How do you think we should tell her?" Annie looked to Jon for guidance.

"I think *you* should tell her."

"I agree," Bree said. "She's waiting for this same news. If someone else tells her, she'll think you are upset or angry. This will be your first chance to begin to heal the breach between the two of you."

How did she go about doing that when in her heart this news had crushed just a little of the life out of her? The gulf between her sister and her seemed insurmountable. Even now she found it hard to think of Taylor as Sarah. Could Annie even look her in the face and call her by her beloved sister's name?

Her chest felt heavy, and she found it hard to think past what the day would bring. "What do I say to her? She knows I didn't believe her, not really. Parts of her story seemed true, but coming here under false pretenses is such a bizarre thing to do."

"Which is why you need to stop with the guilt. You didn't do anything to her," Jon said.

She nodded. "My head knows that, but my heart still sees the little sister I couldn't save. I'd better go there now."

"I'll take Kylie home with me," Bree said. "She can eat breakfast here, and we'll go play a while. Take your time. Say whatever you need to say, but be prepared for this healing to take some time. It's not likely to be resolved today."

That was an understatement with the way Annie felt right now.

/ / /

Jon could sense Annie's agitation at the upcoming confrontation with Taylor/Sarah as he went to call Kylie to come to breakfast. He rapped his fingers on her half-open door, then poked his head in. The sound of the *Pokémon* theme cut off as she turned off her iPad. "Breakfast is ready."

"Okay." She hopped off the bed and came toward the door.

He pushed it all the way open and moved out of the way.

Her eyes widened, and a frown settled on her face. "Why are you wearing my daddy's T-shirt? Take it off right now!"

"I got caught in the storm, and my clothes were soaked."

"Mommy gave you Daddy's clothes?" Her face screwed up as she began to cry. "You're moving right into Daddy's place, aren't you? He's still my dad. No one can take his place. I don't understand why you are doing this."

Jon winced at the pain in her face. "Honey, it's just clothes. Your dad was my best friend. He wore my things sometimes too. He'd jump in the lake with his clothes on when we were horsing around, and I'd have to dig out something for him to wear home. If we looked through his clothes, I'll bet I could find some of mine he never gave back."

"I got him that shirt for Christmas," she wailed. "It was his favorite."

"How about I find another shirt? I'm sorry it upset you. My clothes were dripping with mud."

He backed out of the room, but she followed him. "I'll get a shirt, one that doesn't matter so much."

Her tears continued to roll down her cheeks, but she went to her mom's room and rummaged through the drawer. She rejected several shirts before she settled on a white tee. It had no printing and was completely generic.

He accepted it without comment and pulled off the red tee. Once he'd put on the white one, she didn't seem any happier. What could he say to reassure her? He couldn't deny he was moving into Nate's place. Would she be able to accept the truth once it came out? It was going to be an uphill battle.

"The pancakes are ready. Bree and Mason are here, and Bree is going to take you to play with her kids today."

Kylie wiped her face and made a noticeable effort to stop crying. He tried to put himself in her place. How would he feel if someone seemed intent on erasing his mom's memory? While Dad seemed interested in Martha, she had made no effort to move into Mom's place. It was probably different for a kid who idolized her dad like Kylie did. Her grandparents and her dad had disappeared from her life in one fell swoop. Her emotions had to be in turmoil after trauma like that. It had been bad enough for him as an adult to lose his mom.

He gestured for her to go first, and she headed for the kitchen. Maybe it was time for it all to come out. All this tiptoeing around everything was making him crazy. Get all the drama over with at once. He wasn't a drama sort of guy, and all the upheaval was crazy-making.

He and Annie took their leave as quickly as they could, and they walked around the mud puddles on the way to the parking lot. The sun had burned through the last of the clouds and glimmered on the blue water.

Once they were in his car, Annie gave him a sideways glance. "Kylie made you change the shirt?"

"She got upset when she saw me in Nate's clothes. She said she got him the red shirt for Christmas."

"It was my fault. I didn't stop to think about how much fuss Nate made over the gift. Everything is still raw for her. Two years isn't that long when you lose everything at once."

"We talked it out." He started the car but didn't put it into Drive. "Maybe it's time we told her, Annie." He held up his hand when that stubborn expression landed on her face. "Hear me out. Every time she thinks I'm taking Nate's place, she gets upset.

Wouldn't it be easier to tear the bandage off all at once? Let her know the truth so she can begin to come to grips with it?"

She stared down at her hands clutched in her lap. "I don't know the right thing to do. Every time I think I should tell her, I think about how much she loves Nate."

"I don't want her to forget him, but the truth will come out sooner or later. I'd hate for her to find out accidentally."

"Why would she? No one has any idea. Not yet."

"Well, except for the doctor."

Her eyes widened. "You told Dr. Eckright?"

"I mentioned I had celiac disease, and he already knows Kylie isn't Nate's. I saw the wheels turning as he pieced it together. It just slipped out."

Her blue eyes looked troubled. "He won't say anything." The protest sounded half-hearted.

"But how long are we going to live this lie? I want to be a dad to her. That's never going to happen as long as she thinks I'm only your friend and she has to put up with me because of that. If she knows the truth, I think things would start to shift for both of us. I don't want to pressure you, but I want you to think about it."

He drove away from the marina while she was still looking out the window. It was hard to gauge what she was thinking, but he'd made his case. Now it would be up to her.

TWENTY-TWO

LAKE SUPERIOR'S MOOD WAS TURBULENT. THE STORM had left a huge surf in its wake, and the sound of the waves rose above the ship's engine motoring past. With Jon at her side, Annie walked up the hillside to the little cottage behind the lighthouse. Taylor stood on the wet grass, staring at the waves rolling to the beach.

The sun slanted through Taylor's hair, revealing the yellow glints that grew more obvious every day. That wasn't Taylor standing there. It was *Sarah*. Her baby sister, Sarah. Annie had to pound that into her head because the last thing she wanted to do was slip and call her Taylor. Annie had to show she had accepted the DNA results and was welcoming her home with open arms.

Having Jon with her might not have been a good idea since Sarah was so jealous, but Annie didn't think she could do it alone. Jon's presence steadied her and let her catch her breath.

Squaring her shoulders, Annie walked across the springy grass toward where Sarah stood. Jon gave a slight cough as they approached, and Sarah turned. Her blue eyes widened as she took in the two of them heading her way. She looked toward the water as if she wanted to flee, but she stayed put and her gaze focused on Annie.

Somehow Annie found the strength to smile. "You're Sarah, my little sister, home to us at last."

Until the words spilled out, she hadn't known what she was going to say. Tears filled her eyes, and she wanted to hold out her arms, but the way Sarah crossed her arms over her chest warned Annie the gesture wouldn't be welcomed. Sarah wasn't going to fall into her arms and forgive all of Annie's shortcomings and oversights.

"So you're finally here now that you know. What about the whole past week when you ignored me and told me to stay away from Kylie? I was good enough to be a paid employee but not good enough to be called an aunt? Not good enough to be trusted?"

"You're not being fair, Tay—Sarah," Jon said. "What would you have done if the situation were reversed? What if Annie came to you with a fake name, contacts to change her eye color, and dyed hair?"

Sarah blinked and looked down. Annie wasn't sure if she was trying to understand what Jon had said or if she didn't want to look at her.

Her gaze came up. "And would she have believed me if I'd shown up on her doorstep and announced I was Sarah? She would have tossed me out on my ear."

"That's not true!" Annie took a step toward her. "I told you've I've been looking. Mason sent off a DNA sample after a child's body was discovered just a day or so before you showed up here seeking a job. I never stopped searching for you."

Sarah's mouth twisted, and she shook her head. "I don't believe you."

"Ask Mason," Jon said. "He can show you the email and the record of the DNA sample."

Sarah bit her lip and looked away uncertainly before she turned her back on them. "You've said your piece. You can leave anytime."

"That's it?" Annie took a step toward her. "You plan to know the truth and ignore us? What do you want me to do, Sarah? This situation isn't going away. We're still sisters, even if you're angry with me. Kylie is your niece. Those things are permanent."

Sarah whirled and started for the cottage. "I don't know, but I can't listen to you for one more minute. It's going to take some time for me to figure this out."

She reached the cottage, and the door slammed behind her. Sarah shut the blinds as well, as if she didn't want them to catch even a glimpse of her.

Annie struggled against the tears that misted her eyes. "That didn't go anything like I expected. I thought she'd at least crow about it a little, then demand to see Kylie. It's what she wanted to prove all along, so why not welcome the news?"

Jon embraced her and rested his chin on top of her head. "I think maybe she didn't want you to see her cry."

She pressed her cheek against his chest. "I'm not sure what to do next."

"Maybe some kind of gesture to show her she's part of the family. An invitation to dinner or an offer to go shopping with you and Kylie. Some girl thing."

She lifted her head. "I think I have a better idea. I'll put her name on the marina too. I'll offer to teach her how to run it. I can turn it over to her."

"Whoa, whoa, love. That's radical. What if she shuns you forever, and you have to tiptoe around her at the marina all the time? I think you should think about taking things a little more slowly. You could start by giving her some other family mementos. Pictures of your parents, perhaps. Maybe that stuffed kitty she mentioned, Cocoa. You still have it, right?"

She nodded. "Kylie used to sleep with it, and it's still on her bed."

Telling Kylie what was happening was the next thing she had to tackle. Her daughter would probably embrace the news with joy and want to go see Sarah right away. She wouldn't sense any of the tension and drama going on behind the scenes.

Annie took Jon's hand and turned toward his car. "What if Sarah is mean to Kylie?"

"I'd be surprised if she took it out on Kylie. She seems to really care about her."

How could she make sure that first encounter between Sarah and Kylie went well? "I know! I'll have Kylie give Cocoa to Sarah. It will mean more coming from her anyway, and when she hears Kylie has kept Cocoa safe on her bed all these years, it should soften her attitude."

Jon opened the passenger car door. "We can only hope."

He wasn't any more sure of Sarah's reaction than she was.

/ / /

Rock Harbor's usual summertime bustle had died for the day when Jon walked to his car. Sarah wasn't likely to welcome his questions. He was about to slide into the driver's seat when a woman called his name. He turned to see Anu walking hand in hand with Max toward him.

She wasn't smiling.

Annie got out as Jon went around the side of the car toward

the older couple. The wind off the lake ruffled Anu's short, silvery-blonde hair and blew strands into her reddened eyes. Her smile seemed forced, and his heart sank.

When they stopped in front of her, she released Max's hand and reached out for Jon. He embraced her. "Bad news?"

Her face was buried in his tee. "I just came from Ben's office. The ultrasound is not so good, Jon. I have a mass on my right ovary that has bulges inside it."

Jon tightened his grip on her. "Did he call the bulges papillary structures?"

"Yes. I could not remember that term so well." She drew away and wiped her wet face with the back of her hand. "Since it looks so suspicious, Ben is scheduling surgery immediately with an oncologist in Houghton while he waits for the CA-125."

"That's good. Even if it's benign, it needs to be biopsied to be sure."

Anu straightened, took a step back, and leaned against Max. "Ben hopes if it is ovarian cancer, it will be in an early stage. Thank you for prompting me to be checked."

"Yes, thank you," Max said in a gruff, chastened voice. "I've got this now. Nothing but the best doctors will touch her."

Jon could only hope Max didn't find out money couldn't buy everything. "Thank Milo. He's the real hero here."

Anu put her hand on his arm. "I will give him some peanut butter as a thank-you." She glanced at Annie. "I have a journey ahead of me. But while my flesh is weak, I know my God is strong and will carry me through whatever the future holds. If it's my time, I am ready." She looked up at Jon again. "What would be the best outcome if it is cancer?"

"If it's localized inside that right ovary, it would be stage 1A.

The survival rate at five years out is very high. I'm no oncologist, but I think it's around 94 percent. If it's outside the ovary, that drops a bit to maybe 90 percent, but still very good. I'm hopeful it's in a very early stage."

He didn't try to reassure her that it wasn't cancer. The papillary structures indicated the likelihood, and he didn't want her to face the shock all over again.

Annie embraced her. "I wish you didn't have this challenge, my friend. You've already had so much heartache in your life."

"Life brings good and bad, Annie. We grow our faith through those heartaches. You know this as well as I do, for heartbreak has not passed over you. God has walked with me through those dark times, and his presence has never left me, even when I have not sensed him there. I can look back through every valley to see where he carried me. He will carry me through this. Whether it is into his arms at the end or whether he gives me more days here on this earth, I am content."

Tears spilled down Annie's cheeks. Max moved to embrace them both, and luckily, his arms were long. After a slight hesitation, Jon joined the group hug. They stood together for a long moment until Anu sniffled and stepped away.

She gazed toward Bree's lighthouse home. "I must tell my dear Bree. She will be most distressed at this news." Anu's smile was genuine this time. "I must help her realize once again that as trials come, God is more than sufficient. It is a lesson none of us seem to master."

She patted Jon's arm. "Thank you again. I put you on my HIPAA document so Ben feels free to discuss anything with you, though since you are a doctor, perhaps it was unnecessary. But I want you on my side."

He laid his hand over hers. "I'm always on your side."

She withdrew her hand and went with Max toward the porch. "Pray for Bree and the children."

"Of course," Annie and Jon said in unison.

His heart ached for what was facing the whole family. Mason's family too. The entire town would be pulling for her. Anu was a fixture in town, much beloved by everyone. The residents had watched her pull through the loss of a husband and a son as well. She'd made a success of her shop in the face of almost impossible odds.

Annie stepped closer, and Jon put his arm around her. "I hate this," she said.

"Me too. Ovarian cancer can be a beast, but we have to pray we found it early."

"Thanks to you and Milo. I still can't believe the puppy has that skill. How do we hone it and use it for good? I know nothing about dogs and their medical uses. How did you know about this?"

"Just something I heard at a convention. Milo was acting so weird, and it finally came to me. I wish the ultrasound had proven me wrong, though."

Annie hugged him even tighter around the waist. "You talked about how I cared about people, but look what you did here? Breaking that news couldn't have been easy, but you did it."

"Love faces hard situations. It doesn't run away when circumstances get hard. I know I ran once and regretted it. You can trust me not to do it again. I promise."

She pulled back and looked up at him. "I trust you, Jon. Our breakup wasn't all your fault. We both were young and stupid. I'm not running either."

He kissed her, then inhaled the sweetness of her hair and skin. As long as he lived, he never wanted to take moments like this for granted. The challenge Anu faced was a reminder of the way life could change in an instant.

TWENTY-THREE

A PILE OF PICTURES LAY STREWN ON THE FLOOR around Annie. It had been heartbreaking and yet somehow wonderful to take a trip down memory lane after lunch. They'd had some good times in the years before Sarah was kidnapped.

She showed Jon a picture of the family. Her sister was about two and was sitting on Mom's lap. She wore a goofy grin and had one arm looped around Cocoa, her stuffed kitty. Dad stood behind Mom, and Annie was leaning against him.

Jon studied it. "You all seem so happy. Even your dad. I don't think I've ever seen him looking so relaxed and content."

"He changed after Sarah was taken."

"I can understand why. A dad feels responsible for his children. He's supposed to be their protector, the strong one. Yet he'd been unable to find her. It had to wear on him with every year that went by."

"I can see where that would be true. I'd do anything for Kylie."

In spite of his daughter's standoffish attitude, she was his flesh and blood. His child. Love for her had crept into his heart despite the circumstances. Nate had loved her like that, too, and that thought made Jon a little jealous. He wasn't sure Kylie would ever love him as much as she did Nate.

But maybe that was okay. Love wasn't always reciprocated.

He could take what crumbs she threw his way. At least he told himself he could settle for them. Maybe more would come eventually.

He picked up a picture out of the pile. "You should give her this one. You're braiding her hair."

She took it from his fingers. "I'd forgotten I used to fix her hair. She would have the worst tangles, and she'd cry when Mom tried to brush it. Sarah wouldn't jerk or cry when I'd brush it. You think she remembers that?"

"Probably not, but the pictures might jog her memory." He reached past her and took another one. "This looks like Christmas."

She leaned over his shoulder. "Our last Christmas before everything changed. It was the first year I used my own money to buy presents for everyone. Dad paid me to weed the garden the summer before, and I saved every penny. I got Mom some cologne and Dad a toolbelt. Sarah had a favorite doll, and I got her a cowgirl outfit for it. It came with little plastic boots and everything. There should be a picture of her with it."

She pawed through the pictures and found it. Her eyes misted with the memories. Sarah was holding out the doll dressed in the new outfit. She looked as proud as a new mommy. Would she remember when she saw this?

The back door to the kitchen slammed, and Kylie's voice called out, "Mommy, I'm home."

Annie sprang up to go thank Bree, but her friend and Kylie appeared in the doorway before Annie got more than two steps. Milo, tongue lolling, rushed to greet her, and she knelt to rub his ears.

Bree's green eyes were red-rimmed, and Annie knew hearing

about Anu's health situation was hard to come to grips with. It was one of the things that had bonded Annie to Bree—they'd both been widowed and had gone through major heartache.

Bree shot a glance at Kylie. "How was your morning? Thumbs-up?"

Annie gave her a thumbs-down and shook her head. "Thanks for taking Bug this morning." She hugged Kylie. "Did you have fun?"

Kylie's blonde head bounced up and down. She looked over to where Jon sat on the floor with the pictures spread out. "What are you doing?"

Annie inhaled and squared her shoulders. "Honey, I have something I need to talk to you about." She gestured for Bree to have a seat, then took Kylie's hand. "You've heard me talk about Sarah."

"Your little sister. That's why I'm always supposed to be careful around strangers."

"That's right. Um, I found out some amazing news about her today."

"You found her body?"

Why had Annie thought Kylie wouldn't pick up on her search all these years? She had to have overheard things now and then. "We didn't find her body. We found *her.* Sarah is still alive."

Kylie's eyes widened. "Can we go see her? Where is she?"

"That's one of the really amazing parts. Taylor is really Sarah. She came here to try to get to know us before she told me who she really was."

Kylie's forehead wrinkled as she tried to process it. "My Taylor is your baby sister?"

Annie nodded. Maybe this wouldn't be as hard as she'd

thought. Kylie seemed eager to accept the news. "But she is kind of mad at me."

"Well, you did tell her she couldn't see me. It made me mad too. But she'll forgive you if you ask. I always do."

"I hope so. I want us to give her some things to remind her that she's part of our family. Like these pictures of her when she was a little girl. And I'd like you to give her Cocoa."

Kylie frowned at that. "But Cocoa is mine now."

"She belonged to Sarah first. You've had Cocoa for a long time, and you don't even play with it. I think it will mean to lot to her if you're willing to welcome her and give Cocoa back to her. You have lots of plushies. Sarah has nothing. The woman who took her was not nice to her, and she doesn't own much of anything."

"She doesn't have very many clothes either." Kylie glanced down at Jon. "You changed out of Daddy's clothes."

He got up. "I knew it made you unhappy, and I didn't want to make you sad. Just like you don't want to make Taylor sad."

The light went on in her blue eyes, and she nodded. "I'll get Cocoa. Could we go now and take the pictures and my kitty to her?"

"I think that would be great," Annie said.

Kylie ran from the room, and Annie exhaled. "That went better than I thought it might."

"You handled it well," Bree said. "I'll get out of here and let you gather the things you're taking. You can leave Kylie with me when you're ready to go to dinner. I'll be praying it goes well."

"I think we'll need all the prayer we can get," Annie said. "Especially for Anu. How is the family doing?"

"It's rough. Hilary is beyond devastated. I talked to her on the phone for a while, and I'm heading there now. We haven't told the kids yet. We decided it was better to wait until we know what we're facing."

"That's wise," Jon put in. "We're all praying it's benign."

Bree's eyes focused on him. "But you don't really believe that, do you?"

"Ben sent me the ultrasound, and I took a look. Remember, I'm not an oncologist, just a humble orthopedic surgeon. But no, it looks likely to be ovarian cancer. But I'm hopeful it's contained in that one ovary."

"That's our prayer." Bree touched his arm. "Thank you for caring enough to pursue it." She reached down and scratched Milo's ears. "And many thanks to this guy too."

/ / /

Since they had Kylie, they took Annie's Volkswagen pickup to town to talk to Sarah. Was it as hard for Annie to call Taylor Sarah as it was for Jon? And how easily would Taylor fall into using the name Sarah? She didn't seem to want to meld into the family.

Annie hit the village limits of Rock Harbor and slowed the truck. Jon was in the passenger seat, and he spotted a large SUV maintaining an even distance behind them. Could it be the same one that had tried to run him down?

He was probably jumping to conclusions. "Hey, slow down a sec."

Annie lifted a brow and glanced in the rearview mirror. Her face tightened, and the truck slowed. "The same guy?"

"I'm not sure. Let's see if he goes around us. Maybe pull into Konkola Service Station like you're going to get gas."

She glanced at the dashboard. "I could use some gas anyway."

She parked at the pump. Jon got out and stuck in his debit card. He kept an eye on the traffic moving past. The SUV was black, and it slowed as it passed. The tinted windows made it impossible to see inside, so he couldn't tell if the driver was male or female. By the time he finished pumping gas, it cruised past the other way as if it was going out of town.

He hopped back inside. "Take a roundabout way to Bree's and let's see if the SUV follows."

He glanced in the pickup's back seat. Thankfully Kylie was busy catching *Pokémon* on her iPad. She hadn't paid any attention to what he and Annie were doing.

She pulled out onto Houghton Street, then turned at the newspaper office onto Pepin Street. She took it to Pakala, then turned in front of Naomi and Donovan's house on Cottage Avenue. No one was in the yard or Jon might have suggested they stop. He had Annie turn around in the hardware store's parking lot and go back past Naomi's house to turn onto Pakala again. She took it up to Kitchigami Street, then turned at the jail back onto Houghton.

Then Houghton curved and turned into Negaunee Street. "There he is again," Annie whispered. "What do you want me to do?"

"Nothing. Just drive on out to the lighthouse, where the road ends. If he follows us there, he'll be trapped and maybe I can get a look at him. Or get his license plate."

She nodded and continued on past the Blue Bonnet Bed-and-Breakfast. The SUV maintained its distance behind them. Annie stopped at the curb in front of Bree's lighthouse, and Jon was out in a flash and walking back toward the SUV.

The vehicle stopped in the middle of the road as if the driver had just realized there was no continuing on past. Jon stared through the windshield into a familiar face.

Her gaze collided with his, and she backed away quickly. The SUV careened from side to side as it accelerated away. It reached the drive into the Blue Bonnet, then turned around and sped away. He noted the license number in his phone, but there was no need since he'd recognized the driver.

Why would she be following them?

He jogged back to the truck, and Annie got out with Kylie. "Anything?" she asked.

"It was Idoya Jones." He spoke softly, but Kylie wasn't paying attention anyway.

"What on earth?"

"It makes no sense," he agreed. "We'd better pay her another visit. She knows I saw her, so she won't be surprised when we stop by the shelter."

Annie shielded her eyes with one hand and held a box in the other as she looked up at the lighthouse and the cottage just behind it. "Let's get this done." Her voice wobbled.

He took her hand and squeezed it. "You can do this. I'm here, and so is Kylie."

Her fingers were cold in his. "Sarah wouldn't listen this morning."

Kylie took her other hand. "But I'm here now, Mommy."

"You're a good girl, Bug." Annie lifted her chin. "You have Cocoa?"

Kylie showed her the plushie. "Right here."

"And I've got the pictures as well as Mom's favorite sweatshirt. It still smells like her, so I never washed it."

Jon tugged her up the hillside. They went past the lighthouse and around to the cottage in the back. The breeze blew the fresh scent of the lake into his face. Gulls squawked and flew overhead in the blue sky.

He spotted Sarah sitting on the little porch in an Adirondack chair, holding a book. She rose when she saw their approach.

Her inscrutable expression was a little off-putting, but Kylie didn't seem to notice. She darted forward and ran toward the aunt she'd just discovered existed. "Aunt Sarah! You're my aunt Sarah!" She threw her arms around Sarah, and though the woman hesitated for a moment, she finally embraced the little girl.

Jon held back a few feet in case his presence made things worse. Annie paused at the base of the steps with the box in her hands.

Sarah stepped away from Kylie and stared at her. "You're back a lot quicker than I thought you'd be."

Annie mounted the steps. "We brought you some things."

Kylie thrust the stuffed cat into Sarah's hands. "I brought you Cocoa!"

Sarah smoothed the plushie's fur. "She's a little ratty."

Annie laughed and opened the box. "She's twenty-eight years old, so what do you expect?" She pulled out the sweatshirt and handed it to Sarah. "This was Mom's favorite, and it still smells like her. I thought you might like to have it." She reached into the box and gathered up the pictures. "I thought these might help you remember too."

Sarah glanced at the top picture of the happy family. "I can't do this right now." Her voice quavered, and she turned with her gifts and ran inside. The lock clicked closed behind her.

Tears gathered in Kylie's eyes, and she leaned against the

porch post. Jon moved to lift her in his arms. "It's going to take a little time. She's not mad at you, but she has a lot to process."

Kylie buried her face in his neck, and he felt her tears trickle onto his skin. He had to help fix this somehow.

TWENTY-FOUR

SEATED ON THE LOVE SEAT IN THE LIVING ROOM, Taylor stared at the photo of the happy family. Who was she really? Taylor Moore or Sarah Vitanen? The two were very different women. One had come here for revenge, and one had started life here as the treasured daughter of a popular family.

It was up to her to decide, and she wasn't sure which one to choose. If she accepted her identity as Sarah, she would be welcomed into the bosom of Annie's family and friends. People in Rock Harbor would smile and stop to talk as she walked the village streets. She'd have friends nearly everywhere. And maybe Annie would even give her a job at the marina again. She'd have a place of her own.

If she held on to her previous identity, she could pursue her revenge, a plan she had laid out for years. People would cross the streets to avoid her once they knew what she'd done. She'd have to leave here. Where would she go?

While she had been sure the DNA would show the truth, hearing it from Annie had rattled her. She'd expected Annie to still be standoffish, that she might even try to deny the truth staring her in the face, but she'd come here immediately. And with *gifts*. What did that say?

She laid the top picture aside and stared at one of two little girls. The older girl was braiding the long blonde hair of the smaller one. Taylor ran her fingers through her short hair, which was finally losing the fake color. One of her earliest memories with the woman she called Mother was of her whacking her head with the back end of a hairbrush because she wouldn't sit still. She thought she'd always hated having anyone do her hair, but this picture was proof she'd happily allowed it when she was small.

This picture had to have been shortly before she was taken away. The small Sarah appeared to be around five, the age when she disappeared. She'd heard memories could be tricky, but she hadn't expected to remember only bad and nothing good.

She struggled to remember *something*. The feel of a loving hand in her hair, the sound of another little girl calling her name, squeals of laughter on a swing. But nothing came except more anger and bitterness over what she'd lost. The lack of memories just punctuated what she'd missed for so many years. That time could never be reclaimed. Her parents were gone now. She'd never really known them.

She picked up the sweatshirt that had belonged to her mother and lifted it to her nose. The sweet scent of a cologne made tears spring to her eyes. The memory of sitting on a soft lap and nuzzling into her mother's chest brought emotions surging into her heart. At least it was something, even if it was only a snippet of memory.

She'd been loved once. Really loved. There hadn't been any warmth or cuddles with Mother. Why had she even taken Taylor if she didn't intend to love her? Why snatch her away from her family if she simply wanted a servant?

She'd always felt alone and *different*. Mother had homeschooled her, so she hadn't had any friends. They'd kept to themselves, and the only other person she'd ever been around had been the occasional neighbor. Now that she was out of that living situation, Taylor realized how strange it had been. Since she'd come here and seen how a real family lived, her rage over what she'd missed had grown.

The last picture was one of Kylie and her. She stared into the little girl's face. The plans she'd had to use Kylie to make Annie suffer would rip the little girl out of her mother's arms. In spite of Taylor trying to keep her distance, Kylie had crept into her heart in ways she hadn't expected. Was she prepared for Kylie's tears and heartache?

She would treat her better than Mother had treated Taylor. Shouldn't that count for something?

Her eyes blurred with tears again. Why did life have to be so hard?

Annie hadn't offered any money or property, but then, not many people would give up an inheritance for someone else.

Taylor picked up the picture of the whole family again and stared into her parents' eyes. If only they were still alive. She dropped the picture back onto the coffee table, closed her eyes, and exhaled.

The decision could wait awhile.

/ / /

Annie glanced at her phone to check the time as Jon parked in front of the shelter. "It's five. We have an hour before your dinner meeting. I don't understand why Idoya would be following us. Or why she tried to run you down."

He switched off the engine. "I'm trying not to assume too

much. Black SUVs are common around here, and hers might not be the same one parked by your place. Let's go in calmly and without judgment. Find out why she was following us. We know for sure she was doing that much."

Annie nodded and got out into humidity that frizzed her carefully styled hair and clung to her skin. She'd wanted to do Jon proud when they met his prospective boss, but they would have to take her like they found her.

Jon followed her up the walk to the empty front porch. The scent of sloppy joes and french fries wafted out the screened front window, as did the sound of children giggling inside. She rang the bell, but no one came so she rang it again.

A redheaded boy about Kylie's age opened it. "We're not supposed to talk to strangers."

"That's a very good rule. I'm a park ranger, kind of like a police officer. I need to talk to Idoya. Is she here?"

"She's in her office." He glanced over his shoulder. "I guess it's okay since you're the cops. I can show you."

She didn't want to get him in trouble. "I know how to find her office. I was there once before."

He opened the door, and she shot a quick look back at Jon, who followed her inside. The little boy scampered off to the back of the house where other children talked loudly, probably the kitchen. Annie found her way to the office, but the door was closed.

She squared her shoulders and rapped on it.

"Go away. You know better than to disturb me when the door is shut," Idoya's voice called out.

"Idoya? It's LEO Pederson. I need to talk to you."

There was a flurry of movement from inside, papers shuffling, a chair squealing, then footsteps toward the door. Idoya looked flushed and annoyed. And a little scared. "How did you get in here?"

Annie ignored the question. "This won't take long. You can either invite us in, or I can ask my questions where the rest of the house can hear."

Idoya bit her lip and stepped out of the doorway to allow them in. She shut the door behind them and went to her desk.

"Our visit can't be a surprise," Jon said. "I saw you in your SUV. You followed us all the way through town, even though we took a roundabout route. Don't try to deny it."

Annie took a step closer to the messy desk Idoya seemed to be using as a shield. "I'd like an explanation."

Red spots bloomed in the older woman's cheeks and left splotchy color on her face. "I was hoping you had found Michelle."

"You could have called and asked."

"I didn't think you'd share anything with me. If Michelle was in hiding, you shouldn't tell anyone anything. Not even me."

Annie didn't buy it. The woman wouldn't meet her gaze, and she kept looking around as if the answer to her dilemma was in one of the papers on her desk. "Have you been watching my marina too? Searching for Michelle?"

"Of course not. I don't even know where your marina is."

The woman was a terrible liar. "Someone in a black SUV nearly ran Jon over this morning. It looked like yours."

"I wouldn't do anything like that! I don't even know him. Look, I'd like to find Michelle. Our books are in a bit of a mess, and she's the only one who knows how to figure some of this out. There's a password lock on part of it, and I can't get into it."

That part of her story had the ring of at least partial truth.

But again, why follow Annie when a simple phone call would do? She could tell she wouldn't get much more information out of her, but maybe Mason could dig a little and see what he could find out.

"Did you get together a list of possible run-ins Michelle had with abusive boyfriends or husbands?"

Idoya brightened and shuffled through some papers to triumphantly produce a scrap of paper. "There was only one. The other one I'd thought about moved to Australia six months ago." She handed it over.

Annie glanced at it. The name wasn't familiar. He was local so they could stop and ask a few questions. "Thank you. I'll let you know when we find her. You don't have to follow us for that information."

If anything, the woman seemed more angry and upset when they left than when they'd arrived. Annie knew she was hiding something, but what?

"Where to now?" Jon asked when they were buckled in. "We still have forty-five minutes to kill."

"Let's chat with this guy. Eric Cunningham. He's only a few blocks away." She put the address in her phone and directed him to the house, a neatly kept, modest one-story.

As they got out, the man pulling weeds from the strip of garden along the front porch shaded his eyes from the sun with his hand and turned toward them. "Can I help you?" He was in his thirties with guileless blue eyes.

"Eric Cunningham?" Annie asked.

"Yes."

She introduced herself. "I'm investigating the disappearance of Michelle Fraser, and I hear the two of you had a disagreement."

"Michelle Fraser. I haven't seen her in a long time. Probably at least three months. My wife came back to me in spite of her interference. We're in counseling and working things out."

He turned and went up the steps. Opening the door he called out, and a woman appeared. She linked arms with him and leaned against him. He spoke a few words softly, and she released him to come down the steps.

"You were asking about Michelle? Neither Eric nor I hold any animosity against her. She tried to keep me from going home, you know. She wasn't one to give out second chances, but Eric promised no more drinking. And he's kept his word for the past three months. We're going to be okay."

She glanced up at her husband, and he patted her hand. Annie hated any kind of abuse, but she'd seen men change when alcohol was involved. "Neither of you have seen Michelle in the past week or two?"

"We've actually been to Hawaii and got back yesterday," Eric said. "We were there for two weeks."

"Okay, thank you for your time," Annie said. "And good luck to you both."

She retreated with Jon and he shut her door. "It's possible he could have hired someone to go after Michelle, but my gut says he didn't have anything to do with her disappearance."

Annie buckled her seat belt. "Let's go to the restaurant."

Jon reached over and took her hand. "Thank you for giving me a second chance. Not everyone would do that." He cupped her cheek and leaned over to kiss her.

She closed her eyes and sank into his embrace. While she still didn't know what the future held, everything in her wanted that future to include Jon.

TWENTY-FIVE

JON AND ANNIE ARRIVED AT JOEY'S SEAFOOD & GRILL before his prospective partner did. The aroma of seafood and steak made his mouth water. The wood floors were a nice touch with the tin ceilings. It had kept its Copper Country flavor.

The hostess seated them at a table, and Jon glanced around at the seafood decor. "I haven't been here in ages." He picked up the menu and flipped it open. "Back in the day, I didn't have to worry about gluten. Well, I probably did but didn't know it."

Annie reached over and took his hand. "I know you're nervous. I prayed all the way here. It will work out however it's supposed to. If this isn't the right team for you, you'll know. And God will have something better if it isn't."

He gripped her fingers. "Thanks, love. I'll try to keep that in mind. You look beautiful tonight. But you always do."

She wore a light-blue dress with a V-neck that showed her arms and long neck. It swirled around her legs and ended just above the knee. Her blonde hair was curled around her heart-shaped face instead of straight like usual, and she wore a touch of makeup that enhanced her blue eyes and Scandinavian features.

She touched his navy blazer. "Thanks. You don't clean up so badly yourself."

Since he'd come back to the area, he hadn't had an occasion

to wear a sports jacket, and it felt foreign on his arms. Once he started working again, he would wear one more often. Or maybe he wouldn't. When he'd met with Mike after his appointments for the day, the other surgeon had been dressed in jeans and a casual shirt.

Dr. Mike Willis and a tall brunette trailed after the hostess toward them. Her dark hair touched her shoulders, and she had the kind of expression that made you think you were best friends. Jon began to relax.

Jon sprang to his feet to shake Mike's hand when they arrived. "Good to see you, Mike. This is Annie Pederson."

Annie shook his hand. "Thanks for letting me tag along." Her gaze went to the woman. "I think we've met. You're Priscilla, aren't you? You might not remember me, but I was the ranger who found you when your canoe capsized last spring."

Priscilla's hazel eyes widened. "I remember! You were a godsend that day. My sorority roommate and I were freezing cold from the wind that started after we took that dunk in the lake, and I honestly thought we might die of hypothermia." She settled in the chair her husband pulled out for her. "I'm so happy to get a chance to thank you again."

"I'm glad I happened along," Annie said.

The women fell into chatting about the rescue and the men talked about their joint passion for climbing. They'd both been to Yosemite on trips and shared other adventures on mountains.

Mike sat and picked up the menu, but Jon's stomach was so jittery, he wasn't sure he'd be able to eat. Maybe he should spill what he had to say right away and get it over with. Mike could withdraw considering him for the team, and they could enjoy dinner together without expectations.

But the words stayed locked behind Jon's teeth. How did he bring up such an unusual subject as the situation that faced him back in Rochester?

The server came to take their drink order, and Jon grabbed on to the delay. His thoughts were a jumble as they ordered drinks and appetizers. He ordered clam chowder first. "I almost never see gluten-free clam chowder."

"You have to eat gluten-free?" Mike asked. "Our fifteen-year-old daughter has to eat that way. It can be challenging."

"Our daughter does too. She's eight," Jon said. Once the words were out, he realized what he'd said when Annie's eyes widened, and her face went white. "I mean, Annie's daughter."

Was his subconscious trying to release the truth? Annie was going to kill him. He sent her a pleading glance but tore his gaze away when he saw the shock in her face. What was wrong with him?

Jon exhaled and set down the menu. "There's something I need to tell you, Mike. It came up since I interviewed with you."

He launched into the circumstances around Olivia's arrest and the dire straits of the practice in Rochester. Mike's expression stayed alert and interested, and he showed no real dismay at the news. He nodded a few times when Jon told him about calling and talking to the police.

"I wanted you to know up front about this problem," Jon ended. "I realize it will likely affect your decisions going forward."

Mike leaned back in his chair. "I won't lie and say this isn't a shock, but I won't make my decision based on something out of your control. Let's get to know one another better tonight. I'll take some time to consider what I want to do. It took guts to tell me what happened, and I like courage. Sometimes we surgeons have to make difficult choices, and it helps to know you have some ethics."

Jon's gaze went to Annie, and the color had come back to her cheeks. She smiled at him, so at least she wasn't still furious at his faux pas. At least not publicly. He didn't doubt he'd hear about it when they were alone.

"I appreciate that. If there are any more developments, I'll be sure to let you know."

They ordered their dinners and spent the rest of the time talking about hobbies. Annie told Priscilla about her side hustle of weaving Finnish rag rugs, and Priscilla asked about buying some. Jon mentioned he loved cold-water surfing and discovered Mike was a surfer as well.

Full of seafood and good company, they said their good-byes, and Jon took Annie's hand to walk to his car. "I messed up, Annie. I'm sorry."

She pulled her hand away and stopped to look up at him. "I don't want Kylie to find out about this accidentally, Jon. You've got to be more careful."

"I will," he promised.

He could see she still wasn't ready to talk to Kylie, but he bit back the arguments. Anger had destroyed their relationship once, and he couldn't let it happen again.

/ / /

The road back from Houghton to the marina was dark and winding. Jon didn't have much to say, so Annie was able to stare out at the dark forest zipping by her window and think about the evening.

She knew Jon hadn't had that slip of the tongue on purpose, but it didn't mean it was any less dangerous. Kylie's reaction to hearing the truth accidentally would be devastating. Annie needed to be the one to tell her, but try as she might, those words eluded her.

Kylie adored Nate. Annie had never seen a daddy and daughter any closer. No matter how much she or anyone else might try to reassure Kylie that her love for Nate didn't have to change, it would appear as if Jon was moving into Nate's position. Ten years from now, she might barely remember Nate. That was the actual truth.

Kylie had been six when Nate died. Annie remembered only the dramatic points of her own life at age six. Even all the Christmases had blended together. She remembered getting lost in an abandoned copper mine, but she couldn't quite lay her finger on what year that was. Her childhood ran together in a kaleidoscope of snippets frozen in time.

The memories of Nate and her parents would be like that to Kylie someday, and as much as Annie wanted to preserve every cherished mental snapshot for her daughter, it wouldn't happen. And it hurt Annie's heart to know she had to take a wrecking ball to what Kylie treasured most. Annie knew firsthand what it was like to have your life smashed.

Her phone rang with a call from the sheriff. "Hey, Mason, did you get my text?"

"I did. Thanks for the information. I checked out Chad Smith too. No record of anything. Not even a speeding ticket. And we ran prints on the kayak. We found only prints from Grace."

Annie rubbed her head. "We'll keep digging."

"That we will. Talk to you tomorrow."

Annie put her phone away and sighed. She'd have to figure out what to look into next.

"What's wrong with this thing?" Jon muttered, fighting with the steering wheel. He pulled hard toward the road's shoulder on her side, but the vehicle continued to barrel to the left.

"What's happening?"

"The car is driving itself!" The tendons in Jon's neck stood out in the glare of the dash as he fought hard to control the car.

The tires screamed as the Jaguar rounded a curve. Annie knew this area. The roads curved along thick forest. One wrong turn and they'd smash into a tree. Kylie could lose both her parents in a heartbeat.

Annie gripped the door's armrest. "Just stop the car!"

"The brakes aren't working," Jon gritted out through clenched teeth as he continued to fight the wheel.

Her gaze traveled down his legs to the floorboard, and she saw his foot pressed down hard on the brake. The car continued to scream through the curves as if it knew which way to go to stay on the road.

"Should we jump out?"

He shook his head. "Seventy miles an hour. Too dangerous."

It was dangerous to stay inside. What could cause the car to operate by itself?

She looked around inside the vehicle, trying to find some reason for the car's weird behavior. Nothing stood out. Hadn't she read something about cars being hacked by devious people? Could that really be happening, or was it some kind of computer glitch?

There'd been certain mechanisms hackers used, but she was too panicked to recall what they all were. The only thing she remembered was something do with the door locks. She reached over and unlocked her door. Jon was struggling so hard to control the car, she didn't think he could take a hand off the wheel to do the same to his door. Maybe the key fob.

She snatched it from the console where Jon had tossed it and unlocked the doors. Almost immediately, the car began to slow. At least it wasn't speeding toward certain destruction, but Jon still struggled to keep the Jaguar on the road.

She studied the key fob. The symbols looked to be headlamps, trunk lift, locks, and a panic button. The car lurched and threw her against the door. The fob flew out of her fingers to the floor by her feet, and she scrambled to grab it again.

Jon shot her a quick look, and the desperation in his face scared her. "I'm going to try punching the panic button. Hang on," she told him.

She pressed the panic button firmly, and the car engine stumbled. The road curved to the left ahead, and Jon turned the steering wheel that way.

"It's turning!" The car went slower and slower, and he rounded the curve to the straightaway. "Try another button. I've got to get the brakes back."

Maybe the trunk lift or the headlamps? She didn't want the lights to go out on this dark road so she pushed the trunk-lift button. "Try the brakes now."

He jammed his foot on the brake. "Nothing."

No help for it, she'd have to try the other button. She pressed the button that looked like headlamps, and the lights flashed off and back on again. Jon pumped the brakes again, and the car slowed jerkily.

"It worked!" He pressed down firmly and steered the car to the road's shoulder, then shut off the engine.

He let out a shaky breath. "That was close. How'd you know to try that?"

"I saw it on TV the other day." She laid the key fob back on the console. "I think someone hacked your car, Jon. Why would anyone do that?"

He reached for her, and she leaned across the console into his arms. "I'm shocked we're still alive and in one piece," he said.

"Me too." She could feel he was shaking as much as she was. "I don't think we should drive this thing home. I'll call Kade."

He released her. "Call Mason too. Something is very wrong with what happened. It felt like the car had turned into some kind of malevolent creature. Was it a prank, or did someone want to kill us?"

Good question, and not one with any easy answers.

TWENTY-SIX

THE LIGHTS ATOP MASON'S SUV STROBED ON AND OFF. A wrecker's lights glared though the dark as well. Jon stood with Annie on the shoulder of the road and waited for Kade to arrive. Mason's expression turned grim when he heard about their brush with death.

Jon had no idea when he'd get his car back—or if he even wanted it back. One thing he knew, though: he was going to tell his dad about Kylie. What if he and Annie had died in the Jaguar tonight? Kylie might have had to go to Nate's parents, and he knew Annie didn't want that. Dad might be old, but he was kind and loved kids. He would make sure Kylie was taken care of if the worst ever happened.

The sheriff and Deputy Montgomery stood talking to a state policeman who had stopped, and Jon had a few minutes alone with Annie. Maybe now wasn't the best time to talk about the situation, but that perfect time never seemed to arrive.

He took her hand. "It was a close call, Annie. A very close call."

Her throat tightened and she nodded. "God was with us."

"All I could think about was Kylie and what would happen to her if we'd crashed."

"Me too," she admitted. "I realized you're right. Just before the car went haywire, I was reluctant to tell her. Now I think we have to."

"I'd like to tell my dad tonight."

Her eyes widened. "Tonight?"

He nodded. "Dad already loves her, and he'd make sure she was okay if anything happened to us. Then we can tell Kylie tomorrow. I want her taken care of." He leaned over and cupped her face in his hands. "And I want you both to know I love you."

"I don't think we're going to die tonight."

"We didn't think so an hour ago either, but it could have turned out very differently. If someone is out to get us, we might not be so fortunate next time."

She took in what he said and sighed. "Okay. It's already past Kylie's bedtime, so Bree is keeping her. You want me to go see your dad with you?"

"Only if you want to."

Her expression was unreadable to him as she bit her lip and fell silent. It would be hard for her to admit she'd lived a lie for almost nine years. Society took a harsher view of women than it did men in this kind of situation, though he was sure their friends would be supportive no matter what.

Her fingers tightened on his. "I'll come with you." Her voice was low. "I don't want you to face it by yourself."

"Nothing really to face. My dad will be thrilled. He'll only be sorry Mom isn't here to get to know her granddaughter." He pulled her against his chest. She had always fit so perfectly, like she was part of him. And wasn't that the way it was supposed to be?

Kade's SUV came into view and parked behind the wrecker,

and Jon walked with Annie to his vehicle. Kade's hair was wet like he'd hopped out of the shower and rushed to the rescue.

Kade stared through the window at the officers milling around the road, waiting for the wrecker to haul Jon's car to be examined. "Do you need to hang around?"

"No, we can go."

They were only fifteen minutes from the marina, and they spent the short ride telling Kade all they knew, which wasn't much. Kade dropped them off in the parking lot, and they waited until he disappeared around the curve before heading to Annie's truck.

It was ten, and Jon wanted to get to his dad's before he went to bed. It had been an emotional few hours, both with Mike and then with the horror in the car. Telling his dad felt like what Jon *needed* to do, but he wasn't sure Annie felt the same sense of urgency.

"Want me to drive?" he asked her.

"If you like. I'm still shaking." She went around to the passenger door and climbed in.

He drove as fast as he dared along the dark, curving roads, and his hands perspired as he flashed back to an hour earlier. Stores were closing up, and the last few shoppers lingered under the streetlights as he drove down Houghton Street to Negaunee.

Lights shone out the windows of the bed-and-breakfast, and he spotted his dad sitting in a chair by the bay window. He parked and switched off the engine. "Ready?"

"I have to be." Annie reached out and took his hands in hers. "What if your dad hates me for this? He missed out on all Kylie's early years."

Her cold hands were shaking in his. "My dad isn't like that.

He's the sort of man who counts his blessings day by day. And having a granddaughter will be the best thing he's ever received."

She pulled away and opened her door. "I hope you're right."

He got out and came around the truck to take her hand. "I think I understand why you're hesitant to tell Kylie. It's hard to know where to start. Even with my dad, I'm not sure how to jump into the topic."

"You mean you're not going to march in there and say, 'Hey, Dad, I just wanted you to know you have a granddaughter'?"

He laughed, mostly in relief that she was able to dredge up some humor tonight.

She lifted a brow. "You laugh, but it might come out that way. How else do you bring up something like this except abruptly? You can broach the subject, but I'll be hiding my face in the corner."

He stopped and turned her to face him. "Don't you ever be ashamed, Annie. We've got a beautiful daughter. In spite of how things started, you've done a great job raising her. She's smart and loving. We'll get through the sticky parts."

She came in closer for an embrace. "There's a good reason I was never able to forget you."

He nestled his face into her neck. Things would get better once everything was out in the open.

/ / /

Annie's pulse roared in her ears as she walked into the Blue Bonnet Bed-and-Breakfast with Jon. An apple-scented candle flickered on the fireplace mantel, and the sweet scent of it calmed her jitters. Daniel Dunstan had always been someone she admired. She valued his opinion of her, and tonight they were about to trash it.

Would he ever look at her the same way? Her knees shook, and she blinked at the moisture in her eyes.

Daniel sat at the game table playing chess with Martha. The two seemed cozy and content with one another's company. The lakeshore breeze wafted through the screens in the open windows and brought with it the hum of distant cars in the village.

Jon's dad waved his son over to join him. "Martha is whupping me. I need an opponent I can beat."

Jon chuckled. "Nice, Dad, ragging on your only son."

"Someone has to keep you in line."

Martha rose and glanced at the clock on the mantel. "Anyone need a drink or a snack before I go?" She stepped to the fireplace and blew out the candle.

"We're fine," Annie said. "I know my way around your kitchen. If anyone needs something, I can handle it." She moved to an armchair on one side of the fireplace.

"You certainly do. Good night." Her heels clicked on the shining wood floors as she left them and went up the stairs.

She must have realized a visit this late meant some kind of news they wanted to discuss with Daniel alone. Annie wanted to tell Bree before anyone else in town heard the news, but that would have to wait until Annie figured out what to say. Tonight would be a start on getting the words out, but she wished she could stop this train in the station until she was ready.

She was so not ready.

Daniel sat back and folded his arms across his chest. "You kids are out late."

"We had a close call tonight." Jon told him about the car.

"Things like that make you stop and think about the future. Which means we need to talk to you about something."

"Thank the good Lord you survived. That's a dangerous stretch of road when you don't have control." Daniel glanced at Annie. "You're here to tell me you're getting married?"

Heat washed up Annie's face, and she stared down at her hands clasped in her lap. She couldn't force a word out, so it was up to Jon to navigate this minefield.

Jon glanced over at Annie. "Not yet, but I hope it's coming. It's not easy to tell you this, Dad." He paused and rubbed his head. "This was news to all of us, even Annie, and it all started when the doctor discovered Kylie had celiac disease. The disease has a hereditary link."

Daniel nodded. "Your aunt Jo had it."

"There was no celiac disease in Nate's family, and Annie began to wonder if he was really Kylie's father. She had a paternity test run, and there was no chance Nate was Kylie's father. That only left me."

Confusion clouded Daniel's green eyes. "But you can't have children."

Annie had known that comment was coming. It had been Jon's objection, too, and she didn't know how to explain that part away.

"Something must have healed in my body. Kylie is my daughter and your granddaughter."

"You have DNA to prove it?"

Jon reared back in his chair. "I saw the test that said Nate wasn't her father. Kylie has to be mine."

Daniel rose and paced the living room. "Don't take this wrong, Annie, but don't you think we should have positive proof of this? If only for Kylie's sake. What if she finds out you never verified the results? It shouldn't take long, correct?"

Annie went hot and then cold. "You think I'd lie about something like this, Daniel?" Her words came out more choked and betrayed than she wanted. "I didn't want to think it could be true. Jon had walked out of my life, and I didn't want to consider Nate might not be her dad. It couldn't be anyone but Jon."

"And he's been told he can't have kids. Can't you see how important it is to make sure?"

Jon sprang to his feet, too, and faced his dad. "The only reason we're telling you now is so you can make sure Kylie is taken care of if something happens to both of us. We could have both died tonight, and Kylie would be alone."

Daniel stopped pacing. "You know I want nothing more than to have grandchildren. I would take care of Kylie no matter what, but you need to think things through. I'm an attorney down to my bones. Someday proof might be necessary, so why not run that test now?"

Jon strode past his father and took Annie's hand. "Let's go, Annie. I'm sorry I put you through this."

His immediate defense of her soothed her pain enough that she could see a glimmer of truth in Daniel's advice. Jon hadn't immediately accepted the news either—he'd brought up what he'd been told when he was sixteen after a bad cycling accident.

She laced her fingers with Jon's. "I'll admit your dad's reaction wasn't what I'd hoped, but maybe he's right. Would your extended family have doubts when they hear? And what about Nate's family? When they're told, they might demand more proof than a test that showed Nate wasn't Kylie's father."

Jon stiffened, and his green eyes narrowed. “Are you saying this so you can delay telling Kylie?”

“What? No, of course not.” But she’d take any delay she could get. “It’s only a few more days to have the test showing the proof. There’s nothing wrong with your dad’s suggestion.”

Daniel stepped to her side and put his hand on her shoulder. “I’ve made no secret of how much I care about you, Annie, and that won’t ever change. Whatever you decide is fine with me. I already love Kylie, so it’s not that. I’m trying to look out for your best interests in the future.”

She searched his gaze and saw the truth there. “I know. Thank you.”

A flash of movement at the bay window caught her eye, and she spotted Sarah running off toward the lighthouse. Had she been *spying* on them? And the bigger question was this: How much had she overheard?

TWENTY-SEVEN

JON WASN'T SURE HE WANTED TO PROVIDE A DNA sample. Would Annie think he didn't believe her? If the situation were reversed, he'd be offended.

He had talked Annie into a short walk along the shore, hoping the scent of the trees and lake would blow away his anger. Or was it anger? Maybe more disappointment that his dad hadn't welcomed Annie and Kylie with open arms. Oh, he'd *said* the right things about loving them, but his doubt about what Annie had said was shocking.

The moonlight glimmered on the water as they wandered along the lake's edge. Jon glanced at Annie's profile as she stared toward the lake.

"I'm sorry it went that way," he said. "You're quiet."

She straightened and looked his way. "I saw Sarah outside the window. I think she might have overhead us talking about Kylie."

He absorbed the news. "She might tell Kylie before we do."

"I want to wait until the test comes back. I'll have to go talk to Sarah and ask her not to say anything. It's not going to be easy. I should probably do it now, but I'm not sure what to say. She'll take joy in hurting me." Her voice quavered.

Jon searched her eyes with a steady gaze. "Let's just tell Kylie and make sure she doesn't hear accidentally. She won't ask to see a test, Annie. She's eight. She's not going to question what you tell her."

"She won't take this news easily. I think you're misjudging how much it's going to matter to her."

"And I think you're seeking any excuse to put off telling her." He tried to keep from raising his voice, but his frustration increased.

"I know my daughter," she said stiffly.

"She's my daughter too! You seem to keep forgetting that. I missed out on her first eight years because you didn't want to face the truth. Now that it's here and staring you in the face, you're still putting it off. I'm tired of waiting, Annie."

"I'm not going to talk about it anymore tonight. We're both tired, and we're starting to say things that will hurt later. Go to your room and get some rest. I'll wait until morning to talk to Sarah. I'm too upset right now."

"I don't get why you are so reluctant to spill the truth. Let's just get it over with, push through the mini-drama that will come, and get on with the rest of our lives. I hate how we're stuck in limbo."

She jerked her hand away and headed for the steps up the hillside to the lighthouse. "It's easy for you—you aren't from here. You won't have to face longtime friends and see judgment in their eyes. You don't have to call Nate's family and spill the news." Her voice shook.

He hurried after her. "They never come around anyway. Nothing says you have to tell them."

She whirled to face him. "Which shows how little you know Kylie! The first time Nate's parents call to chat with her, she'll mention it. And they *do* call on occasion. Not often enough, but they have to know the truth. Even if just for Nate's sake, they deserve that."

Annie was so stubborn and sure she was right. He'd been patient, and it was time.

She rubbed her head, and the stiffness around her shoulders slumped. "Maybe you're right. I don't want to, but if Sarah tells her first, it will be even worse. But let me do it by myself. I'll go now."

When she marched up the steps, he let her go and followed at a slower pace. While he would like to be with her, Kylie was still prickly around him. It would be better coming from her mother.

She went inside and he settled to wait on the steps.

Loons warbled from somewhere in the distance, and he shuddered. Hopefully it wasn't a bad omen.

Annie had never been a coward, but he didn't understand why she kept putting it off. Women were hard to understand. They got all bound up in emotions. As a surgeon he was used to seeing a problem and fixing it. It seemed the sensible thing to do with everything in life. Why talk about it endlessly when the solution was to cut to the chase with the truth?

His thoughts transitioned to dinner with Mike tonight. He hadn't told Mike about the problem with his former practice right away either. He'd put it off until dinner tonight, so was he any better than Annie about facing something uncomfortable? Maybe he didn't realize how hard this was for her.

The lighthouse door opened behind him, and he twisted where he sat to see Annie close it behind her. "How'd it go?"

"Kylie was asleep. It will have to wait. I just hope Sarah doesn't tell her first."

He rose and started to embrace her, but she moved past him. "I'm going home. We'll talk more tomorrow."

Her stiff voice warned him she needed space, so he dropped his arms back to his side and watched her walk to her truck. When her taillights vanished around the curve, he started for the Blue Bonnet on the other side of Bree's lighthouse. The path took him past the guesthouse where Sarah stayed. Should he stop and talk to her about what she'd overheard? He stopped and stared at the cottage, but no lights were on.

Waking her up didn't seem a good way to start a difficult conversation, so he continued toward the bed-and-breakfast. He wasn't sure he'd be able to sleep without making it right with Annie, so he pulled out his phone and called her. She didn't answer. He'd have to let her cool off, then he would apologize tomorrow.

/ / /

Tears kept leaking from Annie's eyes and blurring her vision as she made the drive home. Her phone rang, but she tossed it onto the passenger seat when she saw Jon was calling. The argument with him brought back too many bad memories of their final breakup. Why couldn't he see how hard this was for her? She *hated* causing her little girl pain, and this blow would only be secondary to the murder that took Annie's parents and Nate.

Was she being a coward about everyone knowing the truth? She didn't think that was what was holding her back. She kept thinking of gazing into Kylie's trusting blue eyes and telling her Nate wasn't her daddy. And yet, he was too. He'd believed it all his life and had been the best daddy a little girl could want. Shattering that illusion would hurt them all. But waiting wouldn't change anything. That heartbreak was taking aim at them, and they'd be unable to escape the bull's-eye on their chests.

How did she preserve Kylie's memories of Nate and also make room for Jon? It felt like an impossible tightrope to walk. Didn't she owe it to Nate to make sure his memory was still treasured and intact? He'd snatched Annie from despair and given her hope a month after Jon left when she thought her life was over. While she hadn't loved him like she did Jon, he'd been there for her when she needed him most.

She parked in the marina's lot and leaned her head against the steering wheel. Things seemed to be smooth sailing for a while, and now this. Was it the beginning of the end?

Taking her phone from the passenger seat, she grabbed her bag and got out. Her thoughts about the evening ran in a jumble. Who would have the technology to hack into a car? It seemed preposterous. They'd just seen Idoya, but though she'd followed them, she didn't seem to have the technological know-how to hack into a car.

Annie stared at her old truck. Built in 1969, it didn't have any newfangled electronics that would make it vulnerable to what had happened tonight. But could there be any other kinds of danger from it?

She turned on the flashlight on her phone and shone it around the old truck. She checked the rear seat of the crew cab, under all the seats, and the outside bed. Nothing. She dropped to the ground in her dress and lay on her back to scoot under the truck. The light illuminated the truck's structure, and she studied the exhaust system and gas lines. She was about to give up when she spotted a small rectangular box.

She scooted closer and tried to pry it off. It popped off, and she examined it. A magnetic tracking device. Who had put it here and why? Was there one on Jon's car too?

She scooted out from under the truck and turned off the flashlight. Should she call Jon? The clock on her phone displayed the time of nearly midnight. She didn't want to wake him if he'd managed to fall asleep. It could wait, but she hugged herself as she walked slowly toward her dark cottage. If only she'd left on the outside light on the back deck.

The distant sound of a guitar told her a camper was up crooning with friends, and other sounds indicated that the resort wasn't totally asleep and unaware if she needed help. She unlocked the back door and stepped into the kitchen.

Something felt off. A scent, maybe? She set the magnetic tracker on the counter and flipped on the lights. Nothing happened. She flipped the switch up and down again and sniffed the air. The scent was a man's cologne, so she bolted outside again. Should she call Mason or get one of the men camping to help her check the house?

She'd better call. A civilian might get hurt if anyone was inside. She was dressed up so she hadn't brought her gun. Her hands shook as she dialed 911 and recognized the dispatcher with a sense of relief.

"Dana, is that you?"

"Annie? What's wrong?"

Dana had moved to town a few years ago and gotten a job as a dispatcher. She was married to Boone Carter, owner of a small group of cabins on the other side of the county.

"I think someone is in my house, and my lights aren't working. I think he cut the power."

"I'll send a deputy. Stay on the line with me," Dana said.

"I'm okay. Just please send an officer right away."

It would probably be Montgomery, and his sheer size would deter any intruder. She headed for her truck and locked herself inside while she waited. The phone in her hand teased her to call Jon, but she resisted. When a call came in, she assumed it was the sheriff's office, but her spirits lifted when she saw Jon's name on her screen.

She swiped it on. "Jon? I think there's someone in my house. A deputy is on his way."

"Where are you?"

The sound of his deep, steady voice brought tears to her eyes. "I'm in my truck with the doors locked. I'm unarmed."

"You should go where there are people. Is anyone roaming around the campgrounds?"

"Yes, a few people are still up. I came to the truck so I'd see the deputy when he arrived."

"He can text you when he arrives. I don't want you by yourself. I'm on my way. Stay on the line with me."

"How can you get here? Your car is being checked out."

She heard his feet stop. "You're right," he said. "Martha keeps her keys on a hook by the back door. I'll borrow hers."

"Without asking?"

"She's asleep. I'm sure she won't mind."

The sound of his running feet came over the phone again. She hung on as he moved through the bed-and-breakfast to the kitchen.

"Found the keys. I'll be there in a few minutes. Any sign of the deputy?"

"Not yet, but he could have been on the other side of the

county for all I know. Dana didn't say how long it would be until he arrived. I'll go find people."

At least he'd called, which meant he wasn't running from the conflict like he had last time. She found comfort in the fact that maybe, just maybe, they could find their way through the maze in front of them.

TWENTY-EIGHT

DEPUTY DOUG MONTGOMERY HEFTED HIS BULK OUT OF his SUV and yanked on his pants. "You're making a habit of calling for backup, Annie."

"Not because I want to." Annie had called dispatch several weeks back over an intruder, but that man was dead. Whoever was terrorizing her now was a new adversary.

She walked with Doug toward the cottage. "My power is out too."

Doug swerved to the left. "Let me check your box and see if he's thrown the main." He flipped on a high-powered flashlight that lit up the yard like a floodlight.

Annie turned off her phone's flashlight. It was like a tiny night-light compared to Doug's beam. She followed the bouncing light across the grass to the side of the house. The breaker-box cover stood open.

Doug shone his flashlight on the interior. "Main breaker's been thrown. I think you need to get a lock for this box, Annie."

"I'll do that tomorrow," she promised.

He had her hold the light for him while he turned the power back on. The light in the kitchen came on, and its amber glow lifted her spirits.

Footsteps sounded from inside the house, and Doug ran faster than she would have thought a guy his size could move. She followed him around to the front, which was the entry they seldom used. A dark figure burst from inside and jumped off the porch before dashing into the thick forest at the property's edge.

Doug gave chase, but he soon returned panting. "Lost him. He's a spry one. Let's go in and see what he was doing."

She followed him up the porch to her gaping front door. Leaning past him, she switched on the lights. The place was a mess. Lamps were overturned and broken on the floor, rugs pulled up, and every drawer emptied. She moved from the trashed living room to the kitchen and found the same mess.

Her bedroom was the worst. All her clothes were pulled off hangers, and even her jewelry was lying on the floor. The bathroom toiletries were upended on the floor and in the sink, and her cleaning supplies were out from under the cabinet.

"He was searching for something," Doug said. "Do you notice anything missing?"

"It will take some time to figure that out. I'll have to put things away before I can tell. Let me check my safe." She rushed to the gun safe, but it wasn't opened. "It's fingerprint activated so he probably couldn't get in it."

She opened it and withdrew her gun and holster. She buckled the holster around her waist. It would look ridiculous with her dress, but at least she was armed and ready.

Her phone pinged, and she glanced at the screen. "Jon is here. He'll help me put things away. Thanks for coming so quickly, Doug."

He lumbered back to the kitchen, and she went with him out

the door toward the parking lot. "Doug, I about forgot to tell you that I found a tracking device on the underside of my truck. It's on the counter." She got it and handed it to him.

"I'll get out of here and see what I can find out about all this."

Jon's tall figure loped toward her, and she saw the concern on his face when he reached the back-deck light. He stopped to thank Doug, who was walking toward her truck.

"Looks like a robbery attempt," she told him when he moved to her side. "And I found a tracking device on my truck. Doug is going to take it with him. Maybe Idoya had it put there. She sure seems to want to find Michelle."

He embraced her, and she sank into the comfort he offered. It was too hard to be at odds with him. They'd talk more when they had this situation sorted out.

He kissed the top of her head. "I don't think so. It's too coincidental after what happened to my car. Show me what happened inside."

She drew away and led him inside. He winced at all the destruction. "I wonder if he found what he was looking for?"

"But what could that be? I don't have anything valuable. I only have costume jewelry except for my wedding ring. Maybe it's missing."

She took off for her bedroom and checked the jumble of necklaces and earrings. There it was. She lifted up the simple band in triumph. It wasn't worth that much, but Kylie might want to have it someday. Or maybe Annie could have it made into something special for her.

Jon put his hands on his hips and glanced around. "So he wasn't searching for money or anything of tangible value.

What cases are you working on besides Michelle Fraser's disappearance?"

"We're keeping our eyes peeled for any connection to missing hikers in case Sean had any hunting buddies."

"What about Shainya Blackburn?"

"Mason is handling that. I've offered to help, though."

"So several active cases that could possibly be involved."

"I can't see how anyone would want to break into my house because I'm looking for a missing woman."

"Maybe they are hoping you've found some evidence that will lead to her."

"I wouldn't keep it here. It would be with Mason."

"The intruder might not know that."

She thought he was on the wrong track. "Maybe it was kids trashing the house for the fun of it. The guy who ran out the front door was fast. Could have been a teenager."

"Maybe. Let's put things away. Maybe you'll see something that shows his intent."

"I could use the help." She settled on the kitchen floor and grabbed a washtub from under the sink to load the dumped silverware and utensils.

She slanted a glance up at him. "I'm sorry about earlier tonight."

He knelt beside her. "It was my fault. I pushed too hard. We'll take the time you need."

She leaned over and palmed his face. "I'm worried about Kylie finding out. I'm going to grab a test tomorrow and we can send it in. Then I'll tell her even before we get the results. You've been very patient with me."

His green eyes warmed her from the inside out, and she leaned in for a kiss. Give and take. That's what it took to maintain a relationship. She could admit she was wrong even when she didn't want to. And this time she'd been wrong.

/ / /

The sun was barely up as Jon jogged along the water's edge early Thursday morning. The orange and golden hues spread out over the treetops and hillside behind him and touched the water with color. His bare feet slapped against the wet sand, and air pumped through his lungs in a satisfying rhythm. The humid air was a warm blanket against his skin. Jogging helped calm his mind and center his concerns.

And he had plenty of concerns. A lot was riding on what happened today. Annie planned to tell Kylie the truth. If it went badly, would Annie blame him for pushing her into it before she was ready?

He rounded a corner and hit the beginning of a thick forest fronting Rock Harbor. Birds sang good morning in the trees and added to the melody of the waves rolling to shore. The fresh air washed away the ordeal of the night before, and by the time he turned around to run back into the village, he felt ready to tackle whatever the day brought.

The sound of a motorboat blew toward him on the breeze, and someone yelled, "Hey, Doc!" He shaded his eyes with his hand and watched a Boston Whaler head his way. With the sun in his eyes, he couldn't make out the features of the pilot, but the man sounded frantic as he yelled for help.

"I need help, Doc! My girlfriend is injured."

In his jogging shorts he waded into the water as the boat drew as close to shore as possible. The water was freezing cold, and he bit back a gasp at its frigid grip. "What's wrong?"

"Broken leg," the guy called.

Rock Harbor was a small town, so Jon wasn't surprised his identity was known. Everyone knew everyone else's business. "I'm coming."

He had no instruments, but he could assess the woman and immobilize her leg to help get her to the hospital. While he had no privileges at Rock Harbor General, he could turn her over to someone as soon as they got there. He waded out to his waist and grabbed the ladder aboard the boat. He was glad to leave the cold grip of the lake. Superior never really got warm, but it always surprised him how cold it was under the surface.

He clambered onto the deck. "Where's the patient?"

He turned at movement behind him, and his eyes widened when he took in the ski mask on the pilot's face. He barely had time to register the oddity before something came down on his head, and he toppled to the deck. His vision darkened, and he shook his head and tried to regain his focus.

As the man's legs came into view, Jon reached out and snagged his ankle, and the guy fell heavily beside him. Jon shook away the last of his blurred vision and staggered to his feet. The man sprang up, but before the guy could tackle him, Jon leaped over the side of the boat. He slogged through the cold waves toward the shore before he turned to see the man heading to the console. Moments later the boat roared away.

It all happened so fast that Jon couldn't make out any name or number on the boat. All he knew was the brand. There were plenty of Boston Whalers out on Superior.

Why would someone try to grab him? The broken leg was the perfect ruse to get him to come running.

He started back the way he'd come. Sailboats and other watercraft floated off to his right, but he didn't see any other sign of the Boston Whaler. As soon as he reached town, he headed for the sheriff's office.

Mason was exiting the station when Jon arrived, and he stopped when he saw Jon. "You look rough. Your head is bleeding."

Jon touched his temple, and his fingers came away red and sticky. "I was attacked."

Mason's expression was grave as he listened to Jon's story. "I saw a similar story up in Ontonagon. It happened last night to another orthopedic surgeon."

"You mean the guy might have been telling the truth about someone with a broken leg? Why else would he specifically target surgeons who could fix it?" Jon shook his head. "But we couldn't do much without supplies. I wouldn't be able to even set a simple break that didn't require surgery unless I had at least a splint and elastic wrap. Who was the other surgeon?"

Mason named a doctor Jon wasn't acquainted with. At least it wasn't Mike.

Mason jerked his head toward the jail entrance. "Make a formal report, and I'll get it out to other law enforcement. It's a very strange case."

The strangeness of it struck Jon in a new way. "Mason, remember that picture of Michelle? I'm pretty sure she had a badly broken leg. You think it's possible this guy is trying to take a doctor to her?"

Mason frowned. "That's a weird way to handle it when she needs surgery."

"He might think she just needed it splinted. With the right supplies any of us could do that."

"I guess it's possible."

"What about my car?"

"You can have it back. The state tech guys have gone over the electronics and couldn't find out how the perp did it. There was no obvious trail back to who hacked in. They think it was through the power locks."

"That's what Annie thought too. I'll make the report and pick up my keys. It's in the impound lot?"

"I'll have Doug bring it to you while you fill out the report." Mason stopped to send a text to the deputy. "And have someone take a look at that head wound. You might need stitches."

"I'll go see Dr. Eckright."

Mason put his hand on Jon's arm. "Speaking of Ben, I want to thank you for prodding Anu to get checked. She means a lot to me. And of course my wife. But thank you." His voice roughened, and he looked away.

"Annie and I are praying for the best."

Jon watched Mason go to his SUV and drive away before pulling out his phone to text Annie. His head was starting to hurt by the time he finished his report, so he made a beeline to the doctor's office. He might be able to determine if Eckright had jumped to the right conclusion about Kylie's paternity. If he did, Jon would ask him to keep it quiet until the dust settled.

TWENTY-NINE

THIS STUPID LEG. MICHELLE STARED BALEFULLY AT her enormous limb. As near as she could tell, it had been a week since she broke it, and it wasn't much better. The discoloration seemed worse to her this morning, and her leg radiated heat. Had it become infected?

She was no nurse, but she knew she needed a doctor. What if this delay meant she'd be permanently disabled? The thought made her shudder. She'd hoped to have some kind of weapon when her captor came back, but she'd found nothing.

Her despair throughout the week had only deepened. Her situation appeared hopeless, but that couldn't be true. There was always a glimmer of hope somewhere—she just had to find it.

She sat up and slid to the floor, then made her way to the bathroom again. Every trip was more and more of an ordeal, and she always returned weaker with worse pain. On her way back to the bed, she heard the sound of an engine. He was back so soon? He'd been here yesterday.

She managed to return to the cot before the lock clicked and he entered the cabin. The ski mask was in place again, but she memorized the shape of his body. The way he walked, cocky and with his head high, was another tell she could use to identify him if she managed to live through this.

He carried stuff with him. Was that a broken ankle boot? It would be a welcome relief to have some sort of protection for her leg. Maybe she could even manage to hobble on it.

He said nothing but came to stand beside her. He took the boot apart, then lifted her leg to position the back of the boot onto her leg and foot. Her eagerness for help ended quickly when he moved her leg the wrong way and excruciating pain gripped it.

She couldn't hold back the scream, and she pushed his hands away. "Don't touch me! You're not doing it right."

"I watched a YouTube video on how to do it. Hold still and it will be over soon." He reached for her leg again.

She balled up her fist and landed a punch on his nose. He reared back with his fist up, and she cowered.

She held up her hand. "I'm sorry, but I reacted before I could help it. I've had a broken bone before! I know more than you about what to do. You'll make it worse."

"You can't let it heal in this position."

"And you're an idiot! It needs *surgery*. No boot is going to fix this. All it will do is help support it and keep the bones from moving."

"Don't you ever touch me again, or you won't have to worry about your leg hurting."

She shuddered at his low, ominous voice and didn't reply. She released the air in the boot and positioned it on the back of her calf, but her leg was too swollen and out of place to go into the support boot.

She looked up at him. "It's not going to work. Could you get some elastic bandages?"

"Just force it into place. I can do it if you're not going to."

She shook her head. "I think it's infected. We've waited too long to try to splint it. Can't you tell by looking that it won't go into that boot? There's no room, not even with all the air out."

The man's hands clenched. "Look, you're going to take me to where your stuff is stashed, or you'll be dead. This could help you walk out of here."

"I can't get in this one, and even if I could, I'd never be able to walk over rough ground in it." She studied the man's posture. Maybe he was telling the truth and would let her go once she gave him what he wanted. "How about I try to draw you a map?" Not that she knew the distances, but maybe he could find her campsite. "Get me a paper and pencil, and I'll see what I can do."

"I'll have to get some. There's nothing to write on in the truck. You'd better not be stringing me along." The man stalked toward the door and slammed it behind him. Moments later the key clicked in the lock.

Michelle slumped against the cot mattress and moaned. Manipulating her leg had caused the pain to rage even worse, and there seemed to be no end in sight to her misery. What could he want in her belongings? She had no idea.

She shook her head. Even if she complied with everything he wanted, he couldn't let her go. He'd worry that she could identify him. And while nothing about him was familiar, if she saw him walk or talk once she was free, she'd know him instantly. She had always been good with voices especially, and his mannerisms and body type were imprinted in her mind.

She stared at the boot. What if she elevated her foot even more? If she could get the swelling down, the boot would be helpful. Sliding to the floor, she lay on her back on the hard wood and lifted her foot to the cot. The elevation relieved the way it was pounding, but she would be unable to hold the awkward angle for long without the support of a pillow.

She lay there for several minutes until her leg began to throb again. Maybe she could roll up the blanket to cushion her foot. She brought her leg back down and pulled on the blanket until it was beside her. She rolled and fluffed until it appeared to be the right shape, then tried again. It was better, but she would still be unable to keep it that way for longer than a few minutes at a time.

But if she continued to elevate, then rest it, the swelling might come down. She touched the swollen, purple flesh on her foot. It was huge. Hadn't she read something about making sure you could feel the pulse in your foot after a break?

She ran her fingers over her skin and pressed in different areas, but there was no slight pulsing that she could feel. Was that bad? She eyed her leg, which was looking even worse. A tiny slice of skin had opened up and was oozing pus. This wasn't good.

/ / /

Annie read Jon's text as soon as she parked in the lot by Dr. Eckright's office. He was on his way here, too, but he didn't say why. Was he planning to handle the DNA test himself? She'd planned to ask for a test kit to take home. The doctor would know the truth as soon as they asked for a paternity test.

If he didn't already. Dr. Eckright was smart and intuitive. It wouldn't take much explanation.

She'd barely slept after discovering the break-in, and she was eager to get Kylie home. The waiting room was empty when she stepped inside the old Victorian building and glanced around. The receptionist wasn't in her place, but she might be back in one of the exam spaces getting things ready. It was still a few minutes to eight, so the office technically wasn't open.

The door opened behind her and let in the scent of the lake with the breeze. Jon stepped into the room, and she gasped at the blood on his face.

She rushed to him. "Jon, what happened?" She fished a wet wipe out of her purse and dabbed at his face with it.

"Some guy in a boat tried to take me with him to treat a broken leg. The funny thing is, he tried the same thing with a surgeon in Houghton. Luckily, we both got away. He hit me with something, and I think the gash might need stitches. What are you doing here?" Before she answered, his smile dropped away. "You're picking up a paternity test, aren't you?"

"I am, but you'd better get fixed up first." She went to the desk window and rang the bell. "Hello? Anyone back there?"

Dr. Eckright appeared through the open door at the back of the reception room. "Annie, I wasn't expecting you." His gaze went past her to Jon, and his brows went up. "Bring him back right now."

Annie took Jon's arm and they went through the door and into the hall. "Which room?"

The doctor pointed. "First door on the right. Let me get some instruments. I think he needs stitches."

Jon looked a little green, and Annie guided him into the exam room and got him on the table. She stepped out of the way when Dr. Ben came in.

"What happened?" The doctor eased Jon down to lie on his back, then set to work disinfecting the wound.

Annie told him what she knew since Jon was looking more and more out of sorts. He was very pale. "Close your eyes, honey. Rest while the doctor stitches you up."

His eyelids fluttered and closed. "Is he going into shock or something like that?" she whispered to the doctor.

"I think he's got a mild concussion. He'll need to rest today, and he shouldn't be alone. I think we need a CT scan to assess his brain, too, just to be on the safe side."

Jon's eyes opened. "I'm fine, just tired. I didn't sleep well last night. I have a theory about the guy. What if it was the guy who abducted Michelle? He could have been trying to bring a doctor to her so he didn't have to take her to the ER."

"Maybe," Ben said. "But don't think about any of that now. Rest. You need to do what you're told or I'll have you admitted."

Jon's lips twitched. "Yes, sir."

While he stitched Jon up, Dr. Eckright asked him questions to test his memory and recall. Jon didn't stumble with any of the answers.

The doctor finished with the stitches, then dabbed antibiotic ointment onto the seam before he affixed a bandage. "I want you to take an oral antibiotic to avoid infection as well. I'll call the hospital to order the CT. Then home to rest." He glanced at Annie. "Watch for any vision or hearing disturbances, and keep an eye on his balance and coordination."

"I will," she promised.

The doctor put his arm around Jon's back and helped him sit up on the table. "Do you need an ambulance to take you to the hospital?"

"I can take him," Annie said. "My truck is right outside."

Jon looked rakish and handsome with his hair askew and

the bandage on his temple. Annie rose and went to stand beside him. She might as well explain the reason for her appearance too.

"Um, Dr. Ben, we'd like a paternity DNA test for Jon and Kylie."

The doctor glanced at her without surprise. "I see. I suspected this after Jon mentioned he had celiac disease. Let me get a swab. I already have Kylie's DNA."

He left the room and closed the door behind him. At least the initial explanation was over. Once it was sent off, she still needed to face Kylie with the truth. Annie needed no DNA result to know the truth.

Jon tucked a strand of hair behind her left ear. "You doing okay? I didn't sleep well when I got back. I didn't like the thought of you being there alone after the break-in."

"With Kylie gone I had my gun on the bedside table." She didn't admit she hardly closed her eyes all night. She was in law enforcement and didn't need someone to protect her. That was her job.

"That's good. I'm getting my car back today too. They were unable to track who hacked it."

"I don't think you should be driving anyway. I want you to stay at my house so I can keep an eye on you. I'm not sure Martha would have the time to keep checking. And she might not know what to look for."

"I'm really fine, love. I was dizzy for a while and my head hurts, but I can think and see. No double vision or anything like that. A CT is a waste of time."

"But you're going to do it anyway, just to be on the safe side."

He sighed. "Fine, I'll do it for you."

The doctor entered with a swab in his hand. "Let's get this done. You know the drill."

"Results within a week or so," Annie said. "But it's a formality only."

The doctor smiled. "I don't doubt you, Annie. And I make no judgments." The doctor addressed Jon. "Speaking of results. Thank you for urging Anu to get checked. I think we both know it doesn't look good. But I do think it's probably early stage. I'm praying it is."

Jon slid off the table to his feet. "We're praying too."

Annie thanked Ben. At least he didn't doubt her word, but the rest of the town might not be so kind.

THIRTY

TAYLOR SAT ON A GRASSY HILLSIDE OVERLOOKING THE lake. The sun was all the way up, and the humidity climbed along with the sun. The air smelled fresh and clean. Sailboats dotted the blue of the water, and the hum of bees in the dandelions should have calmed her agitation.

But nothing settled her.

What she'd overheard last night had kept her awake all night, and she couldn't decide what she was going to do with the knowledge that Annie, her supposedly wonderful sister, had *lied* for years to her own daughter. So much for her being such a great mom and a good person. She was no better than Mother, who had lied Taylor's entire life. She still wouldn't know for sure who she was if her mother hadn't died and Sean hadn't ferreted out the truth.

Just as she deserved to know her roots, Kylie deserved that too. And maybe she should have a new mother, one who wouldn't lie to her like Annie did. Taylor knew how much lies hurt, and she could raise Kylie herself in a good home, a place of love and acceptance.

It sounded good, but money was the biggest problem. She could get Kylie to come with her willingly, but Taylor only had about fifty dollars in her pocket. That wouldn't go far once she left Bree's cottage. It wouldn't even pay one night for a hotel.

Taylor clasped her legs to her chest and considered her options. She could rob a bank, but with the way streets had cameras these days, she probably wouldn't get away with it. Jon's car was worth a lot of money, so she could steal it and sell it. But she didn't have the title, so she wouldn't get much for it on the black market.

What about kidnapping Kylie and demanding a ransom? Jon was rich, and since he was Kylie's dad, he'd cough up whatever Taylor asked. His father had plenty of money and could chip in too. That might work.

Or she could suck up to Annie and get her to give her half of their parents' estate. Then once she had that, she could sell it and vanish with Kylie.

Taylor shook her head. It would be impossible to hide her disdain for her sister. And besides, she was getting tired of tiptoeing around Bree. It was clear whose side she was on, and Taylor could read the disapproval in her green eyes. Everyone thought Annie was so wonderful. Taylor wanted to be the one to tell Bree what a tramp her dear friend really was. Letting another man believe he was Kylie's father was the height of deception.

What kind of person did that?

Any desire Taylor might have harbored for a real relationship with her sister had vanished when she learned the truth. Now she needed to figure out how to use it to her benefit.

The kidnapping scheme nagged at her thoughts. Was there a way to make it work? She had to make sure no one suspected she was the one behind Kylie's disappearance. And she would need to figure out new identities so they could vanish. How much money would it take to disappear?

Sean would have known, and Taylor had Annie to thank for his loss as well. Would some of his friends be able to help her? Maybe Lissa Sanchez would know of a resource. Taylor had met her a few times, and Lissa might be willing to help for Sean's sake.

"Hi, Taylor. Um, I mean, Aunt Sarah."

Taylor looked around for the small voice and spotted Kylie. "Good morning. I didn't expect to see you here."

"I spent the night with Bree. Jon's car got hacked."

"Hacked? You mean stolen?"

"No, someone took control of it, and he couldn't drive it. So Mommy let me stay with Bree." Kylie, dressed in white shorts and a blue top, settled beside her on the grass. "What are you doing?"

"Just watching the boats out on the lake. It's a pretty day."

If only Taylor was ready to put her plan into action. Jon didn't have a car, and Annie was tied up in the investigation. But wait, why couldn't it work? She could get Kylie away, then call Lissa. A fake ID shouldn't take that long to obtain. And Jon would need a few days to come up with the money.

"I was thinking about taking a hike up the mountain. I'd love to take you, but Bree probably wouldn't let you go. She likes to have all the kids under control."

"Bree is nice. She's not mean or anything. She might let me go if I ask."

"I think it would be better to leave her a note. That way we can make sure we get to go. I thought we'd stop and get ice cream on the way," Taylor added when Kylie frowned.

"The mountains are a little ways off. You don't have a car."

"I have an ATV." Well, Kade had one in the shed he'd been letting her use. It would be a simple matter to duck in there and zoom off into the nearby forest before anyone saw them. "We might be back before Bree notices you're gone. It's a fast ATV. What do you say?"

Kylie chewed her lip, and her blue eyes were worried. "I will probably get in trouble."

"Sometimes trouble is worth the fun, don't you think?"

"I don't know. I hate it when Mommy is disappointed in me. She likes me to obey."

"I'm sure your mom will understand when she knows the whole story. She wouldn't want to deny you a fun day, would she? She seems like someone who wants her daughter to have a good time."

Kylie brightened. "Oh, she does. She's always thinking of fun things to do. Okay. Do you have paper in your cabin? I'll leave a note."

"Sure." Taylor got up and took Kylie's hand. "We can leave the note in my cabin, and Bree will find it there. I'll send her a text and let her know too."

"Oh, that's a good idea!"

And Taylor would make sure that note vanished before they left. She'd call Lissa and have her pick them up in her car. Samson could track them on the ATV, and that couldn't happen.

/ / /

The CT scan showed only a slight concussion, and Jon seemed to be feeling fine, so Annie got him in the truck. "I'll stop and get Kylie on the way out of town. We can go home and binge watch *Little House on the Prairie* all afternoon."

Jon groaned. "How about football instead?"

"It's a Thursday afternoon in June. There's no football."

"There are reruns. I'd even make dinner if you don't make me watch *Little House*."

"You're supposed to be resting. And it would be a good bonding time for you with Kylie. If you're going to be in a household of females, you need to learn to adjust to our tastes. First *Little House*, and by the time Christmas season rolls around, you'll be ready for Hallmark movies."

He moaned. "Oh, the humanity."

She grinned and started the engine. Her phone rang with a call from Bree before she pulled out of the hospital parking lot, so she answered it. "I'm just heading your way."

"Annie, I can't find Kylie! I've looked everywhere. The twins said she went outside while I was throwing a load of towels in the washer, but she's not anywhere."

Annie's heart stuttered along with her tongue. "Wh-what about the beach? D-did you check the water?"

Her greatest fear since Kylie was born was drowning. But her daughter was a good swimmer and knew not to ever go swimming alone.

"Kade and I walked the beach calling out her name."

"What's happening?" Jon asked.

"Bree can't find Kylie," she told him. "Bree, make sure there isn't a bathing suit missing."

"I did already. Hannah has both hers. And there aren't any clothes missing. Just what she was wearing this morning. I'm getting Samson on her trail, but I wanted to call you first. Naomi is on her way with Charley, and several other team members are bringing their dogs too."

"I'll be right there. Call Mason." Annie hung up and squealed the tires as she peeled out of the parking lot. "Bree has called in the SAR teams. That's how scared she is."

She drove the few blocks to Bree's lighthouse faster than allowed, but she didn't care. Let Doug give her a ticket. Tears kept leaking down her cheeks, and her pulse skipped with every few beats. Kylie wouldn't worry them like this on purpose. It wasn't in her nature. She knew Annie's fears for her, and she was always careful to let her know what she was doing and where she was going.

Annie had taught her never to go with anyone unless they knew the secret word *tremolo*. So it had to be that Kylie had wandered off.

Jon scooted over on the bench seat and set his hand lightly on her knee. The comforting touch was enough for her to know he was with her and concerned too.

"We'll find her," he said. "She's a smart kid. Maybe she went for a walk in the woods and got lost. Bree will find her with the dogs."

Kylie had an almost uncanny sense of direction, much like Annie's sixth sense when it came to north and south. Annie didn't think she could get lost, but maybe it was possible. The woods could get you all turned around when you couldn't see the sun.

She screeched to a halt at the curb in front of the lighthouse and leaped from the car. When she started to pause to help Jon, he shooed her up the steps. "I'm right behind you. Don't worry about me. I'm fine."

She nodded and ran up the steps to the porch. Bree was kneeling in front of Samson as she put on his SAR vest. Naomi was there with Charley, her golden retriever, as well. The other SAR members weren't there yet. Urgency strummed through

Annie's veins, and she wasn't about to wait for anyone else to arrive.

Jon came behind her and took her hand. She spotted the shorts Kylie wore yesterday lying on the floor. "Those haven't been washed, right?"

Her expression focused and intent, Bree rose and picked up the shorts. "No, they haven't. And I'm leaving her shirt for the rest of the team to use when they get here."

"Where's Milo?"

"He's inside," Bree said. "She didn't take him out with her. He was climbing around on Samson, and I think she wanted him to have some daddy time. I wish she'd taken him. If she's lost, he would have been a comfort to her at least."

"Where's Sarah?" Jon asked. "She loves Kylie, and she's part of the family. She should help too."

"I knocked on her door to ask if she'd seen Kylie, but she didn't answer," Bree said. "I tried to call her, too, but it went to voice mail."

Jon pulled out his phone. "I can check again." He shook his head after a few moments. "Nope, not answering." He ended the call without leaving a message.

Bree held the shorts under Samson's nose and then passed them to Naomi, who did the same to Charley. "Search!" she told Samson.

Naomi gave the order to Charley as well, and both dogs bounded off the porch and ran toward the hillside overlooking the water. Both dogs ran back and forth, their muzzles in the air. Their dogs weren't bloodhounds but air scenters. They worked in a Z pattern, scenting the air until they could catch a hint of the one scent they sought. Samson's tail stiffened, and he turned and dashed to the right again, then trotted toward the cottage.

Jon had never watched the teams in action. "What are they smelling? How do they know it's Kylie they smell?"

Bree was watching the dogs closely. "Every human scent is different. The skin gives off dead skin cells called rafts. We each shed about forty thousand of them per minute. Every tiny raft has its own bacteria and releases its own vapor that makes up that unique scent we all carry. So believe me, they are tracking only Kylie."

"Looks like maybe she has been at Sarah's," Jon said. "I wondered about that."

"She's not there," Bree called back over her shoulder as she chased after her dog. "I already checked inside, but it looks like she was there at some point. I even checked the closets in case she was hiding."

The dogs nosed around the grass, then headed for the shed. They stopped in front of the door for a moment, and Jon ran past and opened the door. "Isn't there supposed to be an ATV in here?"

Bree peered inside as the dogs went around the walls and sniffed before going back outside. "It's missing."

"Kylie wouldn't have taken it. She doesn't know how to operate an ATV," Annie said.

Samson gave a bark, and his tail came up. He dashed toward the woods, and Bree ran behind him. Why would Kylie go off into the woods by herself? Annie didn't like the implication that someone might have taken her into the forest. Kylie liked being around people. She wasn't prone to wander off by herself, and especially not into the forest.

They followed the trail of the skin rafts the dogs tracked over a mile before they came to a road.

The dogs stopped and whined. Samson lay down at the edge of the road beside the abandoned ATV and put his head on his paws.

Bree eyed the dogs' behavior. "They've lost the scent. They were picked up by a car."

Of course she said *they*. Sarah had taken Kylie. But why?

THIRTY-ONE

IF THIS FEAR WAS PART OF FATHERHOOD, JON WASN'T sure how he'd hold up. His daughter had been abducted, and he felt abandoned on the periphery of the action. His frantic urge to rescue her wouldn't be understood by anyone but Annie.

The band of searchers huddled at the side of the road as they tried to decide what to do next. Mason stood talking to Annie, but he, too, was unlikely to find Kylie quickly, not when the dogs couldn't follow and no one knew what vehicle they were in.

Jon's phone sounded, and he glanced at the screen. Unknown. He nearly didn't answer it, but with Kylie missing, every call might mean something. "Jon Dunstan."

"I have your daughter." The electronically distorted voice didn't sound human.

"Don't hurt her. What do you want?" Jon frantically gestured to Annie and Mason and mouthed, *Kidnapper.* His headache was back in full force, and he felt a little nauseated.

Annie shot to his side, and Mason followed her. Mason pulled out his phone and shot off a text. Jon hoped he was trying to trace the call, but it was likely futile. The kidnapper would be using a burner phone.

"Money. Two hundred thousand dollars. You have three days to get it or you'll never see her again."

A large sum, but his dad would help. And obviously Sarah had overheard the truth of Kylie's paternity since she'd called her his daughter. Did he dare call her out and let her know they knew her identity? Best not to do it until he talked it over with Mason and Annie.

"I want to talk to Kylie and make sure she's all right."

"She's not here right now, but she's fine. But if you don't pay up, you'll never see her again. Understand?"

"Yes. I'll get the money. Don't hurt her."

Would Sarah hurt Kylie? He didn't think so, but what if she simply disappeared with their little girl? She must have someone else working with her or she wouldn't have been picked up in a car. Who could it be? Her only contact had been Sean, and he was dead.

The phone cut off in his ear, and he pulled it away to look at the screen. The call had been disconnected.

Annie gripped his arm. "That was Sarah?"

"The voice was electronically distorted, but it had to be her. She's the only one who could have taken her."

"Unless someone took both Sarah and Kylie," Mason said. "We haven't considered that possible scenario. For all we know, Sarah could have tried to stop Kylie from being abducted and was taken along with her."

Jon glanced at Annie and shook his head. "The kidnapper knows Kylie is my daughter, not Nate's. Sarah overheard me tell my dad last night."

Mason's normally impassive expression went slack before his brows raised. "I wasn't expecting that."

Color rose in Annie's cheeks. "It's a long story."

"Not my business," Mason said. "But this does change things. Is there any chance someone else knows?"

Annie slipped her hand into Jon's. "Only Dr. Eckright. I haven't even told Kylie yet, and I pray the kidnapper doesn't tell her."

Jon gave her fingers a reassuring squeeze. Her worst fears were all coming true on the same day. The news would be all over town in a dramatic way with Kylie missing. Their only real focus was getting their daughter back, but the salacious story would take on epic proportions. He'd stop that if he could, but he was as helpless with the rumor making its rounds as she was right now.

"So what's next?" Jon asked. "The kidnapper is demanding two hundred thousand dollars in three days."

Annie's grip on his fingers tightened. "How can you raise that much money? And you're not supposed to pay kidnappers anyway, right?"

"I'm going to call in the FBI," Mason said. "They have the Child Abduction Rapid Deployment team. CARD has a lot of resources to help us find her quickly."

"I've heard of them." Annie had a note of hope in her voice.

Jon hadn't heard of the unit, but he'd take all the help they could get. "Should I start acquiring the funds?"

"Give me an hour to find out how they want to handle it." Mason strode off toward his SUV and climbed inside.

Jon didn't want to wait—he needed to do *something*. Standing around twiddling their thumbs wasn't accomplishing anything. "Let's get to a computer and see what we can find out about Sarah's past. If we can figure out who might have picked her up, we might be able to locate her."

Annie's eyes were red from holding back tears, and Jon wished he could do something to comfort her. This was agonizing. She didn't resist when he led her back through the woods to Bree's place. He thanked Bree and Naomi before heading to Annie's truck. He could get his car, but that would take more time than they had.

"Can you drive? I can't think." Annie climbed into the passenger seat. "My office is closer, and Kade will help too."

He didn't want to let on how rough he felt. "Yep."

She needed him to be 100 percent, and he was determined to be. If only he could spare her this pain. He started the truck and drove out to her office at the Kitchigami Wilderness Tract where he parked beside Kade's truck.

Kade, his brows drawn together in worry, met them at the front door. "Bree called me, and I've put out a memo to all the rangers to be on the lookout for Kylie. How else can I help?"

Annie gave him a quick hug. "Thank you. We want to find out what we can about Sarah's past. Who she might know, who might have helped her if she called. Sean is dead, and I don't know anything about her other acquaintances."

"I'll run some queries while you do the same."

Kade darted off to his office and Annie led Jon to hers. "There's a spare laptop in the closet. It's not connected to any official government sites, but you can check around on the internet and see if you find anything."

Jon nodded and went to pull it out. At least it would keep him busy while they waited to hear from Mason. Prayer was their best weapon right now.

/ / /

Annie sat back on her sofa and rubbed her aching head. Every second that ticked by without Kylie created an eternity of pain in her heart. There was very little on Taylor Moore, at least not her Taylor Moore. There had been thousands of hits at first, but she'd narrowed them down to some credit reports, an online résumé, and her mother's obituary.

"Nothing," Annie said.

Jon looked up from the chair across the room. "Nothing at all?"

"From what I could find, Sarah led a very quiet life with that woman who took her. Becky Johnson. Why didn't I ask more questions when Sarah was around? There might have been some stray comment I could follow now."

"You were so busy with your caseload, there was no time for social chatter with her."

"All I have are a few comments about her rigid mother's upbringing. That doesn't give me much." Annie looked back at her computer. "The mom. What can I find out about her? Could there be a family friend who might have helped?"

She went back to the search and heard the clicking of Jon's laptop keys as well. Maybe one of them would turn up something on Becky Johnson. They had to. They'd been at this for an hour and were no closer to any kind of lead. Mason should be calling with some instructions soon too. Statistics showed the first three hours were critical, and they were already through one third of that time.

Taylor's mother, Becky Johnson, was an only child according to the obituary. Her only surviving relative was one nephew, Sean Johnson. What all did Annie know about Sean? His parents were dead, and he'd been an only child too. He was well known in town and had worked as a contractor in many of the Rock Harbor homes. They hadn't suspected the darkness in his soul until they were confronted with it.

What else might she discover about him? She typed in his name, and the hits began filling her screen. She grabbed a notebook and pen to jot down the information.

He was an avid fisherman and hunter, having won several contests over the years. He'd been head of several organizations in town, including a well-known youth-mentoring program. On paper, he looked like a fine, upstanding citizen, but in reality, he was a murderer.

"What do you know about Sean?" she asked Jon.

He stopped and closed the laptop lid. "He loved surfing and was a good swimmer. Hard worker and great with his hands."

"What do we know about his activities and acquaintances?"

Jon's forehead wrinkled, and he drummed his fingers on the laptop lid. "What about his hunting partners? He was a big-time hunter."

"Did you ever hear him mention who he went out with?"

"Lonnie Fox and Glenn Hussert were fishing buddies, but I don't know about hunting."

"Glenn is running for office, so I suspect there's nothing to be found in his background. What about Lonnie?"

"During the investigation into the previous murders, we discovered Lonnie's got a rap sheet from his teen years, mostly small-time offenses like breaking and entering and a couple of fights. The charges were dropped. He's a truck driver now, mostly local. Hauling gravel and dirt for one of the businesses in town. And no other priors for the past ten years. He's kept his nose clean."

Nothing stood out. "What about women Sean dated? We know about Lissa Sanchez. Did you ever hear of any other women in connection with him?"

"Half the town. He was a player and dated a lot of women for a short time." He lifted the laptop's lid. "What about Lissa? Sean's relationship with her caused the breakup with Lonnie Fox. Do we know if they continued to see each other?"

"No, but maybe we can find out. A chat with Lissa would be in order. Sarah would be more apt to turn to another woman for help."

"I don't know, love. She's been hurt by women. Maybe she'd be leery of asking a woman for help. We need to consider all of Sean's closest friends. Maybe start with some of his workers and see who he hung out with."

"Mason might have more evidence gleaned from his initial investigation. He wouldn't have necessarily been looking for casual acquaintances like we are. I think I'll call him."

She reached for her phone and placed the call. "Mason, it's Annie."

"I was about to call you. The Child Abduction Rapid Deployment coordinator is on her way. She works out of the Marquette FBI field office. Having CARD on our side will be a big help."

She tried to feel a sense of relief, but Kylie was still gone and not in her arms. Annie had no idea what might be happening to her daughter right now. Her thoughts were crazy-making. For the first time Annie fully understood how her parents felt when Sarah went missing. They'd lived for years never knowing what had happened. How had they gone on every day?

Tears gathered in her throat. "Great. Listen, Sarah had to

have had help. Someone picked her up. The only one she knew in this area was Sean. But what if she contacted a friend of Sean's for help? Did you run into anything when you went through his house? Who were his best friends? Was he dating anyone? That kind of thing."

"We didn't find anything of value in Sean's house. And we don't know for sure Sarah took her," Mason reminded her. "But let me pull my records and see if anything stands out that will give us a lead. We questioned his friends, and we knew he dated Lissa Sanchez at one time but found no other person of interest. I should have something for us by the time you get to my office to meet up with Siela."

"Siela?"

"The CARD coordinator. Siela Cheng."

"Oh, right. Sorry. I am having trouble thinking."

"I know you are. This is very difficult, but we're doing everything we can."

Platitudes. Annie had never realized how much they hurt when you're waiting for answers. "Jon and I are heading in now. What about the ransom? Did she say whether we should start gathering cash?"

"No, she said she'd discuss options when she got here. Her ETA is half an hour."

He must have known for a while she was on her way. At least it wouldn't be another hour. She desperately wanted her baby girl back in her arms, and she'd move the Porcupine Mountains to find her.

THIRTY-TWO

JON COULD FEEL THE TENSION VIBRATING OFF ANNIE as he parked the truck in front of the jail. He leaned over and took her hand. "Hang in there, love. We're going to find her."

She held tightly to his fingers. "Jon, I'm in law enforcement. Seventy-five percent of abducted children are killed in the first three hours." Her voice broke, and tears spilled down her cheeks. "What if she's already dead? Oh, Jon, what if she's dead?"

The wail from Annie broke his heart and echoed his own fears. He gathered her into his arms. "We have to keep the faith, Annie. Try not to focus on the statistics but the fact that God is good and he has us and Kylie in his hands."

Her head bobbed against his chest. "I know, I know. But, Jon, Mason reminded me we don't even know who has her. I had a bit of hope when I was sure it was Sarah. She cares about Kylie, and I didn't think she would hurt her. But what if it's not Sarah? What if someone else has both of them?"

"What's your process when you work a crime?"

"Gather the evidence and stay focused on one step at a time."

"So that's what we do right now too. We need to stay focused on what's in front of us and what we can do in this moment to find our Kylie. You're a good investigator. Do your best to push your fears aside and use those skills to find her. I'm the pot calling the kettle black because I'm scared too. But we can do this together."

Moisture clung to her lashes, and her lips trembled. "I know you're right. We have a little bit to go on. I'm going to assume Sarah has her until we find evidence to the contrary because at least it's a lead. We always look at the evidence as it comes in. It's all we can do right now."

He pressed a kiss on her forehead. "Let's go see what Mason's found out."

He released her and opened his door. The sudden movement made him a little dizzy, but he held on to the door to hide it from Annie. She'd try to get him to rest, and he wasn't going to stop trying to find his daughter.

She came around the front of the truck to join him and watched a black SUV pull to a stop behind them. A woman in her early thirties got out. Dressed in a pair of gray slacks and matching blazer over a white shirt, she hurried toward the jail in sensible pumps. Her long black hair was tied back at her nape, and she walked with a confident stride. She was likely the FBI coordinator Mason had mentioned, Siela Cheng. She probably got grief about her name all the time when she was in high school.

He stepped in front of her. "Agent Cheng?"

Her dark-brown eyes looked him over. "And you are?"

"Kylie's father, Jon Dunstan." He reached for Annie. "This is Annie, her mother. Did the sheriff tell you I received a ransom demand? I've been waiting to find out if I need to begin the process of acquiring the money, and it's already getting late in the afternoon. What should I do?"

"Mr. Dunstan, let's go inside to a room where we can discuss next steps. I'm so sorry you and your wife are going through this. I need to gather some information before I can answer your question. If you'll lead the way, we can get this done quickly."

Her brisk, no-nonsense voice reassured him. "This way." He took Annie's hand, and they walked into the building.

Mason greeted them at the front door and shook Siela's hand. "Agent Cheng, Sheriff Mason Kaleva. Good to meet you. I've got a war room set up. This way."

They went through the inner door and down the hall to a conference room on the left. A whiteboard was mounted at the front of the room, and several people were in attendance. Mason nodded to the group and walked to the front of the room while Annie and Jon found seats.

Cheng didn't wait to be introduced but went to stand beside Mason. "There's no time for formalities. I'm Agent Siela Cheng with the FBI's CARD unit. Mason, if you'll take charge of the whiteboard and list what we know. When we're done with that, I'd like to interview the parents separately."

Jon exchanged a long look with Annie. Alone? Why did she need to get them alone? He didn't like the implications. Did she suspect one of them had something to do with this?

Mason picked up the marker, and it squeaked across the board as he wrote down the names Sarah Vitanen/Taylor Moore. "The first thing to know about in this case is the relationship of the suspected perp. Annie, would you feel up to explaining?"

Annie cleared her throat. "Of course. Sarah is my younger sister. When she was five, she was abducted by an unknown woman and we never saw her again. After all this time, we assumed she was dead. A few weeks ago, Taylor Moore came to town and applied for a job at my resort. At the time I had no idea she was my missing sister."

Cheng's eyes widened. "Interesting. Please continue."

"She finally announced she was my sister, Sarah. That was confirmed yesterday via DNA, but she's very bitter and angry that I was unable to save her from being abducted."

"How old were you?"

"Eight."

"At that age you would've been unable to have taken on a grown woman, of course, but anger and bitterness can blind people. And why would she take Kylie now?"

Annie tucked a strand of blonde hair behind her ear. "To punish me, maybe? We don't know."

"I see. Anything else I should know?"

Jon glanced at Annie. They didn't dare leave out the crucial information that had just come out. It might have influenced Sarah.

He cleared his throat. "We recently found out I'm Kylie's father and not Nate Pederson as Annie had always thought. Sarah overheard me tell my father about it last night. That might have been the catalyst."

"Hmm," Cheng said. "I think it's time I interview the two of you. Annie, would you come with me?"

"You can use my office," Mason said.

Annie stopped at the door and looked back. "Mason, humor me and have someone check on Lissa Sanchez. Sarah doesn't know many people here, and Lissa dated her cousin, Sean. It's possible she might have gone to her. Could we check out her phone records?"

"I have a court order to get the records, but we don't have them yet."

The FBI agent pulled out her phone. "I'll handle it." She sent off a text and beckoned for Annie to follow her.

This was something they had to go through no matter how much Jon wanted to protect Annie.

/ / /

Taylor paced the floor of the cottage. What had she gotten them into? Kylie had finally cried herself to sleep in the back bedroom, and that left Taylor to deal with Lissa. The woman was furious that she'd been drawn into what she called a mess.

Lissa was on the porch berating someone on the phone. Her brown curls bounced as she gestured. "I told you this would get us into trouble." She paced back and forth, waving her hands in the air.

Taylor didn't quite understand why Lissa was so mad, and even worse, Taylor didn't know how to fix it. They had to hide out while they waited on Jon to come up with the ransom, and they needed fake identities.

Maybe she shouldn't have called Lissa, but she'd had no one else to turn to. Lissa lowered the phone from her ear and turned toward the house to come inside. Taylor's gut clenched, and she drew in a deep, calming breath. If there was one thing she hated, it was being yelled at.

Lissa, dark curls askew from the breeze, shut the door behind her and put her hands on her hips as she faced Taylor. "So now there's an FBI agent in town trying to find that kid. Do you have any idea what you've done?" Her brown eyes were narrowed.

FBI? Taylor hadn't considered this case might escalate like that. Why hadn't Jon just gotten the money together like she'd told him?

"That's crazy," she managed to say in a feeble voice.

"What's crazy is that you've pulled me into this. I need to cover your tracks somehow. What phone did you use to call me?"

"It's a burner phone I bought yesterday. No one would know I called you."

"That was smart anyway. You realize you can't collect that money. The cops will be all over you. You need to disappear and not come back. And don't ever call me again."

"I need help to get away. And I'll need the money to care for Kylie."

"You have to give the kid back. That's not negotiable."

Taylor gave a slight shake to her head. This had turned into such a huge problem. She hadn't thought this through. Maybe the problem was she'd gathered her facts about life only from TV shows and her mother. She'd had very little input from real people.

She twisted her hands together. "What do you want me to do?"

"I'll take the girl back to the edge of town and let her go. You're going to call her mother and tell her where to find her. And then I'll take you somewhere so you can disappear."

At least she wouldn't have to face Annie. The longer this had gone on, the more Taylor regretted it. She should have chosen to be Sarah and become part of the family again. Now she'd have no one. She'd *be* no one. The only time her sister would remember her would be when she recalled the terror of having Kylie disappear.

Tears burned her eyes, and she wished she could go back and change what she'd done. Her mother had always said there was no use crying over spilt milk, but then she'd made sure to punish Taylor. Would Annie look for her to punish her too?

"Who were you talking to?" Taylor asked.

"Just a friend. I needed advice on what to do. You realize the girl will be able to identify you. And me. I have to make sure she never sees me again so she can't call me out. I'll have to move away from the place I've lived all my life. I hope you're happy you've ruined my life."

"I'm sorry," Taylor whispered. "I never meant to get you in trouble."

Lissa wrinkled her nose. "Let's get this done. Go get the kid."

"She's asleep."

"Well, wake her up! Good grief."

Taylor gave a jerky nod and rushed to the bedroom door. She scooped up the sleeping child and planted a kiss on her damp blonde hair. Hurting Kylie had never been part of her plan. She loved that little girl. Her niece. A part of her flesh and blood. What had she been thinking? She'd been so consumed with rage that she hadn't realized the consequences of what she'd planned to do.

She carried Kylie out of the bedroom and found Lissa holding open the front door. They exited out to the porch. The breeze teased strands of Kylie's hair, and she stirred. Her beautiful blue eyes opened, and she blinked.

She started to struggle, and Taylor put her down so she could walk. "We have to leave, honey."

"I need to go potty." Kylie turned and raced back inside.

Taylor sat on a porch chair to wait. The air smelled fresh and clean after an afternoon shower, and she wished she could feel as new as that smell. She'd made a terrible mistake.

She rose and went to stand at the steps. What was taking Kylie so long?

Lissa drummed perfectly manicured fingers on the porch railing. "Too bad you couldn't get the money from the kid's dad. Jon had plenty of it, and I think he would have raised it. But we can't risk waiting."

"No, I suppose not. She doesn't know Jon is her real dad yet, so don't mention it in front of her."

Taylor turned at a gasp behind her and looked into Kylie's horrified face. The little girl had heard every word.

THIRTY-THREE

MASON'S OFFICE REEKED WITH ITS USUAL STENCH OF burned coffee. Agent Cheng took out a tablet and stylus. "Let's start off with a physical description of your daughter."

Annie had printed out a recent picture of Kylie in her bathing suit on the dock and slid it across the desk to the FBI agent. "She's eight years old with blonde hair and blue eyes. She was forty-seven inches tall at her last checkup with the doctor a few weeks ago."

Siela picked it up and studied it. "Small for her age. She resembles you."

"She was just diagnosed with celiac disease, and I'm hoping the gluten-free diet will spark her growth." Annie hesitated. "That's actually how we discovered my deceased husband was not her father. No one in his family has celiac, and when I heard Jon had it, I began to wonder. I had been engaged to Jon nine years ago, and we broke up when he left town to go to med school. I married Nate almost immediately after major problems at home with my parents. When I got pregnant right away, I assumed the baby was Nate's. I was wrong."

Annie looked down at her hands. "Sorry, I'm explaining too much, aren't I? This has nothing to do with Kylie's disappearance."

"When a child is missing, there is no detail too slight to be ignored. Is there any chance Nate's family would have taken your daughter? Maybe they fear they won't be able to see her."

Annie shook her head. "They never come to see her anyway. They've only been around her a handful of times since she was born. And besides, they don't know the truth yet. Until last night, only Jon and I knew the truth. Oh, and Dr. Ben Eckright. We told Jon's father last night, and the window was open. Sarah overheard."

"How do you know? Did you speak with her?"

"No, but I saw her. She was running away from the open window. Our voices would have carried clearly through the screen."

Cheng wrote with the stylus on the tablet. "So it's your assumption she overheard."

"Yes. I didn't confirm it. I thought about following her and talking to her, but Jon and I had a disagreement and I was upset."

Cheng's dark eyes narrowed. "A disagreement?"

"His father is an attorney, and he suggested we run a DNA test to have proof Jon is Kylie's father. When I agreed with that, Jon thought I was using it to delay telling Kylie the truth."

"Would he have orchestrated this abduction as a way of forcing out the truth? He *is* the one who received the ransom demand."

"Not in a million years." Annie struggled to keep her voice even. "I know you have to look at the parents first, but Jon would never do something like that. He loves me, and he loves Kylie. I am sure Sarah has her."

"And she harbors resentment, which raises the possibility she took your daughter."

"Yes. She filed a false accusation against Jon as well, and she tried to get out of the charges by revealing her true identity."

Cheng raised her brows. "Interesting. Why would she accuse Jon?"

"She had a crush on him, and he let her know he was only interested in getting back with me. She tried to plant false evidence that would implicate him in a murder I was investigating with Sheriff Kaleva. But Mason saw right through it."

The FBI agent put down the tablet. "We need to take a good look at Sarah and all her acquaintances. Can you think of anyone else who might have taken Kylie? Or has she ever run off before?"

"She would never run away. Even going off with Sarah is very unlike her. She knows she's only to go with someone who knows the secret word *tremolo*. She knows how traumatized I was by my sister's abduction, and she wouldn't want to worry me. She loves Sarah, though, and she's a trusting child. I want us to stay focused and not get sidetracked."

"But we also don't want to be so fixated on Sarah that we miss other clues. Let's talk about Jon and his relationship with Kylie. Are you together? In other words, would there be any reason for him to take Kylie?"

Annie gripped her hands together at the very personal questions. "We love each other, but we're going slowly because of Kylie. She adored Nate, and it will devastate her to find out he's not her father. She has resented Jon for taking his place. But no, like I said, he wouldn't do something like that even if he thought we'd never be married. He's relocating here from Rochester, Minnesota, and we plan to build a life together."

"I know the questions upset you, but I have to examine every possible abductor." Cheng rose. "Could you ask Jon to come in next?"

"Of course." Annie stepped out into the hall and went across to the war room, where she found Jon alone in the room with his head down on a table.

She touched his back. "Are you all right?"

He straightened and glanced up at her with reddened eyes. "Just praying. My head hurts a little, but it's just where I was stitched up."

Her heart hurt at the pain in his face. He was the one person who understood what she was going through. "Cheng wants to talk to you now. Do you feel up to it?"

He rose and embraced her for a long moment, and she clung to him, taking comfort from his love and strength. They were in this together.

"Mason said he'd be right back," he told her. "When he gets back, see if they found out anything about Lissa."

"I'll do that right now. Here he comes."

Mason paused in the doorway. "Annie, you were right. Lissa got a phone call a few minutes before Kylie went missing, and it was from a burner phone. I've asked Houghton PD to pick her up for questioning. I'll let Cheng know in case she hasn't heard from her office yet. She'll want to be the one to question her."

But was it soon enough? Where was Kylie now, and what was she going through?

/ / /

Taylor stared at Kylie, who stood with fists clenched at her sides. Her small face was white with distress, and tears pooled in her eyes.

Kylie let the screen door of the cottage bang shut behind her.

"You're lying! Jon isn't my daddy. Why would you say something like that? It's mean."

Taylor had vowed never to lie to the little girl, and she wasn't going to pretend now. The kindest thing was to let the truth come out. "I'm sorry, honey, but it's true. I heard Jon and your mom telling Jon's dad last night. Your mom found out the truth when you were diagnosed with celiac disease. I know Nate loved you, though. And you loved him. You can still think of him as your daddy."

Kylie shook her head and clenched her hands together in front of her. "It can't be true. My mom wouldn't lie to me like that."

While Taylor wanted Kylie to despise Annie, she couldn't feed more pain into the child's hurting heart. "She didn't lie to you when it was something she didn't know herself until you were diagnosed."

"He's not my daddy!" Tears rolled down Kylie's face.

Taylor approached her with arms outstretched, but Kylie backed away. "Don't be afraid, honey. It's all right."

"Why did you bring me here? You said we were going to go hiking, but we didn't even see the mountains. And you left Kade's ATV along the side of the road. Someone will steal it. We need to give it back to him. You shouldn't have taken it."

The kid's litany of all that Taylor had done wrong spiked her anger. "Look, you're too little to understand, so just knock it off with the complaints."

Lissa went to the car and opened the back door. "Quit your crying and get in the car, Kylie. Now."

The tone was of a woman used to dealing with children, and Taylor thought it had worked when Kylie went down the steps ahead of her. But as soon as she hit the grass, she took off running in the other direction. Taylor didn't have a chance to react before the little girl disappeared into the forest on the right side of the cottage.

Lissa shouted at Taylor to get her, and she finally sprang into motion. "Kylie, come back here!" She ran after her and plunged into the cool shadows of the tall oaks and pines.

She stopped and looked around. "Kylie, where are you? Come here, honey. I'm going to take you back to your mom right now."

Birds resumed their chirping in the treetops, and the scent of pine swirled in the air as Taylor shuffled through fallen spruce needles. Where would the little girl hide? She checked under bushes and pushed back branches while calling for Kylie to come out. But there was no answer.

"Taylor?"

She turned to see Lissa standing awkwardly at the edge of the forest, with one hand behind her. "I can't find her."

Lissa shrugged. "It doesn't matter. She'll run into civilization and get home eventually."

"Lissa, she's a *child*! She could die out there."

"Listen to yourself. We're not that far from town. She's lived near the forest all her life. She'll get home just fine. The biggest problem is getting you away before you're found and they find me. Get in the car, and I'll get you out of here."

"I can't go without Kylie."

Lissa brought her arm around, and Taylor gasped at the gun in her hand. She held up her hands. "Lissa, what's going on? You've got a little girl yourself. How could you be okay with leaving Kylie out here?"

Lissa waggled the gun. "I'm through arguing with you. You

brought trouble on me, and I won't stand by and pay for what you did. Get in the car like I said, or I'll shoot you in the leg and haul you in there bleeding and wounded."

Taylor hesitated, but she had no choice. Lissa's set expression held not a trace of mercy. She'd shoot first.

Dropping her hands to her sides, Taylor trudged past Lissa toward the car. If she had the courage, she'd tackle her and wrest the gun from her hand, but Taylor wasn't the most coordinated of people. Lissa would probably shoot her.

Taylor cast one last glance back to the woods, but no small face looked back at her. This was all her fault. Why had she been so hotheaded and foolish? The minute she got to civilization, she'd call Annie and tell her where to find Kylie.

She got in the passenger seat and fastened herself in. The key was in the ignition, and for a moment she imagined releasing the buckle and sliding over to start the car and drive off by herself, but Lissa got in before Taylor got the courage to act.

Without speaking, Lissa laid the gun in her lap and drove off the property and onto the road. They headed down M-26. Taylor had expected her to head for the airport or a dock so she could escape the area. "Where are we going?"

"To a safe place until I can figure out how to get you out of here."

Lissa's terse voice warned her not to ask too many questions, so Taylor shut up and stared out the window at the passing forest. She must have dozed a little because when she opened her eyes, she was deep in the shadows of thick trees on a narrow dirt track. The bumps must have awakened her.

Lissa shot a warning glare her way, so Taylor pressed her lips together and didn't ask questions.

Lissa parked in a turnaround and shut off the car. "Get out and come with me."

Taylor did as she was told and got out in a cloud of black flies. She waved them away and ran after Lissa, who was sprinting through thick underbrush with an obvious destination in mind. They broke through the vegetation into a small clearing with a dilapidated cabin. The porch canted to one side, and the place looked ready for a wrecking ball.

Gun in hand, Lissa waved Taylor to the porch. Frowning, Taylor went up the rickety steps and stood at the door as Lissa unlocked and opened it. Taylor saw a young woman lying on a cot sit up and stare at her. She had no time to speak before Lissa shoved Taylor inside and locked the door behind her.

THIRTY-FOUR

THE HOUGHTON POLICE HAD PICKED UP LISSA ALONG M-26 heading toward Houghton. The woman was shouting about an attorney as they brought her in. Jon held Annie's hand in the small observation area as Cheng and Mason got her seated at the table. The small interrogation room didn't have enough space for them, and Annie had told him they'd be more of a distraction than a help.

He knew it was killing her to observe instead of interrogate, but she was too close to the situation. They were the only ones in the viewing room, and he was glad for the breathing space with just the two of them.

She took his hand. "You doing okay?"

"Just fine," he assured her despite his pounding headache.

"You're lying. You look pale." She leaned in close to study his eyes. "I think one of your pupils is a little dilated. Jon, you need to go to the hospital."

"I'm not going anywhere. I need to be here."

She palmed his cheeks. "You don't have to kill yourself to be here for me. We're in this together all the way, but I need you to be whole and healthy too."

He appreciated her worry, but he'd power through this. He had to. "Shh, look, they're getting started."

That distracted her, and she leaned forward in her chair as Cheng pulled out her tablet and stylus. The FBI agent smoothed her sideswept bangs out of her eyes. "Ms. Sanchez, do you know why you're here?"

Lissa glanced at her attorney, a nondescript man in his forties wearing a seedy suit. He nodded as if to encourage her answer, and she shrugged. "I have no idea. I wasn't even speeding. Look, I've got a two-year-old I need to pick up from my mother's. I'm already late."

Jon studied Lissa's face and thought fear flashed in her brown eyes. She kept drumming her fingers on the table and moving restlessly too.

"How quickly you get out of here is up to you," Cheng said. "We're looking for Taylor Moore."

"I haven't seen her in quite some time. Not since before her cousin died." She didn't hold the FBI agent's gaze and picked at the fingernail polish on her left thumb.

"She's lying," Annie said. "Look at the tells."

"I think you're right." Even Jon could see the evasive behavior.

"So when we do a sweep of your car, we aren't going to find any stray hairs or other evidence? Better think hard about what you're telling me. A tech is vacuuming your car right now and looking for fingerprints and DNA."

"Don't answer that," her attorney said.

Lissa gave him a wide-eyed glance. "Well, I don't know. She's been in my car, but not in a while. I'm not good about cleaning it up, though, and anything like that would still be there."

Annie pushed her hair out of her face. "Score one for Lissa."

Cheng leaned forward. "So there won't be any fingerprints on the outside door handles either? Anything from before two days ago would have been washed off by the rain. Look, Lissa, we already know Taylor bought a burner phone and used it to call you. We also have a record of a text she sent that told you where to pick her up. You might as well tell me where she is, or you won't be getting your daughter tonight. You'll go straight to jail."

Lissa's face reddened. "I don't know where she is. I picked her up and dropped her off at the Houghton airport. I assume she got a ticket and left."

"And we know that didn't happen either because we tracked the pings on your cell phone. You haven't been near the airport all day. So where are she and Kylie?"

"Who's Kylie?"

"Don't play games with me. You're in this up to your neck."

Jon saw immediately what he needed to do, and he rose. "Come with me, love. We don't need to sit here and wait. Let's ask Montgomery for a list of Lissa's locations today. We can check out a few while Cheng wears her down. It's going to be dark in a few hours. We can't wait any longer."

Annie's eyes went wide. "You're right." She jumped to her feet and glanced through the window one last time before following him out to the hall. They found Deputy Montgomery in his office staring at his computer.

Annie stepped to his desk. "Doug, could you give me a printout of the pings you got off Lissa's phone?"

He barely looked up as he grabbed a paper and handed it to her. "Here's your copy. The sheriff knew you'd be asking. How's it going in there?"

"Slowly. She keeps lying, but Cheng shifts with her. I think she'll wear her down, but we're going to go out searching."

His gaze still glued to his screen, he nodded. "I'll let the sheriff know when he's done."

Jon followed Annie to the hall, and when she stopped to study the map, he peered over her shoulder. He jabbed a finger at a spot outside Houghton. "There were a bunch of pings here, like she spent some time there, but that's not her house."

Annie nodded. "Maybe it's a friend's." She ran her finger in a circle around the area. "This is all forest here. Maybe we could pick up Kylie's scent with the dogs. I'll text Bree the coordinates and ask her to bring her team while we get there and do a once-over first."

The pain in his head had increased until he was having trouble seeing, but Jon nodded and followed her out to the truck. She headed for the driver's side, and he didn't object since he wasn't sure he could manage driving anyway. He couldn't let her know how much he was struggling.

He had to find his daughter. She might be in danger this very minute, and he wasn't about to lie in a hospital bed and not do something to help her.

/ / /

The small cottage was set off by itself with no neighbors. Annie parked in the gravel drive. Towering oak and spruce trees crowded the edge of the lawn and threw deep shade over the ground. The SAR dogs would be here shortly, but she could look around.

She glanced at Jon and saw he was sleeping. Good. Let him rest a few minutes. He hadn't spoken much on the drive up from Rock Harbor, and she didn't like his pasty color. He was stubborn, though, and she knew she'd have no luck convincing him to go to the ER with Kylie missing.

She rolled down her window before she got out and gently closed the door. The late-afternoon sun slanted through the tops of the trees and illuminated the porch of the house. Was it locked? She went up the steps and tried the door. It wouldn't open.

She rang the bell and pounded on it. "Kylie? It's Mommy. Sarah? Are you guys in there?"

When no one answered, she peered in every window she could reach. The place appeared empty. The only window she couldn't see into was a back bedroom. Maybe Jon could help her reach it. Or maybe he could see in.

She retraced her steps to the truck as Jon moved his head and opened his eyes. He saw her looking in the window and managed to smile, but she thought it was more like a grimace. Alarm shot down her spine at his appearance, and she opened the door. "Jon, is your head hurting?"

"A little." He stumbled as he got out. "Anything?"

"Nothing yet. No answer at the door. I checked the windows, but there is one I can't reach." Her terror for Kylie vied with her worry over Jon. She needed his help, but he should be in the hospital.

"Show me." He sounded stronger and walked with his head high toward the cottage.

Maybe he was fine. The doctor said he needed rest, and after they found Kylie, she'd make sure he went straight to bed. She had a feeling their daughter was close, but she couldn't explain it. Mother's intuition, or was it just plain hope?

She scurried to keep up with him. "That window." She pointed out the back bedroom.

He stepped to it, but the ground fell away there, and his eyes barely got to the edge of the windowsill. "I can't see much. Just the ceiling and the posts on the bed. I can't even see the mattress. Let's get you on my shoulders, and you can check it out."

He led her around to the porch and settled on the ground. "You get on the porch and climb on my shoulders."

"Should you be lifting me?"

"Go on. We don't have much time."

She noticed he didn't deny he was struggling, and her anxiety increased. But the sooner they found Kylie, the sooner she could talk him into seeing a doctor.

She climbed the porch steps and went to the side where he sat. Hanging on to a post, she looped her right leg over his right shoulder and managed to clamber onto him. She clung to his hair and could feel the swelling near his right temple. Had it been there before?

"Hang on." He grabbed the posts on the railing and hoisted himself up. Staggering a little, he stopped to steady himself. "I'm ready. Hold tight."

She let go of his head and held on to his chin with both hands. He moved toward the window and stopped under the center of the glass.

She leaned forward a bit and peered into the room. It held a twin-size bed with a pink coverlet. A stuffed animal she didn't recognize lay on the pillow. The cover looked wrinkled as if someone had slept on top of it. She looked around for some sign of her daughter. Nothing jumped out at her at first.

Then she saw a small flip-flop and gasped. "Kylie's sparkly flip-flop is on the floor. It has a *K* on it. I know it's hers!"

She pounded on the window and screamed her daughter's name several times before leaning her forehead against the cool glass and gulping back tears. "I don't think she's in there, Jon. You can put me down."

He carefully carried her to the porch, then bent over to deposit her on the floorboards. Once she was off his shoulders, he sat on the top step and exhaled.

"You okay?"

"Just give me a second. I'm okay."

While he rested, she texted Mason about what they'd found and asked him to check on who owned this property.

Tires popped on the gravel, and Annie looked around to see Bree's Jeep pull into the drive. Her friend hopped out of the driver's door and went around to the back to let out Samson. Naomi climbed out of the passenger side and retrieved Charley. The team joined them at the porch in minutes.

Naomi touched Annie's arm. "I know what you're going through, Annie. Timmy and Emily were missing when Em was eight. It's terrifying."

Naomi's gentle words were a balm, but they also brought tears to Annie's eyes. "We have to find her."

"We will," Naomi said. "Do you have a scent article?"

"Yes, in the car. I've got a pair of shorts." Annie ran to retrieve the clothing.

Each of the women had their dogs get the scent, and they were all heading for the woods to their right in the next minute. Annie and Jon ran after them. As they followed Kylie's trail, the dogs led them to the left. Annie was familiar with this section of forest, and she began to hear the sound she'd been dreading.

"We're near Hungarian Falls," she said. "It can be dangerous for a child to try to navigate the cliffs and rocks." She eyed the setting sun. "Especially in the dark."

Jon's grip tightened on her fingers. "Then we'd better find her fast."

THIRTY-FIVE

TAYLOR HAD YANKED AT THE DOOR SO MUCH THAT HER palms throbbed. The other woman, Michelle, had told her it was no use, but she had to find out for herself.

The crescent moon didn't offer much illumination in the dark cabin, and they had no flashlight. Taylor didn't have her phone either. Lissa had confiscated it.

Michelle reached for a bottle of water. "Here. Rest and let's discuss next steps."

Taylor sank onto the hard wood floor and took the bottle. "Thanks. How long have you been here?" She put the bottle aside and hugged her knees to her chest, which sometimes helped when she was having an attack of claustrophobia.

"Eight days. I think."

"What happened to your leg?"

"ATV accident. What's your name?"

Taylor hesitated. Being Taylor hadn't brought her anything but heartache. She'd thought she could choose who to be, but she'd chosen poorly. "Sarah. Sarah Vitanen."

The name felt foreign on her lips, and she focused on her identity to stem the rising tide of hysteria. Could she be a different person? After seeing Kylie run off into the woods and realizing what she'd gotten the little girl into, Sarah had hated herself. Maybe it was too late to change, but she had to try.

Had anyone found Kylie? If she thought God would hear someone like her, she'd try praying.

"Why are you locked up in here instead of in the hospital getting that leg treated?" Sarah asked.

When Sarah had been brought in during the late afternoon, she'd taken a good look at her fellow captive. Michelle appeared bedraggled and weak. Her brown hair had hung in greasy strings around her face, and circles created shadows under her brown eyes. There were no shower facilities in the cabin, and the woman probably longed for a nice, hot shower. How long was Sarah going to be trapped here too? She'd be looking as rough as Michelle in three days.

Michelle shuffled in the dark, and Sarah realized she had tuned out the first part of Michelle's story. "After a year, I came out of hiding from my husband and was ready to start life again. I came out to the forest to work on a magazine piece about mountain lions, and I found another woman running from her ex. I tried to rescue her, but I had an ATV accident and Grace was killed. Some guy picked me up and brought me here. He brings me supplies, but he won't let me leave. He wants me to lead him to my stuff. Supposedly there's something there he wants, but I don't know what it is."

"What did you take? From where?"

"I'm not sure. I worked at the shelter where I lived for a year, and I do have a copy of some of their records, but that's hardly explosive enough to warrant kidnapping. I keep trying to think of what I took from our house when I ran away, but it was only my personal items—jewelry, makeup, clothing. The laptop. My ex used it some, too, so I wondered if there was sensitive information on it."

"Where is all that now?"

Michelle went still. "Are you a plant to get me to talk?"

Sarah's panic ticked up a notch. "What? Of course not. I need to get out of here and find my niece, who ran off into the woods. She's only eight." Sarah's eyes burned and she blinked back tears. "It's my fault she's out there." She looked out the window into the dark yard illuminated only with a sliver of moonlight. "And it's nighttime. She's by herself." Her voice wobbled. "And I'm claustrophobic. I-I have to get out of here and find some light. And space."

The emotion Sarah couldn't hide must have reassured Michelle because she shifted and touched Sarah's hand. The woman's firm grip helped just a bit, and Sarah wrapped her fingers around the warm flesh. Her panic ebbed a little.

"I just wanted to be cautious," Michelle said. "All my things are at my campsite. I've been camping out since I left the shelter. It's hard to find my camp in the wilderness, but I was going to try to draw a map. There's no way I can lead my kidnapper there. He might go ahead and kill me then. Either way, he's not letting me go." Her voice took on an edge. "We have to save ourselves."

Sarah nodded and set down the water bottle. "Can we get out of a window?"

"I couldn't do it by myself, but I do have a boot now. I've been elevating my leg, and the swelling is down some. Maybe I can put it on. If you can figure out how to get a window open, that would be a start."

Peering through the dark, Sarah walked around the tiny cabin. The biggest window was nailed shut, and she had no tool to pry out the nails. But what about breaking out the glass? She wore sandals, so those would be no help. The water bottle would bounce right off. The only furnishing was the bed, and she couldn't heft it into the window. She could try wrapping her hand in a blanket and see if she could drive it through the glass, but she didn't have a lot of upper-body strength.

Michelle had an orthopedic boot. Maybe that would be heavy enough to break the window.

Before she could suggest they try it, the sound of an engine came from outside. Sarah darted to the window and looked out to see headlights sweep the tree trunks before lasering in on the rickety cabin. She was about to face the guy who was behind this. What was his connection to Lissa?

Heavy footsteps clomped up the steps and, hands fisted, Sarah backed away as the door opened. Silhouetted by the moonlight, the guy seemed strong and rangy. He held a flashlight that he focused on Sarah, and the brilliance nearly blinded her.

She put up her hand. "You don't have to point it in my eyes."

He lowered the flashlight. "Here's the deal, girls. Michelle here is going to draw me a map. If I find what I need, you can leave. If not, I've got your graves already dug."

Sarah fisted her hands at her sides. This wasn't good.

/ / /

Darkness descended early in the deep woods, and Annie could barely make out the others searching for her little girl. The dogs were intent on not losing the trail they followed with their noses held high. Samson's fluffy tail wagged over his back, and he bounded over rocks like a much younger dog.

She heard the roar of the waterfall and smelled the spray, but she didn't see it. Not yet.

She cupped her hands to her mouth. "Kylie! It's Mommy. Where are you?"

She had been shouting so much, her voice sounded hoarse and weak. Would Kylie even be able to hear her? She looked back at Jon, who swayed a bit where he stood. He was pale in the moonlight filtering through the overstory. "Do you need to sit down?"

"No, I'm fine. Let's find her." He shouted Kylie's name much louder than Annie could.

There was a crack up ahead, and Bree fell to the ground. Annie darted forward. "Bree, are you all right?"

Bree sat on the ground with her legs outstretched. "I've sprained my ankle." Her voice was a pained whisper. "Stupid of me not to see that hole."

Samson whined and shot back to nose at Bree's cheek. "I'm okay, boy."

Jon touched Annie on the shoulder. "Let me look at it."

She moved out of the way so he could kneel beside Bree. He gently removed Bree's boot and touched the flesh around her ankle.

Bree gasped in pain. "Sorry. I have an elastic bandage in the first aid kit in my backpack."

Jon reached for the backpack and helped her slide it off her shoulders. "I don't think it's broken. I'll wrap it, and we can see about getting you out of here."

Annie unzipped the backpack, found the first aid kit, and retrieved the bandage. "Here it is." She aimed her phone's flashlight at Bree's ankle.

Jon took the elastic roll and began to wrap Bree's ankle. Annie watched his color come back. Kneeling beside Bree was enough of a rest to rejuvenate him a little. While he worked, Annie stared into the dark woods. Mist curled around the tree trunks and through the shrubs to form an otherworldly scene. The fog would make it harder to find her daughter. Was Kylie out there hunkering down and too afraid to call out for her?

She would welcome the dogs once they found her. Annie turned to watch Samson bump Bree's chin in a worried manner. Charley and Naomi had returned to make sure Bree was all right too. While she understood their concern—and shared it—her bigger fear was for Kylie wandering in the dark so close to the cliffs and the falls. The mist along the ground would make it harder to see drop-offs and slippery rock obstructions.

She curled her fingers into her palms and prayed for Kylie to sense they were out here, for her to feel God's arms around her holding her up. Annie's little girl had to be terrified. This was unfamiliar terrain to her, and she would be completely turned around with no idea how to find her way back to a town or any kind of civilization.

Jon finished bandaging Bree's ankle and stood. "You'll need to stay off it for a few days. And an X-ray would be a good idea just to make sure there's no chip in the bone." He dug into her first aid kit and pulled out a bottle of pain reliever, then shook out some pills and handed them to her with a bottle of water.

She popped the pills in her mouth and recapped the bottle. "It's a little hard to stay off of it right now. I need to find Kylie." Bree reached for Jon to help her up.

He stepped back and shook his head. "No, you lie there for now. Elevate your foot on your backpack or a log. We can continue the search and come back for you when we're on our way out. We'll need some rescue personnel to help us transport you."

When Bree's nod came, it was with obvious reluctance. "Samson will listen to Naomi." She looked over at her friend. "Can you handle both dogs?"

"Of course. But I think we should call for rescue now to haul you out of here. Lying on the damp ground for hours isn't a good idea."

Hours? Tears flooded Annie's eyes. Naomi thought it would be hours before they found Kylie? Annie didn't want to consider that her daughter might be stuck out here all night. She needed her mom, and Annie needed to feel her baby's warm body in her arms.

Why hadn't they already found her? The dogs had her scent. Did she have that much of a head start on them?

She thought back to the events of the day and bit down on her quivering lip. Kylie had probably been out here at least three hours before they had figured out where to start searching.

Naomi shrugged off her backpack and pulled out a satellite phone. "I'll let Mason know your coordinates, and we can continue the search. I'm uneasy about leaving you alone and injured, though. There have been some reports of pumas in the area."

"I'm not afraid," Bree said. "I have a flare gun, and I can scare off any big predators. Would you tell Mason to call Kade too? He'll want to know what's going on."

"You got it." Naomi walked a few feet away into an open space in the trees to place the call.

Annie glanced at Jon and was relieved to see him looking even stronger and more alert. Maybe he was getting past the weakness from the concussion. They all needed to be at the top of their games to find Kylie out there somewhere.

Naomi rejoined them. "Mason is sending help, and he's putting Kade in charge of retrieving you. Anu will watch the kids." She snapped her fingers for the dogs and had them sniff the scent article again. "Let's do this. Search!"

THIRTY-SIX

JON'S HEAD FELT A LITTLE CLEARER AS HE FOLLOWED the dogs with Annie through the mist curling around their feet in wisps. For a while he'd feared he'd have ask to be medevaced out. And he couldn't leave Annie to face this alone. He wanted their daughter back safe and sound.

The dogs' barking took on a frantic tone, and Annie tugged her hand out of his. "Maybe they found her!"

She disappeared into the fog between two large pine trees, and he ran after her. He broke through the rim of trees into a vista looking out over a cliff. It was too dark and foggy to tell if it was rocks below them or water, but he heard the rushing sound of the waterfall. It was very close.

Naomi tossed her braid over one shoulder and beckoned to Annie, who was hurrying toward her. "Be careful. There's a drop-off right here. The dogs have a strong scent. I think she's close."

"She's gone over the edge?" Annie asked, her voice a squeak that was nearly gone.

Naomi surveyed the dogs with their feet planted on the edge of the cliff. "They are stopped at the edge, but they clearly can still smell her."

The caution in Naomi's voice terrified Jon, and he knew

Annie would be petrified. He took her hand and held tightly. She was shaking, and he slipped his arm around her waist.

"My voice is gone," she whispered. "Would you call her?"

Jon cupped his hands around his mouth. "Kylie! We're here. Where are you?"

The waterfall nearly drowned out his words, and the wind howled as if in response. He listened for a moment. Was that a cry?

Annie gripped his forearm. "Did you hear something? Maybe it was an owl."

"I thought I heard something too." He repeated his yell for Kylie to answer.

This time there was a lull in the wind, and he heard a voice. "Jon?"

He released Annie and flung himself onto his belly to peer over the cliff's edge. "Hand me a flashlight!"

Naomi handed him hers, and he shone its powerful beam down into the abyss. At first the light only picked out the waterfall thundering over rocks to fall into the pool far below. If she'd fallen there, she wouldn't have survived. He trained the illumination back closer to the rock face where he lay, and almost immediately he spotted her blonde head.

She was lying on a narrow ledge about fifteen feet below him. How had she survived such a fall? The space was so small, it was a wonder she hadn't hit it and bounced over the side. Only God could have done this.

"She's there!" he yelled back at Annie and Naomi. "On a ledge below."

Kylie huddled on the ledge with her knees drawn to her chest. "I'm cold. Where's Mommy?"

Annie flung herself down beside him. "I'm here, Bug. Mommy is right here. We're going to get you. Don't move."

Her voice was so soft that Jon wasn't sure Kylie could hear it. "Do you see Mommy? She has been calling for you, and her voice is about gone. She's here, though. Don't move. You don't have much room." He sat up and asked Naomi, "Do you have any climbing gear with you?"

"We don't normally do cliff rescues. We locate the missing and call in resources when necessary. I'm not a climber."

"I'll try it." Annie's voice barely registered above the wind. "I'm not a climber, but I'll figure it out."

This rescue would take a lot of upper-body strength, and he was the logical choice. "I'm an experienced climber. I'll get her."

Naomi took off her backpack and unzipped it to retrieve a coil of nylon rope. "Here's the rope I have. I think it's only twenty feet, though, just barely enough to get down to her after you tie it off. This looks dangerous, Jon. The rescue team is on its way to get Bree. We could wait for them." She dug into the backpack again. "I do have some gloves."

"Those will help." He had a plan forming. The best course of action would have been to double the rope so he could rappel the right way, but they didn't have that much. He could make it work, but it would be a challenge, and falling would be a distinct possibility. He had to try anyway.

"Mommy," came the small voice from below. "I'm scared."

Annie tried to call to her daughter, but nothing came out. Jon leaned over. "Mommy's voice is gone, but I'm coming to get you, Kylie. Just stay still. I'll be right there."

Annie reached for him before he could get up. She grabbed a small notepad from her backpack and jotted out what she wanted to tell him. *You're recovering from a concussion. I don't think you should do it. Let me go.*

"You've never rappelled or done any climbing, love. I can do this."

Uncertainty flickered in her eyes. He knew she wanted her daughter, but she also loved him and didn't want him hurt.

"Careful," she managed to rasp out.

"Always." He rose and grabbed the rope. The only tree near enough to hold was four feet away, which wouldn't allow him to get all the way to the ledge once he tied it. And he needed enough length to fashion a loop to slip around Kylie so Annie and Naomi could hoist her up. He tied knots in the rope every foot or so, praying the whole time there would be enough length left to reach her.

It had to have enough. The women couldn't support his weight as he rappelled down the side. He hurried to the large spruce tree and tied off that end of the rope, using as little nylon in the knot as he dared. He yanked on it to test it. It held for now. It would have to do.

He tied a loop on the other end and tested the strength of his knot. Good. If only he had good climbing shoes. At least his sneakers were flexible and nimble. He'd be able to feel the rocks under his feet.

"Keep as much light on the rock face and on Kylie as you can," he told the women. "I'll need to see where I'm going, and I want her to be able to see the ledge clearly so she doesn't scoot over too far to make room for me."

Annie embraced him in a fierce hug. "Praying. Be careful."

He tossed the length of rope over the side of the cliff, yanked on the gloves, then stepped off into space.

/ / /

The humid air in the dark cabin stank of fear. Sarah's dread escalated as she waited for Michelle to respond to the man's ultimatum: draw a map or be killed. It was bad enough to be here with another woman, but she couldn't imagine facing this dark, claustrophobic space by herself.

"You're never going to let us go," Michelle said.

"Try me and see. Just as soon as you give me what I want, you can walk out of here. You haven't seen my face, so you can't identify me. No risk."

He walked farther inside and leaned against the end of the cot as if he didn't care, but Sarah didn't trust him. If she was going to get out of here, it was up to her. The cabin door still stood open, and she made an instantaneous decision to escape. There would be no better time than right now.

She looked over toward the back door. "Who's there?"

The man instantly straightened and rushed to the door. In the moonlight, Sarah caught the gleam of a gun she didn't know he had. But she couldn't let that stop her. She leaped for the door and caught the handle on her way out. The door slammed behind her, and she knew better than to try to pause and figure out how to lock it. He'd be on her instantly.

She ran for the cover of the forest to her left and dove for a thicket in the darkness. She barely pulled her legs under the foliage when she heard his feet pounding down the steps. His angry shouts made her cower, but as long as he couldn't find her, he couldn't hurt her.

She squirreled farther under the leaves and tried to make sure nothing could be seen if he shone the flashlight her direction. His footsteps went past her, deeper into the woods, and she waited until he came back this way. He was cursing under his breath, and she didn't dare breathe as he stomped closer to the cabin.

Had he locked Michelle inside? She suspected he'd been arrogant enough to think he could find Sarah quickly and would lock up Michelle to make sure he didn't have to search for both of them.

A gunshot echoed through the trees on the other side of the cabin, and his shouts grew angrier. Would he give up or call in reinforcements? And what if he randomly fired into the foliage where she hid? She had to get out of here. If more people came and conducted a thorough search, they'd find her.

Since he was occupied on the other side, she pushed her way to the back side of the thicket and emerged into the dark. Which way should she go? The only thing she could do was try to stay as far away from that guy as possible. She used his voice as a guide and kept moving until she couldn't hear him anymore.

She hoped that meant he was a long way away, but it might mean he'd quit yelling, realizing she would use it to pinpoint his location. Her breath came hard in her chest, and her raspy panting filled her ears. She had no idea where she was. Lissa had made many twists and turns along dirt roads, and Sarah wasn't familiar with this area.

Her legs ached, and her head began to pound. Her last meal had been breakfast, and she began to tire. She paused to take stock of her location. Trees, trees, and more trees. They crowded together so closely, she couldn't glimpse a star or glimmer of the moon. She had no idea of the time either, but it would be hours before the sun came up. She'd have to wander out here until dawn, when she might see enough to determine which way to go.

She eyed a large oak tree. If she could climb it, maybe she could see lights in a distant home or fishing lodge. It was worth a try. She placed her left foot in the V of the lowest split and clambered up to the sturdiest branch she could reach. She swept her gaze over the area around her, but the trees were too thick to make out any of the landscape or see more than five feet ahead of her.

A twig snapped and she froze. She desperately needed to sneeze, but she held it the same way she held her breath. A scent wafted her way. Male cologne.

He was right below her even if she couldn't see him. She clung to the limb and waited a long time until the stealthy movements and the scent vanished.

By the time she thought it was safe to climb down, she wasn't sure she had the strength.

THIRTY-SEVEN

ANNIE SCOOTED OUT OVER THE ABYSS AS FAR AS SHE could and still maintain her balance. She shone the light along the cliff wall and watched Jon bounce out from it with his feet as he let himself slide down a few inches at a time to the next knot in the rope. One wrong move, and he'd plummet past Kylie and crash on the rocks below.

What he was doing took incredible strength and concentration. Her pulse roared in her ears, and her hands were slick with perspiration. She moved the flashlight to the other hand and prayed.

Naomi sat on the cliff's edge with her legs dangling over. She aimed her light at Kylie's blonde head. "Just a couple more feet and you're there."

Jon's face was white and focused. The tendons in his neck stood out, and the muscles in his arms bulged with the strain of hanging on to the rope. Annie shouldn't have let him go in his condition, but Kylie's situation was dire. The shelf looked fragile, like it could let break at any moment.

As he neared Kylie, Annie could see he was barely going to make the safety of the ledge. And he would have to lift Kylie up high to get her into the harness he'd created on the end of the rope. Barely daring to breathe, she watched him point the toe of one shoe until it connected with the ledge, then the other one, until he finally released the rope.

It dangled a foot above his head. Getting it around Kylie would be tricky. Maybe they should wait until more help arrived. She moved the flashlight a few inches and gasped. The ledge on the north side had begun to break off.

"Naomi, look." Annie pointed at the crumbling rock.

"Oh no," Naomi whispered. She trained the light on that spot. "Jon, you've got to get out of there! The ledge isn't going to hold!"

Jon tracked the light with his eyes, and his fists clenched when he spotted the danger. He scooped Kylie into his arms and hugged her. "It's going to be okay, Bug. We're going to get you up in that rope there. See it above my head? I'll put you on my shoulders so you can reach it. When you grab it, slip the loop under your arms. Can you do that?"

"You've got to come, too, Jon." Annie's voice barely squeaked out of her throat. He didn't turn his head, so she knew he hadn't heard her plea.

He leaned against the rock face on his left side to steady himself, then lifted Kylie to his shoulders. He slumped a little with the effort, and Annie wasn't sure he'd be able to keep his balance. He was too weak to be doing this. She shouldn't have let him go down there.

Kylie reached above her head and grabbed the rope. She slipped the loop over her head and wiggled it down over her shoulders and then under her arms. "I've got it. I did it, Mommy!" She turned her face up into the light emitted from Annie's flashlight.

"Good girl," Naomi called down. "Mommy is glad, but her voice is gone. Hang on to the rope with both hands, and we're going to pull you up, okay? We'll have to put down our flashlights to do it, though, so don't be scared. We're still here."

"Okay." Kylie grasped the rope tightly.

Annie laid down the light and jumped up to help Naomi pull up Kylie. The rope began to come up easily, and she sobbed at the thought that Kylie would be safe and sound in her arms in just moments. She kept her gaze on the edge of the cliff, and her daughter's blonde hair showed above the grass in a shaft of moonlight. Annie and Naomi gave a final tug, and Kylie was lying on her stomach on the grass.

Annie dropped the rope and rushed to pull Kylie into an embrace. Kylie wound her arms around Annie's neck and burst into tears. Annie wept with her. They might have lost her today. But for Jon, this might have been a very different ending.

Naomi turned on a light so they could check Kylie over. Annie had never seen a more welcome sight than her little girl's blue eyes and sweet cheeks.

She pulled away and ran her hands over Kylie's arms. "Are you hurt? Is anything broken?" she managed to get out in a whisper.

Kylie shook her head. "I just have a bruise here." She showed her a bruise on her right calf.

She gave her daughter a final hug. "We've got to get Jon to safety," she croaked. "Sit here against the tree with Samson and Charley. Good boys," she crooned to the dogs. She set Kylie onto the grass, and both dogs snuggled in, their tails wagging happily. "Don't move," she told her daughter.

She seized the flashlight and focused the light onto Jon's face below. He was seated on the ledge and looked spent. It had taken so much out of him to get down there. She tried to call to him, but her voice was totally gone now. She grabbed the rope and tossed it over the edge. It dangled over his head by a foot.

"Maybe we should untie the loop so it reaches him," Naomi said.

"I'm not sure he can hold on. That concussion has taken its toll."

Naomi leaned over and studied the situation. "But if we don't untie the loop, he's stuck there. And it looks like the ledge has broken away even more. I'm not sure we have time to wait for help to arrive."

Annie followed the beam of light on the ledge. The gap seemed to have doubled in size from a few minutes ago. She nodded and pulled up the rope. Her fingers stumbled as she struggled to untie the knot. Every second counted right now. Jon's life was literally hanging in her hands. There. She finally had it loose.

Naomi swung her light to Jon's face. "Grab the rope, Jon. It's down there for you now."

He laboriously got up and reached for the rope, which ended at his chest now. Annie realized she should have looked for the closest knot. He would need one to hang on to. She frantically made a knot motion with her hand to Naomi.

"Where's the knot, Jon?" Naomi called. "Do you need to tie one?"

Jon ran his fingers along the rope, then wrapped his hand around the rope. "Here's a knot. I'm ready."

She wasn't so sure. She and Naomi got into position. "Let's wrap it around our waists so we aren't jerking on him," Naomi said.

Annie nodded, and the two of them began to wind the rope around their bodies.

"It's working!" Jon called.

Suddenly there was slack in the line. Annie heard something strike the cliff wall. He'd fallen! The rope was totally loose. Her heart in her throat, she ran to the cliff's edge and stared down.

Jon lay spread-eagled atop a spruce tree. Was he dead? She saw no movement, and an overwhelming fear clutched her core. She couldn't lose him. Not ever, but especially not like this.

/ / /

She was out of the cabin. Once the door had opened, Michelle had managed to get the boot on, but it was tight. She hobbled along toward the trees as best she could in her orthopedic boot. The pain radiated up her leg with every step, but she couldn't count on any of his promises. The man would never let her go, and she had to at least try to flee.

She'd stuck two jerky sticks into the waistband of her shorts along with a bottle of water before she hobbled from the cabin, and she adjusted them more securely. The sight of the man's truck had given her pause, and she'd stumbled over to peek in the cab. There were no keys, so she headed for the woods to her left. Once she reached the trees, she found a stick she was able to use as a makeshift crutch. While it helped, having her leg on the ground made the blood flow into the injured tissues, and the pain continued to ramp up. She was unsure how long she could go on this way, but at least she could smell the dew on the leaves and the fresh air.

She wound her way through the massive oak trees and brushed by the spruce spreading their needles and fragrance into her path. If she had to die out here, at least she could breathe in the outdoors she loved so much.

Her intuition had led her to move into the forest on the left side of the cabin, but she had no idea if she was walking straight into danger or heading away from it. She knew better than to call for Sarah. It was hard to know where their abductor had gone.

Since his truck was here, he was still searching out here. And he was armed.

Her senses were on high alert, and she listened for any twigs snapping or anyone moving past branches. There wasn't much wind tonight, but she wished the fog that got heavier with every step would lift so she could see better. But maybe it was godsent. Just as the mist hid the landscape from her, it hid Sarah and her from their pursuer.

It felt like she'd been on her leg forever, though she thought it had only been half an hour or so. She had no way of knowing for sure, but she needed a break. Her leg desperately screamed to be elevated. She peered through the white fingers of mist drifting through the leaves and trees and spotted a downed tree. It would be a good spot to prop her foot, especially since it was partially hidden by a tall shrub.

Using the makeshift crutch, she managed to lower herself to the ground, then hiked her foot onto the obliging tree in front of her. The relief came almost at once, and she sighed and leaned back on her elbows. She closed her eyes and took several calming breaths to help the pain wind back down.

A twig snapped from somewhere, and she opened her eyes and tried to see. The fog had descended even heavier while she'd rested, and she couldn't even see her foot resting on the log. The filmy tendrils obstructed everything.

Another twig snapped, and she heard heavy feet pass very close to her head. She didn't dare breathe. It had to be her kidnapper. There was no sound from Sarah. Had he killed her or simply hadn't found her? She prayed it was the latter.

She barely allowed air to ease from her lungs as she waited to make sure he'd gone on past. A muttered curse came from some distance away, and she closed her eyes with relief. He was on his way back to the cabin. Once he discovered she'd fled, too, he was likely to come back out. Or would he? Maybe he'd leave to get help. Or maybe he'd run. She had no idea what the maniac might do.

She crawled closer to a tree and used it to help her stand. Getting going again after a rest was harder when her leg began to scream again, but she didn't dare lie here and wait for him to find her. Gritting her teeth, she slowly made her way through the dark and fog. It was like trying to move through cotton without any idea which direction her feet were really going.

A hiss came from her right, and she stopped, her heart in her mouth. She knew that sound all too well. An angry mountain lion was warning her off. She stood still, her pulse racing and her mouth dry. She moved her hand to the water bottle and the jerky at her waistband. She yanked the water bottle free. It would be something she could throw. She ran through all the things she'd learned about big cats: face them, look as big and ferocious as possible, wave your arms.

She grabbed an evergreen branch that had fallen and waved it around.

In this moment it seemed ridiculous and futile, but she hadn't come this far to be taken down by the very animal she'd come to learn about. Waving the branch, she shouted, "Go away! Get back!" She banged her stick on a tree trunk.

The puma grumbled again, and then the sound vanished. Had it moved away or come closer to try to take a bite out of her? She yelled and banged some more. No response.

Her heart beat wildly in her chest as she propped her crutch under her arm and began to move away. Her legs trembled and felt weak. Had her noise carried to her abductor? If so, he'd be heading this way, too, but she'd had no choice.

She shuffled through last year's fallen leaves as quietly as possible. It felt like she'd been wandering down here for hours, but she was encouraged by not hearing signs of pursuit behind her. Maybe her yelling hadn't brought the man after all. He'd been gone a little while, and fog tended to muffle noises.

She needed another rest and it took a while to find the right place to shelter, where she hoped she wouldn't be seen as she elevated her foot. Her eyes closed in spite of fighting to stay awake.

A cough filtered through her consciousness, and she opened her eyes to dim the light of morning breaking through. A shuffling movement from above her head made her freeze. Was the cougar back?

THIRTY-EIGHT

WAS THAT THE MAN BENEATH HER TREE PERCH? Sarah's muscles ached and spasmed from being in the tree for so long. She stared down through the fog as a figure moved beneath her. A scream built in her throat, but she stuffed her fist in her mouth and held it back by sheer force of will.

Her foot slipped, and she grabbed at the branch, but it was too late. She plummeted to the ground and landed atop someone. That someone let out an *oomph* in a woman's voice.

Sarah scrambled away into the wet weeds and shoved her hair out of her face in an effort to see. "Wh-who's there?" The moisture from the creeping fog coated her skin and everything she touched.

The other woman's form loomed in the breaking dawn. "It's Michelle. Try to keep it down. I don't know where that guy is. Are you hurt?"

"N-no. He didn't find me. I've been in that tree for hours. Do you have any water?"

Michelle handed over a bottle of water. "Don't drink it all. That's all we have until we find our way out of here."

Sarah took a couple of sips and forced herself to recap the bottle. "I can carry it for you. You don't have any extra hands. How did you get this far on that leg?"

"The tree branch helped. And I rested some." Michelle looked around. "This is beginning to seem familiar."

Sarah shuffled and spun around to view the area. "It all looks the same to me."

"Did you see any cougars?"

Sarah shivered and hugged herself. "No, and I don't want to. You heard one?"

"Yeah. I yelled and waved my arms. I didn't hear it again. When you moved on that branch, I thought you were the mountain lion."

Michelle settled on the ground and lifted her broken leg into the crook of a tree branch a foot off the ground. She exhaled, and a little color came back to her pale cheeks.

Sarah stretched out the spasming muscles in her legs and arms. It felt good to be back on the ground, but she was hungry, tired, and thirsty. She wanted a soft bed and a big breakfast at the Suomi. And coffee with cream.

Would she ever see Rock Harbor again? She was going to be arrested for kidnapping the moment she reached civilization. She settled on the wet ground next to Michelle and leaned against the tree trunk. Maybe she could hitch a ride once they got out to a road. She could go to Wisconsin. Or even Canada. The thought of never seeing Kylie again made her heart hurt.

Had anyone found the little girl, or had she wandered in the forest through the fog? And with mountain lions roaming around. That was a scary thought.

The light of the approaching sunrise filtered through the leaves a little more. Sarah rose and looked around. "Which way should we go to get out of here? You can rest and I can send back help."

Michelle sat up. "I'm ready to move again. I don't want that guy to find me. Once the sun burns away the fog, he'll be able to see much better in the daylight to track us. Footprints and all."

The reminder that the man was still out there made Sarah want to get moving again. "I guess you're right. Is it still looking familiar?" She reached down and helped Michelle to her feet.

"I think so." Michelle pointed to their left. "I think the lake is that way."

"But which way is a road? We don't have a boat, and we could walk for miles along the lake without coming to any kind of town or dwelling."

Annie had often talked about how remote different beaches were that she checked out for campers and fishermen. A lot of them were ATV-only access.

"I don't know which way to go to find a road, but my gut still says to go that way." Michelle fitted her stick under her arm and began to shuffle through the vegetation.

Sarah heard something that seemed to come from the right. She put her finger to her lips. "Shh. Did you hear that?"

Michelle stopped and listened. The wind picked up and scattered leaves from around a tree trunk. Was that all Sarah had heard? She didn't think so. It was more like a cough or something. Was the man back? She and Michelle exchanged a long, frightened gaze.

A flicker of movement caught Sarah's attention, and she stared. Was that a snake in the tree moving its head? She peered through the wispy fog and shook her head. She lifted a shaky hand and pointed to a mountain lion off to their right, on a thick branch about eight feet up. Its tail lashing back and forth was the movement she'd seen.

Its golden eyes stared down at them, and Sarah shivered. She wanted to run, but her feet were glued to the ground.

Another movement just five feet to the left of the cougar drew Sarah's attention. She gasped when she saw the ski-masked man sidling their way. His revolver was in his hand, and his gaze was fixed on them.

"Michelle," Sarah whispered.

"I see it. Don't move and don't run."

"No, look to its left."

Michelle adjusted her gaze, and her jaw tightened. She leaned on her stick, and fear radiated off her—the same fear Sarah felt as the man took another step in their direction.

/ / /

The antiseptic smell of the hospital added to Annie's sense of shock. Jon lay unconscious in a room just beyond that door. Kylie slept in her arms after a doctor checked her out, and Annie feared the worst about the man she had loved since she was a teenager.

What would she do if Jon died? He'd crept back into her heart so quickly, she hadn't been able to put up any resistance. Seeing him spread-eagled in the tree played over and over in her mind. She'd peeled plenty of drivers out of cars after they'd hit trees, and it was never pretty. You'd think a tree would soften the impact, but it was an immovable object.

Dr. Eckright exited a room, and Annie struggled to her feet with Kylie's dead weight slowing her down. He came toward her, and his expression did nothing to soothe her fears.

"H-he's dead?" Her voice hadn't recovered much in spite of several hours of rest, and it came out as a squeak.

Kylie stirred at her words and lifted her head. Her eyes opened, and her arms came around Annie's neck. "Dr. Ben, did you bring Jon a sucker?"

"I'll make sure he gets one, Kylie." Ben put his hand on Annie's shoulder. "He's in a coma, Annie. Some of the smaller branches slowed his descent, but he still slammed into a large tree limb. He's got a couple of fractured ribs, and I'm worried about that concussion. He hit his head again in the fall. He dislocated his left shoulder, but we managed to put it back into place. I'd suspect his climb down to get Kylie resulted in that injury. But he's a tough guy and did it anyway. If he pulls through this, he deserves a medal for saving her."

"He saved me." Kylie's voice quivered. "He can't die."

"We're going to do our best to take care of him," Ben said. "He needs to be moved to Houghton, and I'm arranging for a helicopter to transport him there as quickly as possible."

Annie couldn't take it all in. A coma. What did that mean? "How long before he wakes?"

"There's no way of knowing. Keep talking to him, both of you. We know now that comatose patients often are more aware than they seem. If anything will bring Jon back, it's his love for the two of you. Would you like to see him before he's transferred?"

"Oh yes," Annie whispered. She put Kylie down and took her hand. "Bug, he's going to look pretty bad. He'll have lots of tubes attached to him, too, but don't be afraid."

She led her daughter into a room filled with equipment, and Jon was hooked up to all of it. The beep of the monitors added a nightmarish soundtrack to the scene.

Tears spilled down Kylie's cheeks. "He looks dead."

"He's just sleeping," Annie squeaked out.

Talking to him would be a challenge when she could barely get sounds out of her throat. But if he was in there, he'd hear her. He'd always been such a good listener. Sometimes she thought he could read her mind.

She moved to his side and took his hand, careful not to jerk on the IV in his arm. She caressed the hair off his forehead and leaned over to press her lips against his. She breathed in the scent of him and imprinted it on her memory in case it was the last time she saw him alive.

"I'm here, Jon. Kylie's here. You saved her. The doctor thinks you dislocated your shoulder getting down to her, which was why you couldn't hang on when we tried to bring you up. You're our hero. When you wake up, I'm going to fix you chocolate chip pancakes with whipped cream. I hate baking pies, but I'll find your mom's cherry pie recipe and bake you the biggest one you've ever seen."

Kylie crept closer to the bed. "I'll help her. Thank you for coming to get me. I was scared. Taylor said you're my dad. Is that true?"

At the words Annie swiveled her neck to stare at her daughter. During the emergency, the truth coming out hadn't been a priority.

She knelt beside her daughter and looked into her blue eyes. "It's true, Bug. Jon didn't know about it until he came here. I didn't either. I know this hurts you, and I don't ever want you to think you can't talk about Daddy. In every way that matters, he is still your daddy. He loved you so much."

"I know. I feel him talking to me sometimes." Kylie stared at Jon's white face. "I think Jon must love me too. He came to save me. I haven't been nice to him."

"He does love you, and he understood you were afraid of things changing. He never held it against you."

"He's kind of like Jesus, isn't he? He was willing to die for me."

Tears clogged Annie's throat and made speaking even harder. "He's not perfect like Jesus, but he's always had a big love in his heart for his people."

"And I'm one of his people now."

"You're one of his main people."

Kylie nodded and leaned closer to kiss him on the cheek. "You can't die, Jon. I want to learn to make your mom's pie. She was my grandma, right? And Mr. Daniel is my grandpa."

She sounded pleased, and Annie knew she'd longed for grandparents who paid attention to her. Daniel would gladly fill that void Kylie had always experienced.

She pressed her lips close to his ears. "Come back to me, Jon. You promised you'd never leave me again. Don't break your promise."

Did his hand move? She straightened and looked down his arm to his fingers. They curled around hers, and there was a light pressure. "Jon?"

His eyelids fluttered, and she turned and ran for the door. "Ben, I think he's waking up!"

THIRTY-NINE

BREE HAD TAKEN KYLIE TO GET SOME REST. THOUGH Annie had been reluctant to let her daughter out of her sight, she knew Kylie wouldn't get any sleep in Jon's hospital room with the nurses and doctors in and out since he'd started to come out of his coma.

She'd driven to meet him at the Houghton hospital after they'd taken him by chopper, and he'd been restless for a while until he fell into what the doctor called a natural sleep.

His brain was waking up, but he hadn't clearly seen her or called her by name. Annie couldn't wait until his wonderful green eyes smiled at her. His dad had come to check on him before Jon had been transferred, but Daniel had gone back to the Blue Bonnet after Annie promised to call if there was the slightest change.

She yawned and stretched out her legs. She looked up as the door opened around midnight, and Siela Cheng stepped into the room. She wore the same gray suit and every hair was in place. Her dark eyes were alert, and she carried a printer-paper box.

The FBI agent glanced at Jon. "I thought I'd find you awake. How is he?"

"Out of the coma according to the doctors." Annie's gaze went to the folder. "What do you have there?"

"Mason sent this box of items up for you. They have to do with another case you're working, a Michelle Fraser. He discovered her campsite and retrieved her belongings. And he's unlocked her phone. It was late enough he knew no one was in the office to examine them, so he thought it would give you something to do."

"He's a good man."

"And you're a good mom. You trusted your instincts and you were right. You found your little girl. I'd like to interview her tomorrow, to see what all she noticed and how your sister was able to entice her to leave with her. It will help with future abduction cases."

She must have seen the objection building in Annie's eyes because she held up her hand. "I'm experienced with this. I'll be very circumspect and kind. I won't upset her."

"Okay. Can I be there?"

"Of course. It will be at your convenience." She set her slim fingers on Annie's shoulder. "And again, good job, Annie."

"Thank you."

Once the FBI agent left, Annie dove into the box. Inside was the cell phone and a file folder. She started with the phone. There weren't any recent text messages, so she went to the pictures, where she hit pay dirt. The last picture taken was clearly of Grace Mitchell. The young woman appeared ill. She was very pale and had dark circles under her eyes. Her lips were twisted like she was crying.

The next picture back was of trees and cat scat. Many more pictures came of the woods, then she got to one of a desk with a page from a logbook. There were passwords and login information to several websites, including what appeared to be an accounting program.

This must be what Idoya was so desperate to get back. Annie

would have to text her the information in the morning. Lifting out the file folder, Annie riffled through the pages. The top set looked like a dissertation on mountain lions. Lots of research there. She checked every page, and it all flowed perfectly until she got to the last page.

It had a list of withdrawals. The total was nearly a million dollars. What did that mean? Nothing jumped out at her, but her curiosity was piqued. She grabbed Michelle's phone again and scrolled back to look at the page of logins.

After grabbing her computer, she went to the online site and logged in with the password on the page. She got in immediately. It appeared to be the books for the women's shelter. She'd taken a course or two on forensic accounting, so she decided to look at the last year of the books. Jon still slept, and she had a lot of hours before morning. She began to see large sums of money deposited into the bank account. And large amounts withdrawn.

The recipient was none other than Glenn Hussert, who was running for state senator. What did that mean? Fraud, graft? Was Sarah mixed up in it, too, through Sean? Had Glenn taken Michelle to hide his crime?

She glanced at Jon, who was stirring in the hospital bed. "Jon? Can you open your eyes?" She'd recovered her voice after rest, but it was still a little raspy.

She couldn't do anything to figure this out until she knew Jon was going to be all right.

/ / /

Annie's voice. Jon swam up from the deep recesses where he'd been floating. She was counting on him, and he had to get to her.

Something was wrong. He heard it in the quiver of tears and the thread of fear in her voice. He wanted to open his eyes, but they seemed so heavy and he was so tired.

There was a pressure on his hand as if someone was holding his fingers. He tried to hold on, but he wasn't sure he could. Part of him wanted to slip into the warm light around him and sleep. Maybe for just a little while. But Annie's voice tugged at him, and he couldn't ignore her.

He made another try to open his eyes, and he caught a movement through his slitted lids. Annie's worried face hovered above him. Kylie was there, too, and a nurse. Dr. Ben too.

He closed his eyes again, and the sound of beeping went wild in the room. Going back to sleep to escape seemed a good option.

When he opened his eyes again, dim daylight filtered through the windows. Annie was curled up in a chair by the bed, and her blonde hair was disheveled around her face. She breathed evenly in her sleep.

He looked around the room. He was in the hospital. The events at the gorge came flooding back, and with it, pain made itself known. His shoulder and head throbbed, and it hurt to breathe. The steady beeping of the machines around him was a soothing rhythm. It had been dark at the falls. How long had he been here?

He yawned and flexed his jaw. His headache eased a bit, and he desperately needed a sip of water. His mouth felt like it was full of sand.

He'd fallen. That horrible moment when he couldn't hang on any longer. The plummeting through the air, expecting oblivion when he struck the ground. The fear combined with his joy in knowing his daughter was safe in Annie's arms. He'd known going down that rope that his return was unlikely, but he'd willingly offered his life for his little girl. And in that moment when he was falling to certain death, he'd been content knowing at least Annie wouldn't be alone. He'd expected to see his mother in heaven in the next instant.

And yet here he was. Alive with Annie sleeping next to him. How had that happened?

He drank in the sight of his beautiful Annie. So faithful, so determined, so loving. How had he won such a prize? He was a lucky man, and he'd never take her for granted again.

She rustled and lifted her head. Her gaze met his, and joy flooded their blue depths. "Jon? You're awake!" She leaned in closer and kissed him.

The taste of her was better than the finest chocolate. Ignoring the stab of pain in his ribs, he wrapped his good arm around her and pulled her half onto the bed. Her soft lips were a reminder that he was alive by some miracle.

He reluctantly let her go. "Have you been here all night?"

"Yes. Kylie was here for a while, then Bree came and got her for me." She hesitated. "You probably don't remember anything we said to you before you woke up, do you?"

Bits and pieces came back in a jumble. "Not really. I just knew you were here, and I wanted to get back to you."

Her eyes filled with moisture, and several tears leaked out. "You were in a coma. Ben wasn't sure you were going to live. He told us you dislocated your shoulder climbing down to get Kylie."

He remembered. "I did. I was pretty sure I couldn't climb back up, and I didn't want to risk trying to do it with her in case I took her into the falls with me."

"Sarah told her you're her dad. I think Kylie's willing to open up to you. At least a little. It's progress. She compared you to Jesus. She said you were willing to die for her."

His throat tightened. "That's a name I can't live up to. But I love her, and I'll always do my best to let her know how important she is."

"She kissed you last night before she left." Annie leaned over and cupped his face in her hands. "I was so scared I was going to lose you, Jon. Don't ever scare me like that again."

His lips quirked, and he turned his head to kiss her palm. "I'll try. It's kind of out of my hands. When I was trying to get back to you, I'd promised you I'd never leave again. And I didn't want to break that promise."

He pressed the button on his bed to raise his head. "Could I have water?"

"Just sips," she cautioned him. She held the cup and straw under his chin.

"Hey, I'm the doctor here."

"Yeah, the doctor with a concussion who refused to go to the hospital. I'm discovering that doctors make the worst patients."

"Shh, you're not supposed to know that."

"Kylie told us Lissa made Sarah leave. She had a gun. I think Sarah is in trouble."

"Does Kylie know why Sarah took her?"

"She doesn't know, but she's scared for Sarah." Annie's eyes narrowed. "Sarah doesn't deserve any sympathy, not after taking Kylie."

His gaze fell on file folders and a box. "What's all this?"

"Mason found Michelle's campsite. I think I might have figured out what's going on! I examined the books for the women's shelter. I think there's fraud occurring. It appears to be Glenn Hussert who's involved. It might be a huge lead."

"That guy has always rubbed me the wrong way."

"I know." They exchanged a knowing look. "The first thing I want to do is check his properties and see if there's a place he might have stashed Michelle. Remember when we saw Lissa talking to Glenn in his driveway? She was crying and upset, so I think they are connected in more ways than we know. And if Lissa is involved, she'd know his safe places. Maybe she took Sarah to one of his properties."

"What are you doing here then? Go find her!"

She hesitated. "I didn't want to leave you. Mike took over your case, by the way. He checked out your shoulder and ribs but said you didn't need surgery."

He glanced around. "I'm in Houghton?"

She nodded. "They brought you by chopper. You've been here since about midnight. You really think I should go search for Sarah?"

"You have to. She has no one else."

Her blue eyes were still troubled, but she nodded again. "Your phone is in the drawer. Text or call if you need me, and I'll come right back."

His head was feeling fuzzy, and his eyes were heavy. "I think I'll just sleep."

FORTY

THE OVERCAST DAY WOULD MAKE FOR A LITTLE COOLER search. Annie's phone had the coordinates Mason had texted over. He'd found three properties Glenn Hussert owned in the forest. One was the cottage where they'd tracked Kylie. The second was a lake cottage on Sleeping Bay, and the third was in the deep woods between Twin Lakes and Fourteen Mile Point.

The dogs hadn't searched for Sarah at the first cottage, only Kylie, but Kylie had told them Lissa had taken Sarah somewhere else. Annie thought it smarter to focus on the second and third properties.

The lake cottage was closer, so she'd followed Bree and Naomi with their dogs to the turn out near Sleeping Bay. There was a road, but it was potholed and too rough for the trucks. The gasoline fumes jetting out of the ATVs they rode mingled with the scents of pine and wildflowers as they followed the dogs through the forest toward the glint of Lake Superior in the distance.

The dogs hadn't caught a scent yet, so Annie wasn't hopeful.

The dogs broke through the trees into the clearing, and Annie paused at the pretty picture in front of her. The blue-and-white cottage was a single story with dormers and a small porch. A well-tended flower bed meandered up the stone walk.

Bree and Naomi had their dogs go to the porch. After

presenting the scent article to them again, Bree told Samson to search. The dog did his Z-pattern search in the front yard with his nose high, but no happy bark or any other sign revealed that he'd gotten the right skin rafts.

With a gloved hand Bree returned the shirt to the paper bag. "I don't think she's been here. Where are the other coordinates?"

Annie rattled them off to her, and Bree put them into her GPS in case they got separated. "Fifteen miles away," Bree said. "As the crow flies. As the ATV wanders along fire roads, it will be longer." She checked the time on her phone. "Ten o'clock. Let's get going."

This time, Bree and Naomi had the dogs on the machines with them to save time. The clouds grew lower in the sky as they drove the ATVs back the way they'd come. The foliage was thick and black flies plentiful as they navigated the fire trails and pushed through on unspoiled terrain when it looked safe.

An hour later, Annie shut off her ATV and consulted her GPS. "There's no road or driveway to this next property, and the forest is thick. Let's get the dogs out and let them search as we walk in."

Bree shut off her machine and dismounted. "I was thinking the same thing."

Annie eyed the glowering sky and pulled out her rain gear. She shouldered a backpack with water and jerky. Luckily the rain wouldn't affect the search. Moisture only enhanced the ability of the dogs to detect scent.

The other women gave their dogs the command to search, and they all took off quickly into the deep woods. A patter of raindrops on the leaves alerted Annie to the shower before she felt moisture on her face. She pulled on her rain poncho and tugged up the hood. The path quickly became slippery, and mud began to form.

To her left she heard the eerie yodel of a loon. The *oo-AH-ho* warble made her shudder and took her right back to the night twenty-four years ago when Sarah was taken. Annie shoved away the prickle of sympathy rising in her chest. Sarah didn't deserve it after what she'd done.

Annie stopped and consulted her GPS. Another mile that would be drudgery in this rain. At least it was warm.

Samson's ears came up, and he gave a happy bark. Charley followed suit, and the two of them shot forward in an easterly direction. The property was more to the north, but that didn't mean much if the dogs had a scent.

The women followed after the dogs, and Annie kept a sharp eye out for any movement in the gray mist hovering around the forest. This could be it. Even if Sarah continued to hate her, Annie would know she'd done everything she could to save her this time, unlike the last time.

The thick forest pressed back against them as if resisting their search. Annie squeezed between two intertwined spruce trees and listened for the sound of a human voice. "Sarah!"

She'd lose her voice again after another long search, but it would be worth it if she found her sister.

Samson shook his wet fur, and his ears canted forward. A growl rumbled from his throat, and his dark eyes looked fierce. Annie had never seen him like that.

"What's wrong with him?"

Bree paused and looked around the wet and dreary forest. "Maybe a wolf or another predator. Any other animals should be hunkered down in this weather, though."

They followed the dogs deeper into the thick trees for a while. Annie began to hear a deep rumble. A man's voice? "Bree, do you hear something?" she whispered.

Naomi was on the other side of Bree, and she nodded. "Sounds like a guy," she whispered back. "Let's be careful."

Annie pulled her gun from its holster and took the lead. Kylie had said Lissa had a gun, and if Hussert was here, too, he might be armed as well. They might be nearly to the property.

Squinting through the drizzle, she advanced until she could clearly hear the guy.

"You've given me a lot of trouble," the man said.

Annie peered through the screen of wet foliage and spotted a man in a ski mask waving a gun toward two cowering women. A movement above the guy caught her attention. She nearly gasped when she saw the puma creeping toward him on a large branch just above his head.

There was no time to shout a warning at him because the big cat's muscles flexed, and it launched itself onto the unsuspecting man below.

/ / /

The big cat's snarl made Sarah scramble back as it leaped from the branch onto the man. He screamed and flailed his arms as the puma's mighty jaws clamped on to the back of his neck. The scream became choked as the animal tightened its grip and hunkered down on his back.

Sarah's first inclination was to grab a stick and rush to poke at it, but Michelle grabbed her. "Let it alone or it might go for you. The cougar has a death grip on him already."

Before Sarah could protest at the thought of leaving the guy to the cougar, two dogs and several figures burst through the vegetation toward them. Samson and Charley. Both dogs rushed at the cougar, and Samson sank his teeth into the animal's hindquarters.

The big cat let go of its prey and screamed its anger as it crouched on the man's back and defended itself. Its claws lashed out at the dog, but Samson danced back and missed the deadly swipe. Charley dove in for an attack on the other side, and the cat snarled and angled a paw that direction.

That attack made Charley yelp, and Annie rushed forward with her gun ready. "Call back the dogs!"

Bree and Naomi gave orders to their dogs, and both Samson and Charley backed away with obvious reluctance. Their volleys of barks continued as Annie planted her feet to take aim.

Michelle staggered forward with her crutch. "Don't shoot! Don't hurt the cat."

The distraction was enough to allow the big cat to leap into the canopy of leaves overhead. The vegetation shook, and the puma vanished before Annie could fire a shot.

Unslinging her backpack from her shoulders, Bree rushed forward to check on the man while Naomi tended to her injured dog.

Michelle collapsed to the ground and sat rocking back and forth with pain. Sarah's knees were weak, and she wanted to join her on the ground, but the puma might be back any second. Eyes wide, she checked the branches to make sure the cat wasn't about to pounce again before she made a move toward Annie.

Annie turned toward her, and her eyes went soft when she locked gazes with Sarah. "Are you all right?"

Her sister shouldn't look at her so kindly. Sarah wasn't fit for her to even speak to, not after what she'd done. Tears welled in her eyes. "Annie, you've got to search for Kylie! She ran off into the woods, and I couldn't find her. I'm so sorry."

Annie approached and squatted by her sister. "I've got her, Sarah. She's fine. Are you injured?"

"No, no, I'm not hurt. But Michelle has a badly broken leg. Can you help her?"

"Bree has a first aid kit with ibuprofen. We'll call for help and get you both to the hospital." Annie went to where Bree knelt by the man.

Sarah followed close behind. She wanted to see who had terrorized them, but she didn't recognize the man even without the ski mask on. He lay in the wet leaves with his eyes closed. She didn't think he was breathing.

Bree rose and stepped back. "He's in a bad way. The cat nearly suffocated him."

Michelle stirred and lifted her head. "That's how cougars kill their prey. They strangle them from the back of the neck. Who is he?"

"Glenn Hussert," Annie said. "He owns the Bunyan Fisheries and is running for a state senator seat."

"I don't know him," Michelle said. "But he is a terrible man. He found me in the woods after my ATV accident and kept me prisoner in an old cabin even though I told him I needed a hospital."

Bree went to tend to Michelle. "Broken leg?" She dug into her backpack and pulled out ibuprofen. She shook out four tablets and handed them to Michelle along with a bottle of water. She gave Sarah a bottle of water too.

Michelle swallowed them down, and Bree produced some

pistachios for both women. Sarah's stomach rumbled at the sight of food. When was the last time she'd eaten? It seemed an eternity ago.

She was beginning to realize she'd been saved from one predicament only to face another. What she'd done to Kylie wasn't going to go away. Even if Annie forgave her, she'd have to face the law. She'd abducted her niece. Looking back, it was hard to believe she'd made such a stupid decision.

Her throat burned with unshed tears, and she wanted to beg Annie to forgive her, but the words wouldn't come. Nothing could change what Sarah had done.

"Naomi, how's Charley?" Bree called.

"He'll be all right. The cat got him, but it's bleeding well, and I have him patched up. I already called for help. We'll need a litter for Michelle and Hussert. Paramedics should be here in about an hour."

"Does Kylie hate me?" Sarah forced the question out past her tight throat.

"Of course not. She was worried about you and told me I had to find you. She'll be relieved to hear you're all right. Hussert didn't hurt you?"

Annie still hadn't made a move to embrace her or touch her, and why would she? Sarah had hurt her in the worst possible way. She'd inflicted the same kind of pain on her sister that had come to their parents, and to Annie herself. Why hadn't Sarah thought about the consequences of her plan before acting? The bitterness and hurt had destroyed her ability to think clearly. She'd wanted to hurt Annie, and while Sarah had done just that, she'd also hurt Kylie. And herself.

"No, he didn't hurt me," Sarah said.

She'd give anything if she could go back a few days. She would welcome Annie's overtures and let go of the past. But it was too late. She'd ripped apart Annie's feelings for her and shown she wasn't worthy of the Vitanen name.

FORTY-ONE

THE RAIN FINALLY STOPPED, AND THE FRESH AROMA in the air felt like a new beginning to Annie. Her baby girl had survived her ordeal and so had Jon. And even her sister was alive and whole. It could have turned out much worse.

Mason was first on the scene with the rescue team. The paramedics rushed to assist Hussert and Michelle, and Annie walked over to meet the sheriff. His sharp gaze raked over Sarah, and he started that way until Annie put her hand on his arm. "What kind of penalty is she facing?"

"She committed a felony. Here in Michigan it's punishable by imprisonment for life or any term of years, or a fine of not more than fifty thousand dollars, or both. Serious charges."

And Sarah deserved the full extent of the law. What she'd done was unforgivable. But life imprisonment after Sarah had already been imprisoned for most of her life struck a soft chord somewhere in Annie's heart. "What do you think will happen?"

Mason shrugged his bulky shoulders. "Hard to say. It will depend a lot on what evidence we uncover. We know she's unstable. This could have turned out much worse."

She winced. "That's true enough. The trauma of her earlier life warped her somehow, Mason. Do you think she's beyond hope?"

"I'm not in the hope business, Annie, and the law isn't God. God is in the forgiveness business, but the law is about justice, not grace."

Was there good left in Sarah after her experiences growing up? Annie wasn't sure.

Mason's gaze tracked the paramedics transporting the injured man out of the forest. "I hope Hussert is going to make it. I really want to have a chance to interrogate him."

"Me too. He has to have been behind everything—the hacking of Jon's car to try to kill us, the break-in at my house, Idoya following us. I think it's likely he was trying to see if we had the incriminating evidence you found at Michelle's campsite."

Mason nodded. "I've got the state boys working on uncovering what they can about all of it." He pulled out zip ties and went to take Sarah into custody.

She watched him arrest her sister. This was not how she'd thought finding her sister would be. Not standing by and watching her go to jail for a terrible crime like kidnapping. Kylie would be very upset about it all. She loved Sarah.

And Annie was shocked to discover even her sister's terrible behavior hadn't completely rooted out the love she felt for Sarah. Annie hadn't thought it was there, had thought that the way Sarah pushed at her had ripped out any tender feelings by the roots. But real love was hard to kill, and she'd spent a lifetime loving her sister. Even when she'd thought Sarah was dead. So a tiny flutter of love still germinated deep down.

At least Mason had zip-tied Sarah's hands together in front of her to make it easier to walk out of here. Annie moved to intercept them. "Sarah."

A softness resided in her face that Annie hadn't seen since

her sister had come back to her. "I'm so sorry, Annie. I care about Kylie."

Annie gave a jerky nod. "I know you do."

Sarah's lips trembled. "Tell Kylie I'm sorry. I never meant to hurt her."

"I'll tell her."

Annie stepped out of the way, and Mason guided Sarah out toward the fire road. The paramedics had gotten Michelle out as well, and only Annie and the SAR teams remained to trail out of the woods.

Annie accepted a small bag of pistachios from Bree and split one with her thumbnail. She couldn't remember the last time she'd eaten.

"Let's get out of here. I want to let Kade know the case is over."

Annie nodded. "I need to check on Jon, too, and see how he's doing. And I want to be in on Mason's interrogation of Idoya."

Bree shouldered her backpack, and Annie, Naomi, and she began the trek out to the fire road. "Idoya doesn't seem the type to take the fall for Glenn," Annie said. "She will likely tell Mason all she knows as soon as he picks her up."

Annie was ready to hear the full story. And she was ready to try to build that new life with Jon.

/ / /

Who knew an orthopedic injury could be so painful? Jon's arm was in a sling, and a bit of the wrapping around his ribs peeked out the top of his hospital gown. Now that he had to wear a wrapping, he understood his patients' complaints. But he was glad to be alive.

Annie and Kylie sat beside his hospital chair. Kylie was intent on her *Pokémon Go* game, and he leaned over to admire the Frillish she'd just caught. The window was open and looked out on Lake Superior.

A movement caught his eye, and he looked up as a woman came through the door. "Good morning, Agent Cheng."

Annie tensed, and he knew she dreaded the upcoming interview. She hadn't wanted to stir up any fear in Kylie after her ordeal, but he'd urged her to let Cheng do her job. He felt Kylie needed to talk about it and let it all go. Just like Annie should have done years ago with her own trauma.

Cheng smiled when she saw Kylie. "I love *Pokémon Go*. My buddy is a Pikachu. Mind if I join you?"

Kylie showed her the Frillish too. "Look at its stars."

Cheng pulled up a chair. "A hundo."

The woman knew the *Pokémon Go* lingo, which impressed Jon. He was just beginning to figure it out.

"I had a few questions about your day with your aunt."

"Okay," Kylie said.

"Did you go see your aunt Sarah, or did she come find you?"

"I saw her when I was in Bree's yard and came over to talk. She's lonely. We're her only family." Kylie shot a cautious glance at Annie as if to ask if she was allowed to talk about such personal things.

Annie nodded to let her know she could talk about anything. Jon took her hand.

"That's sad. So you feel sorry for Aunt Sarah?"

Kylie nodded. "I wanted her to feel better. I didn't really want to go hiking when she asked, but she had tears in her eyes. I wanted to make her smile again. I thought if we went for a walk, she'd laugh more. And she said we could get ice cream."

"That's always important," Cheng said. "How was the hike?"

"We didn't go at all! And I didn't like taking Kade's ATV. Aunt Sarah left it by the side of the road. That's not a smart thing. I'm glad no one stole it."

"I'm sure Kade would have been sad," Cheng agreed. "Did you hear your aunt talking to the woman who picked you up?"

Kylie shook her head. "I cried when we left the ATV behind. The other woman was mad at me, but Aunt Sarah kept telling her to leave me alone. I was sleepy, and when we got to the house, they let me take a nap in the bed."

"I'm sure it was all very scary."

Tears filled Kylie's eyes and spilled down her cheeks. "And Mommy told me never to leave with anyone without telling her. It's my fault Aunt Sarah is in trouble now."

Annie opened her mouth to contradict her, but Jon pressed her hand in warning and shook his head. She closed her mouth and gazed down at her lap. Jon wished he could make it easier for her.

"It's not your fault, Kylie," Cheng said. "She planned what she wanted to do. But we have to be smart about what other people want us to do. We always have to stop and think about how it's going to affect others. If someone asked you to go somewhere without telling your mommy, what would you do next time?"

"Say no. Talk to my mommy." Kylie voice grew stronger. "I would refuse to go, and if she tried to make me, I'd yell for help."

"Good girl. And you did a good job getting away. Why did you run into the woods?"

"I knew the falls were that way. I'd seen the sign when we drove in, and I knew if I found the falls, I could find people who would call my mom. Besides, I didn't want to go anywhere with Aunt Sarah. I was upset when I heard her tell that Lissa that Jon was my dad. I thought she was spreading lies."

Annie shot Jon an apologetic glance. "She shouldn't have been telling anyone that," Kylie said.

"No, she shouldn't," Cheng agreed. "Any information like that should only come from your mommy or daddy."

Kylie looked up at Jon. "But it's okay. He saved me when I was on the cliff. I prayed, just like Mommy and Daddy always told me to do when I was scared. And God sent a little bird to sit with me. It was a goldfinch, which was my daddy's favorite bird. So I knew someone would come. And then Jon came to get me."

This was the first time Jon had heard anything about a goldfinch coming to be with her. He hadn't seen it. Nate was a birder, and he loved the bright-yellow bird. Jon's heart squeezed at the things Kylie was saying. The fact they'd all survived was an amazing miracle.

Cheng patted Kylie's hand. "You were so brave, and we are all very proud of you."

"I won't ever go again, though. Not unless someone knows the secret word."

Cheng rose and gestured for Annie and Jon to follow her to the hallway. As soon as they were out of earshot, she stopped. "She's going to be all right. She talks easily about it, and she knows what she did was wrong. This event has a happy ending."

Jon noticed the sadness in her eyes. "And you don't see that often."

"Not often enough." Cheng smiled and headed down the hall.

Jon took Annie's hand as they went back into the hospital room. "The goldfinch story was something else."

Tears hung on Annie's lashes. "I'd like to believe Nate was looking out for her."

"Me, too, love. Me too. And if God could send a raven to feed Elijah in the desert, he could send a goldfinch to comfort a little girl."

FORTY-TWO

ANNIE YAWNED AS THE SUN BEGAN TO LOWER OUTSIDE Jon's hospital window. It had been a long couple of days. She hoped he'd get out tomorrow, but it would be Mike's decision. He hadn't come in yet today, and since it was Sunday, she wasn't sure if they'd see him or not.

Jon hadn't spent much time in the bed today. He sat in the chair by the window and sucked on his cherry Popsicle. "You should go home and spend some time with Kylie."

"I will. I told Bree I'd get her after dinner." She grinned at his red tongue. "You've had, like, four of those today."

He winked at her. "Five sounds like a good number."

The door opened and Mason came in. "The patient is still here, I see."

Jon tossed his Popsicle stick into the trash. "We're hoping the warden springs me tomorrow."

"I'll put in a good word for you." Mason settled in a chair by Annie. "You cracked that case, Annie. When Hussert wakes up, we're charging him with fraud. It's obscene how much money he's milked from the shelter. I'm sure he was terrified Michelle was bringing his lucrative little scheme down around his ears. His hacking of Jon's car was on his computer too. He was behind all of it." Mason crossed a leg over his other knee. "I wanted to talk with Idoya, but she's disappeared. I've got a BOLO out for her, but she might have slipped into Canada."

"How could Glenn know how to hack the car?" Annie asked.

"We'll have to ask him. Maybe he has someone working for him who used his computer," Mason said.

"And Lissa Sanchez?" Jon asked.

"She's cooperating, but she doesn't seem to know anything about the shelter or have any knowledge that Hussert had Michelle confined in the cabin. She'd picked up Sarah because she was Sean's cousin, then panicked when she realized Sarah was trying to take Kylie. She took her to the cabin to give Hussert time to get out of the state. At least that's what he told her. She passed a polygraph test about it, but I'm still considering charging her. I hope to know more when Hussert regains consciousness. It appears he's going to survive."

"And Sarah?"

"She's in jail, but you can get her out on bond. Child abduction charges."

Annie closed her eyes and hung her head. It would take a miracle to get Sarah out of this trouble. And Annie wasn't even sure if she wanted to have anything to do with her sister now.

"I wanted to make her smile again." Her daughter's words echoed in Annie's mind. Children found it easy to forgive and go on. It would take Annie longer, if she even managed it.

Jon reached over and took her hand. "We're grateful for all you've done, Mason."

Mason unfolded himself from the chair and rose. "Glad this all ended well." He paused a moment. "Anu said it was okay to tell you—her CA-125 was 553."

Jon winced, and Annie knew that meant bad news.

"Some women with other inflammatory issues have an elevation of CA-125," Jon said. "But coupled with the ultrasound, I'm glad she's going in for surgery."

"It's next week." Mason headed for the door. He passed Mike in the doorway and eased the door shut behind him.

Mike eyed Jon sitting in the chair. "The nurses tell me you're the demanding sort, asking to be let loose. Let me see how your lungs and heart sound, and we can see about that."

He unslung his stethoscope from around his neck and listened to Jon's chest and back, then replaced the scope. "You're a lucky man, Dr. Jon Dunstan. When you're fully recovered, we'll talk more about you coming to work with me. For now, rest and recuperate."

Annie straightened and reined in her jubilation. Having a new position would go a long way to making Jon settle in here. She knew the uncertainty weighed on him.

Jon's green eyes gleamed, and he sat up straighter. "Thanks, Mike, that sounds good. Can I get out now?"

"You don't want to wait until morning?"

"I'd like to sleep in a comfortable bed tonight."

Mike turned toward the door. "I'll write the release order. Come see me in a week."

Once the door shut behind him, Annie rose and leaned over to kiss him. His beard was a bit scruffy, and his brown hair stood on end, but his kiss was as loving and steady as she could ever want. He pulled her down onto his lap to kiss her properly. She sank into his embrace and felt truly safe for the first time in weeks.

His green eyes smiled when he finally broke the kiss. "Things are looking up. I might be able to support you after all."

"Maybe I'll support you," she teased.

He rested his chin on her head. "You can do anything you set your mind to do." His expression faltered. "Unless Olivia's problems follow me here."

His breath warmed her as he nuzzled her neck. "Let's get you home, Dr. Dunstan."

"How about your place? I don't feel like having Dad and Martha hover over me. We can have pizza and popcorn. I'll even promise to watch *Little House on the Prairie* without complaint."

She chuckled and circled her arms around his neck. "I think that can be arranged. Kylie has been sleeping with me anyway, and you can have her bed."

She'd focus on the future once she found out what role Hussert played in the events of the past few weeks. Now that Kylie knew the truth, Annie could finally see a path through the trees. It was a future she had only been able to dream of for so long. But maybe it was actually coming their way.

A NOTE FROM THE AUTHOR

Dear Reader,

Twenty years sounds like such a long time, but it's passed in the blink of an eye for me. In 2002 I was just learning how to write the mysteries I loved to read so much, and I wasn't even a grandmother yet. That seems impossible to believe now!

Yet here we are twenty years after *Without a Trace* was picked up by Thomas Nelson (HarperCollins Christian Publishing) and my local museum just installed a permanent display about my career. I didn't even have to die first, which is a good thing since I feel like I have many more books in me yet. ☺ In fact, I'm making notes on several new ones even now.

I'm so thankful for you, Dear Readers! Thank you for taking this journey with me through story and for your support. I hope you enjoy this new series in Michigan's Upper Peninsula. Let me know what you think!

Colleen
colleen@colleencoble.com

ACKNOWLEDGMENTS

TWENTY YEARS AGO AS I WRITE THIS I SAT ON THE floor outside a writer's workshop and pitched *Without a Trace* to Ami McConnell Abston at Thomas Nelson. At the time I was full of hope but very little real belief the book would find a home there. After all, they were the best publisher out there, and Ami was a legendary editor. But a few months later, I was staring in disbelief at an offer letter in my inbox. That was the beginning of a long partnership that has brought me only joy and blessing.

Thank you, team HarperCollins Christian Publishing, for all you have done for me through the past two decades! Dear editor Amanda Bostic has been with me through thick and thin and has set my suspense free to fly. My marketing/publicity team is the best out there, and no one has better covers than me. ☺ The love and support I've felt travels all through every department all the way up to Mark Schoenwald himself.

Julee Schwarzburg is my freelance editor, and she has such fabulous expertise with suspense and story. She smooths out all my rough spots and makes me look better than I am. I learn something from her with every book!

My agent, Karen Solem, and I have been together for twenty-three years now. She has helped shape my career in many ways, and that includes kicking an idea to the curb when necessary.

My critique partner and dear friend of nearly twenty-five years, Denise Hunter, is the best sounding board ever. Together we've created so many works of fiction. She reads every line of my work, and I read every one of hers. It's truly been a blessed partnership.

I'm so grateful for my husband, Dave, who carts me around from city to city, washes towels, and chases down dinner without complaint. But my Dave's even temper and good nature haven't budged in spite of the trials of the past year.

My family is everything to me, and my three grandchildren make life wonderful. We try to split our time between Indiana and Arizona to be with them, but I'm constantly missing someone. ☹

And I'm grateful for you, dear readers! Your letters and emails make this journey worthwhile! God knew I needed you to be whole.

And speaking of God, this was all his doing. He knew the plans he had for me from the beginning, and I'm thankful for every day he gives me.

DISCUSSION QUESTIONS

1. Have you ever had to deal with someone abusive in your life? How did you handle it?
2. What is the difference between justice and grace?
3. Do you find it hard to tell if God is directing you or if you're listening to what you want to do instead? How do you tell the difference?
4. I love kids and always have (taking care of younger siblings molded me into a nurturer). Are you a kid person or do you shudder when you hear a baby cry on an airplane?
5. Dietary restrictions seem to be all around us. Do they drive you crazy or are you one of those who has to deal with them? How do you feel about them?
6. Why is it so easy to rationalize holding back full truth/disclosure?
7. Have you ever done something impulsively you regretted bitterly a few hours later? What makes us give in to those types of moments of insanity?
8. Annie isn't sure how to forgive Sarah for what she did. Would you be able to do it?

Read the entire

ANNIE PEDERSON SERIES

FROM USA TODAY
BESTSELLING AUTHOR

COLLEEN COBLE

Coming July 2023

THOMAS NELSON
Since 1798

Available in print, e-book, and audio

ABOUT THE AUTHOR

Photo by Amber Zimmerman

COLLEEN COBLE IS A *USA TODAY* BESTSELLING AUTHOR best known for her coastal romantic suspense novels, including *The Inn at Ocean's Edge*, *Twilight at Blueberry Barrens*, and the Lavender Tides, Sunset Cove, Hope Beach, and Rock Harbor series.

/ / /

Connect with Colleen online at colleencoble.com
Instagram: @colleencoble
Facebook: colleencoblebooks
Twitter: @colleencoble